PREVIOUSLY LOVED
TREASURES

The Serendipity Series Book Two

BETTE LEE CROSBY

Previously Loved Treasures

ISBN-13: 978-0-9891289-5-7

BENT PINE PUBLISHING
Port Saint Lucie, FL

Published in the United States of America

ALSO BY BETTE LEE CROSBY

THE TWELFTH CHILD
The Serendipity Series Book One

♥

CRACKS IN THE SIDEWALK

♥

WHAT MATTERS MOST

♥

SPARE CHANGE
The Wyattsville Series Book One

♥

JUBILEE'S JOURNEY
The Wyattsville Series Book Two

♥

To read more about the author and see other books, visit:

www.betteleecrosby.com

Dedicated to the memory of
JoAnn Braunn

Special Friendships are Forever

IDA JEAN SWEETWATER

1989

I fell in love with Big Jim when I was seventeen and never stopped loving him. He was the kind of man you can't stop loving. He was like his name says: big. As a baby he was born big, and as a boy he grew into a man with a fullness twice the size of life itself. When Jim laughed you'd swear it was a roll of thunder coming down from heaven, and once he'd made love to you, you knew there'd never be anybody else.

There was never a day when I didn't love Jim, but there were plenty of times when I also came within a hair's breadth of hating him. During the summer of fifty-five I couldn't find a kind word to say to him. Even though he was only partly at fault, I blamed him for what happened. More than once I wished he'd walk out the door and never come back. Those were the bad years, but somehow we got through them.

I suppose that's how marriage is. When the preacher says it's for better or worse, you're so blinded by the possibility of better you fail to see the reality of worse. Maybe that's a good thing. If I had known about the heartache that lay ahead I might have turned my back and walked off. I could have avoided the misery, but I would have missed out on a whole lot of happiness too.

Nineteen fifty-four. That was the year our boy, James, stood toe to toe with his daddy and said it was his life and he'd live it however he damn well pleased. James was just like his Uncle Max, wild and irresponsible. One word led to another, and pretty soon it blossomed into an argument that could've been heard fifty miles away. Finally James just turned and walked out the door. That was the last I saw of our boy. He was nineteen.

I pleaded with Jim to go after James and bring him home, but it didn't happen. Jim was big on a lot of things, but the one thing he wasn't big on was forgiveness.

This afternoon I said goodbye to Jim, and as I stood there watching them lower him into the ground I decided to do what I should have done over thirty years ago. When that first thump of dirt landed atop his casket I said a prayer asking Jim to please forgive me, but the truth is I know he won't. As I told you, Jim was not a forgiving man.

THE SILENT HOUSE

In the weeks following Big Jim's funeral Ida began making plans for her future. Even though Jim was gone, she could set things right by finding James.

The last time she heard from him he was living in Plainview, a town ninety-seven miles north of Rose Hill. A place she'd never before been to. Plainview was where she would start her search. No major highway ran by the town, but a back road wound across a seemingly endless stretch of flat land. Land that was barren and without a gas station or roadside stand where you could stop for a sandwich or cold drink. Ida took a bottle of Pepsi Cola from the refrigerator, tucked it into her purse, then pulled on her sensible walking shoes and climbed into the car.

When she started out Ida felt optimistic, certain she'd find James and just as certain that he'd welcome the thought of returning home. Never mind that thirty years had passed; never mind that he was now a man in his fifties. Ida pictured him as only slightly older than the nineteen-year-old lad who left home, his hair still dark, his face without the creases of age. She even imagined the possibility he could be married and she delighted in thoughts of a grandchild, a feisty little tyke who would scatter toys throughout the rooms and bring the sound of laughter back to the empty house. In her handbag Ida carried a picture of James. She had taken it the week after graduation; it was the one where he leaned against the side of his green Pontiac and smiled the smile of a man without a care in the world.

Ida arrived in Plainview shortly before noon, drove to the center of town, and parked the car on Market Street. Once she stepped onto the street, the thought of "What next?" settled on her and ripped loose a bit of the optimism she'd started out with. The town was bigger than she thought it would be and busier. Much busier.

A few doors down Ida spied a coffee shop where people hustled in and out. That seemed as good a place as any to start. She walked in, sat on a counter stool, and waited. Her thought was to start up a casual conversation with the waitress and then work her way around to asking if the girl knew James, but she never got the chance. Before she could pull the picture from her purse, a group of businessmen came in hungry for lunch and in a hurry. Moments later three ladies followed, and before long every seat in the luncheonette was filled. Ida waited, thinking the rush would slow and the girl would have time to talk. But it didn't. As soon as one group left, another took its place. After lingering over a single cup of coffee for nearly a half hour, she climbed off the stool and left.

Her next stop was the drug store, where the pharmacist shook his head and said that he couldn't recall ever seeing such a man. It was the same at the dry cleaner, the hardware store, and the library. Ida had considered the library a long shot anyway, since James wasn't one for reading. After she'd thumbed through the Plainview telephone directory and stopped in every store on Market Street, Ida drove crosstown to the post office. She handed the elderly clerk the last postcard she'd received from James. On the face of the card was a picture of the three-story Elgin Hotel but no street address.

"I'm looking for a young man who may have been living at this hotel," Ida said. "Of course by now he's most likely moved into a more permanent residence, so I was wondering if you might—"

"The Elgin burned to the ground years ago," the clerk replied.

"Years ago?"

He nodded. "In fifty-eight, or maybe it was fifty-nine."

That postcard was the last time she'd heard from James; maybe it was because— "Oh my God, did anyone die in the fire?"

The clerk shook his head. "Not to my recollection."

"What about injuries? Was anyone severely injured?" Ida conjured a picture of James, still a young man but sitting in a wheelchair, incapable of speech, unable to call out for her.

"Unh-unh, the place was empty. It closed down a year or so before the fire. When Hilda Wilkins owned the Elgin it was a nice hotel, but after she died it pretty much went to ruin."

After a good fifteen minutes of chit chat about how the town had changed and not for the better, the clerk agreed to check and see if they had a listing or change of address for James Sweetwater. He disappeared into the back room and after a lengthy absence returned, only to say there was nothing.

"Nothing?" Ida repeated. "No address? No change of address?"

It was late in the day when Ida left the post office. By then her legs were tired, her feet ached, and her heart was weighted with more than thirty years of worrying about James.

On the drive home the sky turned from day to dark, and the road seemed to grow longer. The weariness of the years spread throughout Ida's body. It made her arms heavy and her legs feel as though they had turned to stone. The sorrow of all that had been lost plucked her heart from its rightful place and dropped it into the pit of her stomach.

That's when she began to sob. She'd been so determined, so convinced she could find James, that the disappointment now felt unbearable. When she pulled into the graveled driveway the house appeared even larger than it had when she left. Larger and emptier. She climbed from the car and walked toward the door with shoulders hunched, pushing her into a slow step-by-step movement. Once Ida opened the door the only sound she heard was that of a grandfather clock ticking, counting off the seconds, minutes, and hours of loneliness that lay ahead.

Not thinking of food, she climbed the stairs and fell across the bed she'd shared with Big Jim. In the fifty-six years they'd been married she had never once slept apart from him, and now apart was all there was. While the sky filled with stars and the moon rose, Ida wept. She thought back on the night it all began…

It was in the spring of 1954, when Big Jim told the boy if he wasn't going to college he'd have to get a job and pay ten dollars a week for board. There'd been a big row over it, and James, in that cavalier way he had of talking down to his daddy, said life was too short for nothing but work.

"There's a lot of fancy living outside of this little peapod town," James said, "and that's what I'm after." Then he continued with the statement that ultimately pierced his daddy's heart.

"I'm too smart to end up like you, Daddy. Way too smart."

Such an attitude rankled Jim to the core. He'd grown up poor and gone to work when he was not yet thirteen. As a boy he had loaded trucks during the day, tended a gas station at night, and worked in the print room of the *Rose Hill Chronicle* on weekends. It mattered not that it was long hours or demeaning work; what mattered was that in time he'd made something of himself. Now when Jim owned the largest house in Rose Hill and had enough money to send his son off to college, the boy looked down his nose at such an opportunity.

Angry words flew back and forth for nearly two hours. Finally James turned and walked out the door. He stopped for one brief second, looked back, and said, "Bye, Mama."

Ida had held on to that fleeting moment all these years. She told herself James hadn't wanted to go, and for a long while she blamed Jim for allowing such a thing to happen.

During the first year or two Ida searched for James numerous times. She called the friends he'd known, the places he'd frequented, even a few young ladies who occasionally came knocking on the door. It was always the same story: James had been there and gone. When there was no longer a trace of where he'd been, she held to the belief that he would sow his wild oats and then return home. The months became years and years turned into decades, but still there was no word. With the passing of time, Ida settled into the unhappy realization that the boy did not want to be found.

Although in many ways they were different, Big Jim and his son were very much alike—both of them proud and stubborn. On bad days when the sky was black and her heart heavy, Ida told herself that in time even the most stubborn heart would grow weary of carrying such a grudge. But it never happened.

Ida lay on the bed sobbing long into the night before her tears ran dry and sleep finally overcame her. In the morning she woke with her eyes crusted and her hair matted, but during the night she had come to the realization that she needed help if she wanted to do anything more than simply wish for James to come home.

She called Sam Caldwell first. He was not someone she knew but simply a name taken from the yellow pages of the telephone book. "Investigations and surveillance" the ad said. Then it told how Sam had been in business for more than twenty years and was registered with the county and state. But it was the tagline that convinced Ida to make the call. At the bottom of Sam Caldwell's ad in a seemingly hand-written script it read, "Missing Persons Specialist."

When Ida Jean Sweetwater walked into Sam Caldwell's office she was prepared to answer questions about her missing son. She'd brought along a picture and a shirt she'd taken from his closet. She thought she was prepared for anything, but she wasn't prepared for the sizable price tag hanging on Sam Caldwell's services.

"It's an eight hundred-dollar retainer to cover the first two weeks," he said, "then three hundred a week for as long as I'm actively working the case."

Ida gasped. "Doesn't that seem rather high?"

"Not really," Sam answered. Then he explained that expenses were extra.

Ida hesitated for a moment, picturing the balance in her checking account. "How long do you think it would take to find James?"

Caldwell shrugged. "Could be days, could be months."

Ida pictured the bank account again. There had been so many expenses: Jim's illness, the doctor bills, the funeral. She could swing two months if she cut back on groceries and Sam's expenses didn't cost too much.

"Okay," she said. "You're hired."

She pulled out the checkbook that still had Jim's name on it and in a shaky hand wrote the check for eight hundred dollars. She had never in all her life written a check for that much money.

That night Ida heated a can of chicken rice soup for her dinner then sat down at the table with her checkbook and stack of bills. On a yellow tablet she wrote columns of what had to be paid and what could wait, what was necessary and what could be considered a luxury, and in very small box at the bottom of the page she added up any income she expected. With Jim gone the Social Security would be considerably less, and most of their savings had gone to pay doctors during Jim's long illness.

On a second sheet of paper Ida began to list the things she might do to make some money. First she'd sell the little bit of jewelry she had, all but the thin gold band Jim placed on her finger the day they were married. That she'd never sell. It no longer fit her arthritic finger, but it dangled from a chain around her neck and nested in the crevice between her breasts. As the hours of the evening slid by, Ida added any number of other thoughts to the list: babysitting, sewing, light housework, homemade pies.

When she crawled into bed that night Ida knew that somehow, someway she would find the money to pay Sam Caldwell for as long as it took to find James. Whatever she had to do, it would be easier than living with the silence of the house.

PIES, LIES, & MAX

A week passed before Ida heard back from Sam Caldwell, and even then it was just a piddling bit about how James had left Plainview in 1958 and moved to Lodi, New Jersey.

"He left Lodi in sixty," Sam explained, "and it looks like he moved down to Nashville."

"That's quite possible," Ida answered. "James always liked music. In high school he played a saxophone in the band."

When Ida began to sound a bit too optimistic, Sam said, "Bear in mind this was twenty-nine years ago. A lot could have changed by now."

"Oh." Ida sighed. "I'd rather hoped…"

"Don't worry, I'll find him. It's just a question of time."

Although she didn't say it aloud Ida thought, *Time and money.* Hopefully she wouldn't run out of either before he found James.

Two days before she had to make her first three-hundred-dollar payment to Sam Caldwell, Ida walked into Suzanne's Bake Shop with two pies, one apple and one peach. She set them on the counter and said, "I thought you might be interested in ordering some homemade pies."

Suzanne laughed. "I sell pies, not buy them."

With her bank account going down faster than the lake in a drought season, Ida reached down to the soles of her feet and hauled up enough courage to say what she'd come to say. "You don't sell pies like these."

Suzanne chuckled. "Says who?"

Ida pulled a pie server and small china plate from her tote bag. First she cut into the apple, which was her particular favorite, carved off a good size slice, and handed it to Suzanne. "Taste this. If you don't agree, I'll leave and not bother you again."

The bakeshop owner forked a bite into her mouth and chewed. After what seemed to Ida an excruciatingly long time Suzanne looked over with a raised eyebrow. "You make this yourself?"

"Yes, indeed," Ida answered. "And there's plenty more where that came from." She explained that she wanted three dollars each for pies that could easily be sold for six. "I've got apple, peach, and blueberry, and I can do nine pies a day."

"No question the pies are tasty," Suzanne replied, "but three dollars?"

Ida then did something she'd never even imagined herself capable of. She told a barefaced lie. "The Muffin Tin didn't think so. In fact they said—"

In the space of that few minutes Suzanne had already dug into the peach pie and was busily chewing a sample. "Hold on a minute," she garbled. "I'm willing to pay the three dollars, but I want an exclusive."

Ida tried to imagine herself as Big Jim. He was such an admirable businessman, so strong and staunch. She hesitated a moment, then spoke as she believed he would have. "An exclusive's more."

"Three-twenty-five per pie," Suzanne offered, "and I can take up to twenty a week."

Ida smiled. "You've got a deal."

As she drove home Ida began singing along with the radio. She was certain Big Jim was looking down and feeling mighty proud of her. As a matter of fact, she felt pretty proud of herself.

Later that night Ida sat down at the table and tallied her income and expenses again. "Oh dear," she said. Although the pie money helped, she was still way short of the amount needed. One day at a time. She would simply have to take it a single day at a time. That's all she could do. Tomorrow she would post a notice on the supermarket bulletin board announcing that she was available for babysitting.

Two days later when Ida was up to her elbows in flour and Crisco, the doorbell rang. She slid the fourth peach pie into the oven, swiped her hands across her apron, and hurried to the door.

She'd expected it to be a neighbor or perhaps a harried

mother responding to her babysitting services sign. But when she opened the door there stood Alfred Maxwell Sweetwater or Max as everyone had come to know him. A large brown suitcase stood alongside of him.

"How's my favorite sister-in-law?" Max pulled the bewildered Ida into a bear hug that left his brown shirt dotted with flour and bits of pastry dough.

Ida wriggled loose, then backed up and looked him square in the eye. "What are you looking for, Max?"

That may have seemed a harsh question, but in truth it was quite appropriate. Max was Big Jim's younger brother, and they were as different as day is from night. Jim was hard working, generous, and faithful as a Baptist preacher. Max was none of those things. He'd go a mile out his way to avoid work, was selfish to the core, and a scoundrel with the ladies. Before he turned forty he'd been married to four different women, and after those marriages went south he took to living with first one woman and then another. There were no shades of grey where Max was concerned; he was the blackest of black sheep.

"What makes you think I'm after something?" Max grinned. "I just got to worrying about my big brother's wife being here all alone and thought I'd come and check on you."

"With a suitcase?"

"I was figuring to maybe stay a while."

"Well, you can figure again. I'm too busy for your nonsense, and I've got no money to lend you."

Max saw a window of opportunity and jumped on it. "That's exactly why I'm here. To help out financially."

"Help out financially?" Ida repeated dubiously. "How?"

"Well, you've got this big house and all these empty rooms. I was thinking I could move into one of them, help keep an eye on things, and pay a bit of rent."

The thought caught hold in Ida's head. "How much rent?"

"Fifteen, maybe twenty dollars a week."

"Twenty-five, and you get the small guestroom at the end of the hallway."

"That include meals?"

Ida eyed Max. He was small and skinny. How much could he possibly eat?

"Okay," she said. "Meals, but nothing fancy, just home cooking. And no ladies in the room."

"Why, Ida," Max said, "I'm surprised you'd think such a thing of me."

Ida wanted to tell him she didn't think it, she knew it, but by then he'd grabbed his suitcase and was halfway down the hall.

The first three weeks of Sam Caldwell's search uncovered very little other than the fact that James spent a considerable amount of time moving from place to place and apparently got tangled up with a singer named Joelle Williams in Nashville. But following such a haphazard trail of breadcrumbs involved a considerable amount of traveling from state to state and subsequently a larger-than-anticipated amount of expenses. In addition to the three-hundred-dollar fee for that week, Ida had to pay one hundred and seventy-three dollars in expenses.

On top of that, not one person had called for babysitting services.

At the end of his first week Max handed Ida twenty-five dollars, and that's when she got the idea. If she could rent a room to Max, why not rent out two or three of the other rooms? That afternoon she typed up a new sign and took it down to the Piggly Wiggly.

Ida removed the babysitting services sign and posted her new one.

"Room for Rent" it read and stated that the price was $30 a week with meals included.

Before nightfall she had received two calls.

IDA SWEETWATER

I suppose you can tell I don't have much use for Max, and given his history such a feeling is justifiable. Max and Jim had different daddies, and you knew it just by looking at them. Jim's daddy was a carpenter, a man who got up every morning, went to work, and provided for his family, but the Lord called him home when Jim was only five years old.

With Mama Sweetwater being a grieving widow I guess she was easily suckered in, because along came a slick-talking salesman and before she could reconsider what she was doing they were married. He moved in, parked himself in the front parlor, and started calling for her to bring him a cold beer. A year later the poor woman had Max and a husband who'd run off with a waitress from the diner.

An experience like that most likely soured Missus Sweetwater on any further thoughts of marriage, because once Max's daddy was gone she raised both boys by herself. I know that's neither here nor there, but the problem is Max is just like his daddy. He's a man who don't know how to keep his pants zipped. When you meet a man like Max, you've got to keep a sharp eye on what he's up to.

I know you're probably wondering why I'd let a scoundrel like that move in; I know if I was you I'd be wondering.

I could say it's because he's Big Jim's brother and let on like it's a family responsibility, but that would be a flat-outt lie. The truth is having a bad egg is better than having no egg at all. Since Jim's been gone, my ears ache from the sound of quiet. Max is company. He's somebody who I've got to get up and make breakfast for, somebody who's sitting across the table at dinnertime.

I miss Big Jim more than I ever thought humanly possible. If I take a cup from the cupboard, I think about how he liked his coffee. If I put clothes in the washing machine, I start wishing I had one more pair of dirty overalls to wash. But most of all

13

I miss the sound of him playing the television too loud and I think back on how I used to holler for him to turn it down. If I had my Jim back I'd never again say a word about how loud that television was; in fact, I'd sit down alongside of him and watch those football games.

You just never know how much you're gonna miss someone until they're gone. And then it's too damn late to do a thing about it.

The Rosewood Bed

Nine days after Max arrived Ida Sweetwater took in her second boarder. She'd hoped it would be a gentleman, not a forty-six-year-old widow with hair the color of a chili pepper. But when Harriet Chowder came knocking at the door, her face was creased with misery and her eyes rimmed with a color close to that of her hair.

"What am I to do?" Harriet sobbed. Then she told of a son-in-law who was dead set against relatives living in his house. "*His* house," she reiterated. "It's Sue Ellen's house the same as it's his, but did she say a word? No, not a word. The fact that I'm her mother didn't make a bean of difference. Sue Ellen just stood there nodding while Walter, in that snooty way he has of talking to people, said I should find another place to live."

With Harriet teetering on the brink of tears, Ida simply didn't have the heart to turn her away. She did, however, give her the upstairs bedroom, far away from where Max slept; hopefully the distance would be enough to discourage any funny business.

Ida charged Harriet five dollars more than Max but felt justified in that Harriet's room had a new bedspread and a writing desk. Besides, Harriet had not even questioned the amount. Moments after she'd seen the room, Harriet began hauling two large trunks up the stairs and down the long hallway. She made one last trip back to the car and carried in a little transistor radio. Before she'd unpacked her clothes Harriet found a music station that blasted out the golden oldies and started singing along. Every so often the announcer screamed out, "You're at WXRM, all music, all day, every day, so stay tuned!"

On the third day of listening to golden oldies, Ida was about to mention how for the past two nights the music had kept her awake long past her bedtime, but as soon as she said, "I heard the music last night…" Harriet grabbed the conversation and ran away with it.

"Isn't it wonderful?" she gushed. "Such a happy sound. I hear music like that, and I've just got to sing along."

"I've noticed," Ida answered, then said nothing more. Listening to a bit of music seemed a small sacrifice in return for having a regular income.

Other than the music, which was way louder than Big Jim's television, the first few days went quite well. Harriet had nothing but glowing things to say about the room. Her view of the backyard was lovely, such attractive curtains, the meatloaf was one of the best she ever tasted. And, much to Ida's delight, Max made no advances, even though Harriet was a reasonably attractive woman.

Now that she was selling her homemade pies and collecting rent from two boarders, Ida thought she would have enough money to keep Sam Caldwell searching for James. That was, until she received the second bill for his expenses.

"Three hundred and eighty-seven dollars!" Ida gasped. "Isn't that a bit much?" What she meant was that it was exorbitantly high but she held back on saying it because such a statement could sound antagonistic. One thing Ida did not want to do was antagonize Sam Caldwell, especially when he was so close to finding James.

After her conversation with Sam, Ida returned to the table and recalculated her cash flow. That's when she realized she was nowhere near having the amount of money she needed. Since renting rooms was working out so well, the most obvious answer seemed to be to take in a few more boarders. If you had to cook dinner anyway, Ida reasoned, it simply meant you'd set out another plate or two.

That week Ida began to ready the house. She cleaned and polished even the most forgotten corners of rooms that had long gone unused. She scoured yellow grime from the top of the refrigerator, swept away the dust balls at the far back of the closets, and dusted beneath bric-a-brac that hadn't been disturbed in more than a decade.

With the help of a young man who lived three doors down, she made room for a bed in the sitting room and set the burgundy velvet sofa out for the trash man. At one time that sofa was the most beautiful piece of furniture she'd ever seen, but that was forty years ago, before James left home and left a hole in her heart. As she returned to the house Ida glanced back for one last look at the sofa, and for the flicker of a second she saw James jumping up and down on it.

During the night Ida heard the rumble of thunder, and then came the rain. It didn't start as a drizzle but came rushing in like an angry river. Ida thought of the sofa. It was old, not worth much perhaps, but the thought of it sitting out there in the rain pained her heart. She climbed from the bed and stood alongside the window, watching. Remembering the good times. Regretting the bad ones.

The next morning when she awoke, the sofa was gone. There was no trace of it ever having been there.

That afternoon Ida went shopping for a bed. The downtown area of Rose Hill was hardly what one could consider a downtown. It was little more than a scattering of stores that stretched along the last four blocks of Hillmoor Street. For as long as she could remember, Ida had shopped up and down Hillmoor and she knew every store on the street.

That's why she came up short when she saw the carved headboard in the front window of a store that had sat empty for decades.

Two days ago the store was nothing more than a black hole behind soot-covered glass. It had been that way for more than twenty years. Ages ago it housed a silver shop, an elegant place where a dark-eyed young woman sold silver tea sets and bracelets that jangled. It was rumored that the girl was a gypsy and the silver came from the graves of her ancestors, but such rumors are seldom more than old wives' tales. That's what the residents of Rose Hill told one another, until the morning they found the girl with a silver dagger stuck straight through her heart.

After that no one dared rent the store, and it remained empty. Two years later Parker Henry, the thirty-two-year-old owner of the building, suffered a massive heart attack and died. That was enough to convince the residents of Rose Hill that the rumors were true. So the building sat there, an unclaimed eyesore, for decades.

Ida squinted at the bright gold lettering stretched across the front of the store. "Previously Loved Treasures," it read. In the bottom corner of the front window there was a row of tiny letters too small for her to read from where she stood. She crossed the street and walked up to the glass. It was not just clean, it was sparkling, and the words she'd been unable to read from a distance read "Peter P. Pennington, Proprietor." Ida touched her finger to the glass and felt a pulse, a heartbeat almost.

"Oh," she said, and stepped back so quickly she almost stumbled.

A hand reached out and steadied her.

Ida thought she was alone; she'd not seen anyone coming. Yet there he was, standing in back of her lest she topple over. "Where on earth did you come from?" she asked.

The man was small with the slight build of a boy and heavy wire-rimmed glasses. Despite the warmth of the Georgia sun he was wearing a black suit, white dress shirt, and red bow tie.

"I pop up whenever I'm needed," he said and gave a mischievous grin. He extended his hand. "Peter Pennington."

Ida laughed and returned his handshake. "So you're the owner of this store?"

"Yes, ma'am." He nodded proudly.

Ida eyed the front window display. If you looked only at the beaded vest you might think it a clothing store, or the crystal perfume bottle might mean an apothecary, but then there were several other unrelated things and in the window was the carved rosewood headboard, none of it the sort of junk you'd find in a thrift shop.

"What exactly are previously loved treasures?"

Peter Pennington pushed the heavy glasses back onto the bridge of his nose. "They're the things you need, things other people no longer needed."

"How would you know what I need?" Ida said doubtfully.

"I read the need in people's face," he replied. "Right now I can see you're in need of a bed, and you're considering this rosewood beauty in the window."

Ida laughed. "Read the need, indeed. You saw me looking at that bed from across the street."

"That may be," he said, "but you have to admit that I did have the bed here ready and waiting when you were in need of one."

"Oh, I get it." Ida chuckled. "You tell me the bed was special ordered for me, then charge twice what it's worth."

He shook his head side to side. "No, ma'am. That bed is fair-priced at five dollars."

Ida's jaw dropped open. "Five dollars?"

He pushed the glasses back onto his nose a second time and nodded.

"Five dollars is not fair-priced," she said indignantly. "I may not be wealthy, but I'm certainly not looking for charity!"

"And I'm not giving any," Peter replied. "You've got to understand, when people sell previously loved treasures it's not about the money. It's about finding the right home for something they've spent years loving."

The dubious look remained on Ida's face. "Okay, so you charge me five dollars, and I give the bed a good home. Then what? You charge two hundred for delivery?"

"Delivery's free."

"Free?" Ida thought back on how Big Jim always said, *You get what you pay for,* and she searched her mind for what the catch might be but could not find one. Again she clarified the terms. "So this is a one-time payment of five dollars, and you deliver the bed free?"

Peter nodded. "That's the deal, Missus Sweetwater."

"How'd you know my name?"

"I make it my business to know the names of people in town."

Ida could feel a ball of suspicion pushing against her chest, but she was torn between heeding such a warning and wanting the bed. After several more questions, she followed Peter Pennington inside the store, pulled five dollars from her purse, and paid cash for the bed. As she turned to leave, the funny-looking little man said, "I think you might also need a picture for that room."

"Picture?"

"Yes." He reached beneath the counter and pulled out a framed photograph of a young man. "This one."

"Ha. Seems your 'read the need' is no longer working. I have no need of a picture like that."

"Oh, but you do," Pennington assured her. "You just don't know it yet."

Ida laughed so hard her belly bounced. "Well, when I figure out what I need it for, I'll be back," she said and left the store still chuckling.

On the way home Ida again found herself singing along with the radio. Peter P. Pennington was indeed a strange little man, but despite the suspicions picking at her she liked him. And the rosewood bed was every bit as beautiful as the burgundy sofa she had let go.

AND THEN THEY WERE FIVE

L ate in the afternoon a van pulled into Ida Sweetwater's driveway. There was no name on the side of the van, and it was painted a shade of green that made it almost invisible when it rolled to a stop alongside the azalea bushes. With flickers of sun bouncing off the grill, even the letters of the license plate disappeared into nothingness. Peter Pennington stepped out, still wearing his three-piece black suit. When he spotted Ida standing at the door, he announced, "I've come to deliver your bed."

"By yourself?" He was a small man and not one she would have thought capable of lifting a bed of such heft.

Pennington nodded, circled around to the back of the van, and hauled out the rosewood headboard. He carried it as though it was made of nothing more than balsa wood. After setting it down in what was once the sitting room, he returned to the van for the other pieces.

When he came through the door with a mattress wrapped in plastic, obviously fresh from the factory, the first thing that popped into Ida's head was *You get what you pay for.*

"I didn't buy a mattress," she said.

"It's included."

"Included? That mattress is new, never before slept on—it's not a previous loved anything. It's brand new!"

Pennington ignored the comment and circled the bed, making certain the latches were latched and the set up was sturdy. Once he was satisfied that everything was as it should be, he thanked Ida for her business and started to leave. He had one foot out the door when he turned back and said, "I think you need that picture to finish off this room."

Although she was delighted with the beautiful bed, a blunt needle of suspicion still prickled Ida. "No, thanks," she said and closed the door before he had the chance to explain why she needed the picture.

After the van disappeared down the driveway, Ida called three of her neighbors. Not one of them had ever seen or shopped at the Previously Loved Treasures store. Nina Mae, a woman whose husband had grown rich selling used cars with faulty engines, said, "It sounds like that Mister Pennington is up to no good." She advised Ida to make certain her doors and windows were locked when she went to bed for the night.

For three days and nights Ida remained in the house with all of the doors and windows locked tight. On the second day Maxwell went down to the Owl's Nest after dinner, and when he returned hours after midnight he had to pound on the door for a good twenty minutes before Ida answered. When she finally opened the door he was snorting like an angry bull.

"You locked me out!" he steamed.

"I didn't do it intentionally," Ida said. "I was just being cautious."

"Cautious about what?" Without really expecting an answer he started down the hall, listing to the right after his evening of drink.

"Burglars," Ida said to his back. "Burglars and shifty swindlers."

Max stopped and turned around. "Ha. In Rose Hill? Not likely." After that he stumbled into his room and fell asleep still wearing the day's clothes.

The next day Ida drove down to the hardware store and had six keys made. She gave one to Max and one to Harriet Chowder. The remainder would be for new guests when she added them.

After the transformation of the sitting room was complete, Ida stepped back and admired it. The five-dollar rosewood bed was a thing of beauty, making this room by far the nicest in the house. This room had to be for someone special. For this room she would charge forty-five dollars a week.

That same day Ida called the *Chronicle* and placed an ad offering a spacious room with a wood-burning fireplace at forty-five dollars a week, including delicious home-cooked meals and desserts. She'd added desserts thinking it would be easy enough to pop an extra pie or two in the oven.

The first call she received was from a truck driver named Louie Marino. "Friday's my last run," he said. "I'm retiring and looking for a place to settle down."

Ida simply could not picture a gruff-voiced truck driver sleeping in the rosewood bed. "I'm afraid the room advertised is more of a lady's boudoir, but I've other rooms if you're interested."

"The other rooms, they come with the same cooking?"

"Oh, yes," Ida assured him. "A hot home-cooked breakfast and dinner. Lunch is mostly salads and sandwiches."

"The sandwiches ain't those little bitty tea room things, are they?"

"No, sir. I believe in feeding folks proper. You'll never walk away from the table hungry, that's for sure."

"I'll take it," Louie said.

"But you haven't seen the room or asked about the rent—"

"I'm in Pittsburgh today," Louie said, "but I could come by tomorrow night."

By the time Ida hung up the telephone she'd decided that since the cost of rent seemed of little importance to Louie Marino, she would offer him the upstairs bedroom with a connecting bath and charge the same forty-five dollars she planned to charge for the sitting room now dubbed the Rosewood Room.

The second caller was a silky-voiced woman who spoke with the slightest touch of an accent. She introduced herself as Laricka Marie McGuigan Herrman.

"Good gracious," Ida said. "That's a lot of name for one person."

The woman laughed. Not a guffaw, but a soft chuckle that made Ida want to like her. "I know. But I hang on to each of those names because they mean something. My father worked in a Cuban cigar factory and named me after their best cigar. It was called La Ricka, meaning the rich one."

"Oh, so you're a wealthy woman?" For a fleeting moment Ida wondered if forty-five dollars was enough to be asking for rent.

Laricka laughed. "In some things, yes. But when it comes to money, unfortunately no."

The answer put a quick end to Ida's thoughts of higher rent.

That afternoon when Laricka came to look at the room, twin grandsons who appeared to be ten or eleven accompanied her. Although Ida was none too happy with the boys since they constantly poked and jabbed at each other, she was overwhelmingly pleased with Laricka herself. The woman was soft-spoken and pleasant, the type Ida could see as a friend. As Laricka walked around the room oohing and awing at most everything, Ida was already picturing them lingering at the breakfast table long after the others had departed. She could almost hear bits and pieces of conversations about planting flowers, needlepoint patterns, and recipes.

"I love the room," Laricka said wistfully, "and it's so close to my daughter's house…" Her smile slid into a downward slope. "But with being on a limited budget I can only afford forty."

Ida hesitated. It was the most beautiful room in the house, and the bed was almost majestic. It was worth forty-five. She knew she should stick to her guns, but the truth was she had already pictured Laricka sleeping in the rosewood bed. She'd already imagined the conversations they'd have. Letting her walk away would be like losing a friend.

"Okay," she said. "It's a deal."

The next morning Laricka moved in with nine trunks of clothing, a sewing machine, and Bobo, a yappy little dog who nipped at Ida's heels.

"You never mentioned a dog," Ida said.

"I didn't?" Laricka filled the dog's bowl with water and set it on the kitchen floor. "I can't imagine how I forgot a thing like that."

With Bobo's constant yapping, Ida could no longer hear the conversations she thought she'd be having with Laricka. She now wished she'd stuck with her request of forty-five dollars for rent.

By the end of the week Ida had five boarders. Louie moved into the upstairs room with a connecting bath, and the last bedroom she rented to a bachelor dentist who pompously referred to himself as Doctor Payne. Although he was a bit uppity for Ida's liking, he was willing to pay forty dollars for a much smaller room with no fireplace and no private bath. The only bedroom not occupied was the one that belonged to James. Ida had purposely not rented that room.

On Friday Sam Caldwell telephoned Ida with the news that he had a lead on Joelle Williams. "She gave up her apartment and left Nashville with James. The two of them moved to New Orleans and lived together three or four years, but there's no record of them ever being married."

"Living together and not married?" Ida replied. "That doesn't sound like my James."

"We'll know soon enough," Sam said, "because when Joelle Williams moved from New Orleans she left a forwarding address for Cherry Hill, New Jersey."

"Did James move with her?"

"I don't think so. According to the superintendent of the building they lived in, James had been gone for five or six years before she left."

"Well, then, shouldn't you be looking for him instead of this woman?"

"I haven't been able to find anything on him, but I think Joelle may know where he is because they had a kid together."

Ida gasped. "My James has a child?"

"That's what it looks like. The superintendent said the girl was about eight or nine when Joelle moved out."

"This girl," Ida stammered, "she's my granddaughter?"

Sam laughed. "So it would seem." He said he would go to Cherry Hill in the coming week, and there'd be plane fare involved.

"Do whatever you have to do," Ida said, disregarding the ridiculously low balance in her bank account. She knew somehow things would work out. She had a full house now and a successful pie-making business. Things would work out.

On Saturday evening after she'd delivered the week's pies and collected all of the rents, Ida sat down at the table and again calculated her finances. Her earnings came to a total of two hundred and forty-five dollars, which didn't take into account the two dollars for the newspaper ad and the additional groceries she'd been buying. As things now stood she would need to withdraw another two hundred dollars from what had quickly morphed into a very meager savings account.

They were so close to finding James and his family, Ida knew she had to continue. She wrote the check to Sam Caldwell, slid it into the envelope, and began thinking of what else she could possibly sell.

The bits of jewelry she once owned were already gone. The house was comfortably furnished but contained nothing of great value. The car, which was cranky about starting anyway, was worth next to nothing, and if she sold it she'd have no way to get around. Ida began to consider the possibility of doing yet another thing she never thought she would do: take out a mortgage on the house Big Jim had long ago paid for.

If she took in another boarder, she could make it through two more weeks, maybe three. Although she wouldn't rent out the room that belonged to James, she was willing to move into the tiny attic room and rent out the master bedroom she'd shared with Big Jim. And she could reduce the household expenses—turn off lights that weren't being used, cut back on groceries.

Ida sat there late into the night planning menus that would be filling enough and yet inexpensive to make. Meatloaf replaced baked ham on Tuesday's menu, and Wednesday's roast turkey became stuffed peppers. Friday's baked fish became a macaroni and cheese casserole.

After she'd replaced the Sunday morning sausage and cheese omelet with homemade biscuits and gravy, Ida felt she had the makings of a workable plan.

IDA SWEETWATER

*L*ast night when I started to think about mortgaging the house, I half believed Big Jim would send down a lightning bolt to strike some sense into my head. He wasn't in favor of such things, that's for sure.

Jim was a self-made man, and he took a whole lot of pride in not owing anybody anything. *Ida, he used to say, if anything happens to me, you won't have a worry in the world because this house is bought and paid for!*

That's how he was, practical to a fault. Jim never did understand the difference in owning something and having it own you. Because of that he couldn't find it in his heart to forgive our boy for leaving home. He thought James was walking away from the most important thing on earth. And James, well, he was every bit as obstinate, because he believed he was headed toward whatever was most important. The two of them were like telephone poles on opposite sides of the street, and I was the wire stretched between them.

The funny thing is both of them were wrong. What you own or where you go has nothing whatsoever to do with what's really important.

I only wish I could tell Jim how wrong he was. Having this house is like having a fistful of hundred dollar bills in my pocket. Those bills are nothing but bits of paper as long as I hang on to them, but once I start spending them I can buy a whole bunch of happiness. The same is true of the house. An old woman like me doesn't need a big house. Without Jim, all I need is a narrow bed to sleep on and an oven for baking pies.

The truth is I'd give this house and everything I own just to see James and his family. I know, I know, Sam Caldwell said they might not be married, but that doesn't sound like my James. He might be the biggest flirt ever, but he wouldn't be that disrespectful to a woman. For now I'm going to keep right on believing they're married and that little girl is my granddaughter.

Granddaughter. Just saying the word puts happiness in my heart. How can I not believe in something that makes me feel this good?

THE GIRL

On Sunday afternoon Ida moved all of her things from the big bedroom she'd shared with Jim into the attic alcove where there was a narrow single bed, a chest of drawers, and a cord strung from one rafter to the other for hanging clothes.

With the steep staircase she had to stop and rest every four or five steps. It was almost six o'clock when she carried the last of her nightgowns and underwear up the stairs and set the basket down. Before she could catch her breath she heard the hallway clock chiming six gongs.

Minutes later Louie's voice came hollering up the stairwell. "Hey, Ida, there's no supper on the table!"

"I know, I know." Ida came bustling down the stairs as fast as her arthritic hip would allow. "I was busy moving things around, so supper will be a bit late tonight."

"A bit late?" Louie repeated. "It's already late, and I'm hungry."

"I'll bring you a bowl of chips or some pretzels," Ida said as she hurried toward the kitchen, but as she passed the dining room she saw the other four residents already sitting at the dining room table. No dishes, no glasses, no salt and pepper shakers, just four hungry-looking faces staring back at her.

Before Ida got halfway through her feeble excuse, Laricka suggested she could whip up her famous black cake if Ida had any cocoa in the kitchen.

"Cake?" Louie echoed. "I don't want cake. I want meat and potatoes."

"I could do without the potatoes," Harriet said. "A green salad maybe."

"Meat and potatoes!" Louie reiterated. "I signed up for meat and potatoes, and that's what I want."

Doctor Payne stood and held up the palm of his hand. "Just a minute!" he boomed with an air of authority. "The question of the menu is not debatable. The issue here is time." He eyed his wristwatch then glared at Ida. "It is now six-twenty. Dinner was supposed to be served at six, which means it is officially late!"

Louie guffawed, "Hey, Doc, you sure you ain't a brain surgeon?"

Oblivious to the crackle of tension between the two men, Laricka leaned over and whispered loudly, "He said he was a dentist."

"I realize dinner is late," Ida replied patiently, "but it will be ready in twenty minutes." She turned and left before more arguments could erupt.

Doctor Payne stood, checked his watch again, and announced, "That would be precisely six-forty-two, by my watch." He turned and started off.

"Ease up, Doc," Louie said. "There ain't nobody hungrier than me, but dinner's coming. Instead of acting like the Big Ben timekeeper, why don't you stick that watch up—"

Harriet let out a raucaus roll of laughter. "That's telling him, Louie!"

Doctor Payne sneered back at the two of them, then walked off.

"I think he's angry," Laricka said.

Harriett let out another roll of laughter.

Once in the kitchen, Ida realized she had a bigger problem. In the hustle and bustle of moving she'd forgotten to defrost any meat. The hamburger was a solid chunk of ice, and the only piece of meat not frozen was a single pork chop. After shifting things from place to place and searching through the back of the refrigerator, Ida remembered the storm supplies Jim packed away last summer. She pulled the large brown box from the bottom shelf of the pantry and found seven cans of Dinty Moore Beef Stew.

She opened the cans, emptied them into a baking dish, and popped it into the oven.

In what could be considered record time, she mixed a salad, set out a basket of biscuits, and put dinner on the table.

Louie spooned a large helping onto his plate, but before he lifted the first bite to his mouth Laricka joined hands with Doctor Payne and Harriet and began the mealtime prayer.

"Father God," she said, "please bless this food and this house and all who enter, and those who do not have—"

"Speed it up," Louie grumbled. "I'm hungry."

Although Laricka usually included a long list of those in need of blessing, she ended with a quick "Amen."

Louie shoveled up several bites of stew then looked over at Ida. "You sure can cook. This stew was worth waiting for."

Ida smiled and said nothing. Late that night she gathered the Dinty Moore cans she'd hidden under the sink and carried them to the outside garbage can. From that day forward she was careful to plan ahead, and even on the busiest days when Ida baked pies supper was on the table at the dot of six.

After the bedroom she had shared with Big Jim was cleaned and polished, Ida ran a second ad in the *Chronicle*. By week's end she had rented the room to Wilbur Washington, a retired lawyer with silver hair and a soft-spoken manner. He moved into the master bedroom with a single suitcase, a shopping bag filled with books, and a grey cat named Miss Abby.

On the first evening of Wilbur's residence, Ida was about to set a bowl of string beans on the table when she caught the image of his face from the corner of her eye. For a fleeting moment she could see Big Jim sitting there. It wasn't so much Wilbur's features but something in his mannerisms, the gentle tone of his voice, even the way he would stretch out a long arm and fetch the salt shaker for Laricka who sat next to him.

The days of the weeks that followed rushed by and left little time for worry. Every morning Ida got up before six and had breakfast on the table by seven. After the six residents had eaten and the dishes were cleared away, Ida began making pies. But even as her hands flew from task to task, she pictured James and his family. Although the years told her that James would be a man well into his fifties, in her mind he remained young. The wife, Joelle, was faceless. The granddaughter, she imagined as a bouncy teenager who would bring new life to the tired old house.

"Grandma," Ida muttered every so often, trying on the name for size. It fit perfectly.

Oddly enough she did not hear from Sam Caldwell at all that week, and she also did not receive a bill for his services. Ida simply assumed he was in Cherry Hill tracking down James and his family, which was all well and good with her.

On Sunday evening Sam Caldwell telephoned. "I've put together a report on my findings. Would it be okay if I stop by tomorrow morning to go over it with you?"

Ida had waited thirty years, and another day seemed too much to bear. "Did you find James?"

"I'll give you all the details tomorrow," Caldwell replied.

"Why can't you just tell me now?" Ida asked, but instead of giving a reason, Caldwell just said he'd be there at eight the next morning and hung up.

That night sleep was impossible for Ida. She was too hot with the blanket on and too cold with it off. The pillow seemed lumpy, and the ticking of the bedside clock became a troublesome distraction. After listening to the tick, tick, tick for more than an hour, she wrapped the clock in a flannel nightgown and stuffed it into the bottom drawer of the chest.

Even with the clock gone, Ida twisted and turned. There were brief moments when she could imagine Caldwell had found James. Not just James, but his entire family. When that happened the warmth of happiness settled over her but it was always short-lived, for the fear of truth followed close behind. It came, clamped an icy claw around her throat, and screamed in her ear.

Ida kept asking herself if Caldwell found James and his family, why didn't he say so? Why didn't he simply say where they were and how much she owed him? It was never a good thing when someone was hesitant to present their bill. *You get what you pay for.*

She thought back on Big Jim's last visit with Doctor Morgenstern. That day the doctor Jim had gone to for more than fifty years hung an X-ray on the wall and explained how he would refer Jim to an oncologist. When they got ready to leave the office, Jim pulled out his wallet. Doctor Morgenstern shook his head and said, "No charge." It was the only time Ida ever remembered such a thing happening.

When worry and apprehension rose from her stomach into her throat and threatened to choke off her breath, Ida climbed out of bed and went to the kitchen. Before dawn she'd baked two peach pies plus the mincemeat she'd planned to add to her merchandise offering in the fall.

At seven o'clock the residents came for breakfast. Ida had a box of Cheerios, a box of corn flakes, a gallon jug of milk, and a peach pie on the table. "Help yourself," she said, then turned and went back into the kitchen.

"Where's the coffee?" Louie said, but by then Ida was gone.

As the others began to eat, Wilbur rose and headed toward the kitchen. He found Ida standing in front of the sink with a stream of tears running down her face.

"Do you want to talk about it?" he asked.

Strangely enough he used the same words Jim would have used. Ida turned and fell into his arms sobbing.

"I know something is wrong," she said. "Something horrible." She poured out the story of James leaving and Sam Caldwell's search for the boy.

"Maybe it's too early to start crying," Wilbur said. "You haven't even heard what this Mister Caldwell has to say."

"If it was good news," Ida sniffled, "he'd have come right out and said it. So if it's not something good, it's got to be something bad."

"Not necessarily," Wilbur replied. "A whole lot of life falls between good and bad."

"That's true," Ida conceded.

"Of course it is," Wilbur said. "Getting married and having babies, that's good. But all the in-between days of washing diapers, cleaning house, getting out of bed, and going to work, they're neither good nor bad, they're just life."

Ida gave one last sniffle and nodded.

Once she'd stopped crying, Wilbur volunteered to clean up the breakfast dishes and suggested she go freshen up before Mister Caldwell arrived.

At five minutes after eight the doorbell rang, and when Ida opened the door Sam Caldwell stood there with the same blank face he always wore, not happy, not sad, not telling anything. "Morning."

Ida invited Sam in and called for Wilbur to join them as she led the way to the dining room. The three of them sat at the corner end of the table.

"I've got good news and not-so-good news," Caldwell said.

Wilbur slid his chair a bit closer to Ida's and reached for her hand. "Why don't you start with the good news?"

Caldwell fumbled through his briefcase, pulled out a sheaf of papers, and laid it on the table. Paper-clipped to the folder was an invoice for eight hundred and forty-seven dollars.

Ida smiled. *You get what you pay for.*

"Starting at the beginning," Caldwell said, "James met Joelle Williams when he was working at a club in Nashville. While he was in Nashville he was living at her place, and when he left for New Orleans she went with him. There's no record of them ever being married, but they did have a child together and the girl was given the Sweetwater name."

"James didn't marry the child's mother?" Ida asked, her disappointment apparent.

Caldwell shook his head. "It doesn't appear so. He stayed with Joelle for almost five years, then took off. The woman who lived upstairs from them at the time said he claimed to have a job in Mexico, but there's no proof of it."

"But he came back, didn't he?"

Caldwell shook his head again. "Afraid not. Joelle raised the child herself."

"Oh, dear Lord," Ida murmured.

"Were you able to locate Missus Sweetwater's son or this Joelle?" Wilbur asked.

"There's no further trace of James. I was able to follow him out to California and ultimately into Mexico, but after that there's nothing. Mexico's a place where a person who wants to get lost can do so easily."

Wilbur nodded knowingly.

Sam hesitated a moment, then continued. "Joelle remained in New Orleans for another five years. After that, she and the girl moved to Cherry Hill. She remained there until her death in nineteen eighty. Once the mother was gone, the daughter moved to Philadelphia."

"Were you able to find the daughter?" Wilbur asked.

Caldwell nodded. "Her name is Caroline Jean Sweetwater. She's single, got a job as a copy editor at *Back Roads and Byways*, and living with Greg Markey, the features editor."

"Caroline Jean," Ida repeated. "Jean is my middle name," she added wistfully.

"From what I've been able to ascertain Caroline barely remembers her father. I doubt that she has any idea of where he went or where he might now be, but if you'd like to talk with her——"

"Well, of course I want to talk with her, she's my granddaughter!"

Wilbur let go of Ida's hand, and she reached for the folder Sam Caldwell offered. Inside there was an address, telephone number, and five photographs of Caroline coming and going from the *Back Roads and Byways* office building. The profile beneath the pictures said Caroline Jean Sweetwater was twenty-eight years old, never married.

A tear fell from Ida's eye. "Caroline's older than James when he left home. Imagine me having a grandbaby all these years and never having the joy of knowing it."

"It's never too late to start," Wilbur said.

"That's true." Ida nodded, but in the back of her mind she wondered if there was still a chance she would one day find James. She tried to tell herself she no longer cared, not after his selfish ways had robbed her of a grandchild. But the sad truth is that a mother's love never dies; it forgives and forgives and then forgives again.

With a heavy heart Ida began to envision all the things she had missed. She tried to see the young woman in the picture as a baby and then a toddler. She tried to hear the sound of the child's first word, see the courage in her first steps, feel the apprehension in her first day of school. But all those things were gone. Gone forever. Caroline was a woman now. A single woman living with a man, making decisions Ida wished she could have influenced.

Although Ida said very little in her heart she decided that although she had failed James, she would not fail Caroline. She had little other than love to give, but sometimes love was all a person needed.

In Philadelphia

Caroline Sweetwater was sitting at her computer when the telephone rang, and, believing it was Greg, she purposely ignored it. Earlier that morning before he left for work he'd asked her to write an article, which was already overdue. An article that would carry his byline.

"I won't have time," she answered. "I'm working on my novel today."

Greg rolled his eyes in that condescending way he'd mastered. "You're gonna blow me off for that piece of trash?"

Trying not to hear the ugliness in his tone, Caroline replied, "To you it's trash. To me it's a love story."

"It can wait," Greg argued. "This article has to be on Tom's desk tomorrow morning."

"Then write it yourself," Caroline answered flatly.

Of course such a statement angered Greg to no end. He flew into a rage, ranting about her ingratitude after all he'd done for her, and how he could no longer love someone with such an attitude. When pleas and threats failed to change her answer, he angrily slammed his fist against the wall and stormed out.

Such a scene was nothing new. It had happened countless times before; different days, different projects, but always the same bitter accusations and demands. For three years Caroline had written most of the articles appearing under Greg's byline. Early on he'd promised that in time she would have her own column, but it never happened. When he moved into the corner office she remained in a cubicle, proofreading, editing, and writing his words.

It started innocently enough. Four years ago he'd asked for her opinion on the Hampshire Inn article he'd written, and she'd made a number of suggestions.

"Great ideas," he'd said, flashed a smile that was irresistible, and invited her to dinner to show his appreciation. One dinner led to several more, and when Greg lost his lease a year later he moved into Caroline's studio apartment.

"This is just short-term," he promised, "because with two of us, we're going to need a larger place."

Caroline, who by then had fallen madly in love with Greg, imagined that come Christmas he'd be slipping an engagement ring on her finger. Instead she received a pair of pearl earrings. She moved her expectation of a ring ahead to April. But when her birthday arrived, he gave her a computer he'd bought at a discount.

By then Greg had begun to find various reasons to stay late at the office. There was always a last-minute conference call with the West Coast affiliate, or a strategy meeting, or a dinner with an important advertiser. During those empty evenings Caroline started something she had long wanted to do: she began writing a novel. At first it was little more than a title page, but in time it grew and blossomed into a love story. And if you looked closely and read between the lines, it was easy enough to see it was the love story she hoped to be living.

Caroline would close her eyes and see the story unfold; then she'd transform her vision into magical words that fairly danced across the page. She and Greg became the fictional Claire and Matthew. But, unlike Greg, Matthew was madly in love with Claire.

While Greg found other things to do, Caroline spent evenings pouring her heart into page after page of the novel she'd titled *Someday*. The lonely weeks turned into months, and the months became years. In time a wall rose up between Caroline and Greg. Bricks of resentment, thoughtlessness, and anger were laid one on top of another until the wall reached a point where hope could no longer slide through the cracks.

But even the most hopeless love doesn't disappear like a shadow in darkness. It clings to you and hangs on with every last thread of possibility until one day you see the ugly truth of what it is: something that never really was. When that finally happened, it was too late. The ill-tempered and vengeful Greg was Caroline's boss. For her there was no longer an easy way out.

When the telephone rang a second time, Caroline grabbed the pillow and covered the phone to muffle the sound. When a softer ring came from beneath the pillow, she moaned, "Go away," and covered her ears. The answering machine finally clicked on and the caller hung up. Obviously Greg.

Caroline buried her face in her hands. Every ounce of common sense screamed let this be the end of it, but there was a pinprick of possibility poking through her resolve. She thought back to a week earlier when they'd fought over precisely the same thing. She'd refused to write his article on the Delaware Water Gap, and Greg had stormed out saying he'd not be back, ever. But he did come back. He came back with flowers and a feeble apology. He'd kissed her mouth and held her close until she crumbled.

"I wouldn't ask if I weren't in a bind," he said, "but this is the last time, I promise."

Caroline had remained at the computer until two in the morning finishing that article. In the morning he'd scooped up the pages and dashed out the door with little more than a peck on the cheek.

Before a half-hour had passed, the telephone began ringing again. Caroline threw Greg's leather jacket over the pillow, and the ring became little more than a soft buzz. She knew what would happen if she answered the phone: he'd say he was sorry, tell her how much he loved her, and ask if she'd meet him at some little out-of-the-way restaurant so they could talk. When the telephone finally stopped ringing, Caroline gathered her resolve, pulled Greg's suitcase from the closet, and began packing his clothes. "Not this time," she sobbed. "Not this time."

The telephone continued to ring off and on for most of the day; still Caroline refused to answer it. Shortly after nine she heard a key in the door. Greg.

He came in obviously tipsy and carrying a bouquet of flowers that had already started to wilt. "I'm sorry," he said and offered the flowers. "It's the stress of the job. It makes me crazy."

Caroline did not turn to look at him.

"You know what it's like. Deadline after deadline. My life is hell. If I didn't have you—"

"You don't have me," she said crisply. "I'm through."

"Through with what?"

"You." She motioned to the suitcase standing in the hall. "Take your stuff and get out."

"You're kidding."

The words stabbed at Caroline's heart, but her expression remained flat. "I'm not kidding. Go."

"No way!" he shouted. "I paid half the rent, and I'm staying." He suddenly sounded a bit more sober. "Okay, you're mad, I get it. But we'll work this out. By tomorrow——" Greg lifted the suitcase onto a chair and began unpacking his clothes.

"Please don't do this, Greg," she said. "Our relationship is not working. I need to get on with my life. You don't care a thing about me——"

He turned and looked at her. "That's not true. I do care about you."

Caroline heard the words, but this time she also heard the truth behind them. *He cares about me, but he doesn't love me.*

Without saying another word, she turned away. Tomorrow she would go in search of a new job and a new apartment. Even as that thought ran through her mind, a nagging voice whispered, *But if he says he loves you? What will you do then?*

IDA SWEETWATER

I didn't get twenty minutes worth of sleep last night. *I just couldn't stop thinking about how I've got a granddaughter I never knew existed. A number of times I squeezed my eyes shut and tried picturing sheep jumping over a fence. Counting sheep is supposed to make a person sleepy, but it doesn't really work. Not if you've got something more important on your mind. I'd get to three or four sheep, then I'd go back to thinking about Caroline again. I was imagining her smile and her laugh, and I was wishing she'd have that same happy-go-lucky laugh James had.*

Yesterday I tried calling her twelve different times, but all I got was an answering machine. It would be downright impossible to tell a machine the things I've got to say. Wilbur suggested I ought to leave my name and number with a message for her to call back, but I was afraid to do it. What if she's already decided she wants nothing to do with her daddy's family? If she feels that way she might not bother calling back. I can't take that chance.

James is still my son, and I can't find it in my heart not to love the boy, but I surely am ashamed of the way he treated his family. If he loved that Joelle enough to be living with her, he ought to have loved her enough to marry her and introduce her to his family. I can't begin to imagine the hardships the poor woman went through because of James. Married or not, if I'd have known about Joelle all those years ago I would have invited her to come live with us, no questions asked. And knowing the kind heart Big Jim had, I think he would have agreed. He might have been angry with James, but Jim wasn't the type to take it out on others.

I'm going to keep right on calling Caroline. Sooner or later she'll have to answer. When she does, I'll tell her how sorry I am about what James did. I'll say that wasn't the way his daddy and I brought the boy up. Hopefully she'll understand and be forgiving.

With me being right there on the telephone, I think she'll at least give me the courtesy of listening. It's a lot harder to hang up on a real person than on a machine.

THE TELEPHONE CALL

Monday morning Greg Markey was in the foulest of moods, and it got worse when Caroline told him she was not going to work.

"I've a terrible headache," she said, "and I'd be useless anyway."

"I need you to write that article," he replied. "I'll take you to breakfast on the way; then you'll feel better."

"I don't think so," Caroline answered and looked away.

To allow Greg to reach out and pull her in again would be the undoing of her resolve. He had that power. His eyes made promises he had no intention of keeping, and the sweet words he spoke left a bitter aftertaste.

Were it possible, Caroline would have made a clean break, ripped herself free of him like the quick yank of a Band-Aid from tender skin. But after three years of being together their lives were braided in a tangle that could only be undone one strand at a time. Today she would start unwinding the strands.

As soon as Greg was gone, Caroline hurried to the corner newsstand and bought the *Philadelphia Inquirer*. Returning to the apartment, she poured a cup of coffee, sat at the table, and turned to the "Help Wanted" section. By nine-thirty she had circled three ads that looked promising.

The first listing was for a marketing manager in a sporting goods store. It wasn't something Caroline had experience in, but she felt she could do the job. Unfortunately, the store manager had other thoughts.

"I won't even consider someone without at least three years of sporting goods experience," he said.

Caroline moved on to the second listing, copywriter at the Palmer Ad Agency. A young woman answered, and Caroline quickly launched into an overview of her qualifications.

"Wow," the girl said, "you sound perfect for the job."

"Would you like me to come in for an interview?" Caroline replied.

"Oh, I'm not the one doing the hiring, that's Mister Sorenson. He's out right now. I could have him give you a call when he gets back."

"That would be great," Caroline said, then rattled off her telephone number.

On the third listing there was no company name, just a job description and telephone number. A machine answered. "If you are calling in reference to the editorial position, please leave your name and telephone number. We will get back to you."

"Good morning," Caroline said to the recording. "My name is Caroline Sweetwater, and I've had more than four years' experience writing for—" A shrill beep interrupted her words and signaled the end of the message. She redialed the number and hurriedly left her name and telephone number.

Shortly after ten the telephone sounded, and Caroline grabbed it on the first ring. Using a tone she hoped would sound professional, she said, "Caroline Sweetwater here."

There was a moment of silence; then Ida gave a deep sigh. "Caroline Sweetwater," she drawled. "Lord have mercy, I never dreamed—"

"Beg your pardon?"

"You've got nothing to be pardoned for," Ida said. "It's your daddy's doing. I don't hold you one bit responsible, not one bit."

"Responsible for what?" Caroline asked. "Who is this?'

Ida chuckled. "I'm your grandma."

Caroline gasped. "My what?"

"Your grandma," Ida said. "Your daddy's mama."

"You must be mistaken," Caroline replied tersely. "I don't know that my daddy had family. Anyway, I haven't seen or heard from him in almost twenty-five years."

"I know," Ida said sadly. "I haven't heard from him for over thirty." She continued with the story of how James left home and after a few postcards that first year they hadn't heard from him again.

"That sounds like Daddy," Caroline replied. The disdain in her voice was obvious.

"You've got every right to be angry with him," Ida replied. "I'm angry with him myself. If I had James here I'd sure—"

"Well, if you're expecting me to tell you where Daddy is, I can't help you."

"Oh no," Ida said. "That's not why I'm calling."

"Then why are you calling?"

"Because I'd like to get to know you," Ida said. She wanted to say, "Because I'm hoping you'll come and live with me, let me love you the way I would have loved your daddy if he'd have let me," but she heeded the wariness in Caroline's voice.

"Missus Sweetwater, I'm real sorry that Daddy did you as he did, but I honestly don't know where he is. He disappeared without—"

"I know," Ida cut in. "I paid good money for a private investigator to go looking for James. I know he can't be found, but I'm happy Mister Caldwell found you."

Caroline laughed. "I'm not that hard to find."

"Thank the Lord." Ida sighed.

"It's sweet of you to say that," Caroline replied, "but the sorry truth is you don't know a thing about me, and I don't know a thing about you."

"I know," Ida replied sadly. "And I'm to blame. I should've hired Mister Caldwell years ago. I waited too long, that's the problem."

"Well, I don't know that I'd say—"

"Yes, indeed, it's my fault!" Ida said emphatically. "When James stomped out the door I should have insisted Big Jim go after him, but I didn't." The years of regret made her words seem weighted and heavy. "You never want to believe a person is what they are, so I kept telling myself James would come home. I sure never figured him for one to abandon his family."

"Neither did Mama." Caroline's voice was tinged with resentment.

"I know," Ida said. "The investigator who found you told me about your poor mama. All those years." She sighed again. "If only I'd known…"

"I doubt there's much you could have done," Caroline said. "Mama was crazy in love with Daddy. No matter how much dirt he dumped on her, she'd forgive him. She hated New Orleans but stayed there 'cause she kept thinking he'd come back."

Even though Ida's heart already knew the answer, she asked, "Did James ever send money? A letter maybe?"

"Are you kidding?"

"Not even a telephone call?"

"Nothing. The last we heard from Daddy was the day he walked away."

A whoosh of disappointment gushed through the telephone line.

As they spoke Caroline found herself talking about things she hadn't spoken of for years, not since her mama's death. "Living in New Orleans was almost worse than dying," she said. "Mama cried all the time, and the place stank of tears, sweat, and whiskey. In the summertime there wasn't a breath of air in that apartment, and sweat dripped off my face even if I was standing still. 'Please, Mama,' I used to beg, 'let's move to New Jersey so we can be close by Aunt Pauline.' Mama was just as miserable as me, but she wouldn't move. She kept right on believing Daddy was gonna take a turn for the good and come running home to save us."

"James is my boy," Ida said sadly, "but I'm mighty ashamed of him. It's not right for a man to treat a woman such a way. "

"It sure isn't," Caroline answered, thinking also of Greg.

The minutes turned into hours as they continued to talk, Caroline asking about James and Ida asking about Joelle. You might think it would be strained or unusual, but that's not at all the way it was. Shortly after she finished telling a story about the year Big Jim built a scarecrow to keep watch on the five stalks of corn he'd planted in the side yard, Ida asked if Caroline would consider coming to live in Rose Hill.

"Live in Georgia?" Caroline stammered.

"I know it's sudden," Ida said, "but I'm getting on in years and there's no telling how much time I've got left." She paused, then added, "You'd like it here, I know you would."

"I'm sure I would," Caroline answered politely. "But I've got a job and…" As the words slipped from her mouth, thoughts of what she really had in Philadelphia settled in her head. She had a job she was on the verge of leaving and a boyfriend who was unfaithful. It wasn't all that much to stay for.

"Rose Hill's a real nice town," Ida said. "I've got a big house, and I make the best peach pie you've ever stuck a tooth in."

The thought of leaving blossomed like a flower in Caroline's mind. Having a grandmother was like having warm soup on a cold day; it was being loved instead of being used. Her voice turned mellow. "This is kind of sudden, are you sure? You've never even met—"

Ida laughed. "I don't need to have met you. I already love you."

"You do?"

"Of course I do. You're my granddaughter, my own flesh and blood."

Although she had not yet said yes Caroline found herself nodding in agreement with sentiments the new grandma offered, and she mellowed at the mention of things like home-baked pies and crocheted doilies.

When Ida asked again if she would come to Rose Hill Caroline stumbled over a few feeble excuses about her job and the apartment, but as she listened to her words they had a familiar sound. "I can't leave because…"

She recognized the voice. Perhaps it was those remembrances of New Orleans or maybe it was her recollection of a daddy whistling as he walked off leaving her mama behind, but Caroline suddenly envisioned herself wearing her mama's shoes. She knew that if she stayed she would, in time, forgive Greg and they'd go back to the same life. He'd lean on her to do the work he should have done, and he'd come home late smelling of perfume and alcohol. Years from now she would be her mama, a woman used up and left behind.

Caroline closed her eyes and tried to imagine herself driving south on Route 95. A silken cord was tied to the back of the car, and as she started to move the cord grew taut. For a few moments it stretched like a giant rubber band and threatened to pull her back, but when she pressed hard on the accelerator the car sped up and the cord snapped. It was the final tie to a love that never was.

Breaking free is never easy. There are no baby steps in walking away. There is only one gigantic leap. You take it or you remain forever rooted to a life of unhappiness.

Caroline took a deep breath and made the leap. "I can be ready to leave this Wednesday."

CAROLINE SWEETWATER

I *can't believe I'm actually doing this. Me, a girl who's never been particularly*
adventurous, leaving home to live with a woman I've never even met. Of course
I have questions, I'd be crazy if I didn't.

But strange as it may be, the truth is I feel good about doing it. I like myself better
than I have in a very long time. Maybe it is irresponsible to just up and leave, but I
like having a grandma and I feel that for once in my life I'm doing what I want to do.
It's funny, I talked to Missus Sweetwater for a few hours but in that short time she
made me feel better about myself than Greg ever did, and I've been living with him for
almost three years.

On second thought, it's not so funny. It's actually quite sad.

I told Missus Sweetwater about the novel I'm writing, and do you know what she
said? I'm proud of you honey, *that's what she said, and I could tell she really*
meant it. You know what Greg said about my novel? He said it was trash. Of course,
he's so insensitive he wouldn't know a love story if it rose up and smacked him in the
face!

At first I thought I was giving up everything, but thinking about Mama
and the misery she had I realized I wasn't giving up anything. This apartment
is no more mine than Greg is, and as far as a career goes mine's laughable. For the
past three years I've been telling myself that one of these days Greg is going to want to
marry me, but it's never going to happen. He's not going to propose, and he's not going
to make me a columnist. He can't. Greg has to keep me small so he can be big; how
sick is that?

I can't say for sure if Ida Sweetwater is my real grandma or not, but I'm choosing
to believe she is. Why else would she want me to come there and live with her? It's not
like I have a lot to offer.

I'm not telling Greg I'm leaving, and I'm not telling him about Grandma

Sweetwater either. I'll leave a note on the table and by the time he gets home Wednesday night, I'll probably be somewhere in South Carolina.

Once I get to Georgia I'll have plenty of time to finish my novel, and hopefully I'll sell it to a big publisher for a million bucks. If that happens, I think I'll send Greg a copy with a sticky note that says, So now how do you like those apples?

THE BED AND THE BEAR

By the time Ida hung up the telephone, she was already thinking through plans for Caroline's arrival. The only unoccupied room in the house was the one awaiting James' return and while it was once the most vibrant room in the house, it was now nothing more than a worn-out reminder. A room darkened with the weariness of waiting and deafened by the sound of silence. It needed to come alive again.

Forgetting the arthritic hip that ached from the too-steep stairs, she hurried up the steps and flung open the door to the closed-up room. It was exactly as James had left it thirty years ago. Through the years the magazines on the floor had yellowed with age, and the curtains, now weighted with decades of dust, hung limp.

Ida could no longer remember the last time she'd stepped inside this room. It had been ten, maybe twenty years. After James disappeared she could not bring herself to move one thing, not even the worn sneakers hanging from the bedpost. With everything left untouched the room was a shrine of sorts, a place where she had gone to sit and breathe in the scent of him being there. The sheets on the bed remained unwashed, and a scattering of laundry still remained on the floor of the closet.

Decades ago Ida closed the door to the room and put her thoughts of it in a memory box that was too painful to open. She moved through the years, not thinking of the room and not allowing herself to step inside and reopen the box of memories. And now, oddly enough, the room was not at all the way she'd remembered it.

In one fell swoop Ida snatched the coverlet from the bed. She spread it on the floor and began to toss in all the things that should have been thrown out ages ago. Sheets, pillowcases, old clothes, gym shorts—one by one they landed in the center of the coverlet. When the closet and all the drawers had been emptied, she gathered the four corners of the coverlet together and hauled it down the staircase one step at a time. Thump. Thump. Thump.

Hearing the commotion, Wilbur poked his head out into the hall. "You need help?"

"No, thanks, I'm doing fine." Ida thumped down another step.

"Wait a minute!" Wilbur hollered. "I'm coming."

"I told you I don't need help."

"I heard what you said. The thing is you do need help, you're just too stubborn to ask for it." Without another word of argument he squeezed past her and grabbed the other end of the coverlet. "Go on now, I've got this end."

When they got to the bottom of the staircase, Ida opened the front door and they hauled the coverlet to the curb. Since it was way too big to fit in the garbage can, Wilbur tied the four corners together and closed the bundle.

As they started back to the house, Wilbur said, "You got another new boarder coming?"

Ida gave a wide grin and a nod. "I sure do. My granddaughter."

"So you got hold of her, huh?" Wilbur replied. He looked almost as happy as Ida.

Once the room was emptied out, Ida began thinking about how she'd decorate it. The rosewood bed would have been perfect, but, of course, it was now sitting in Laricka's room. If Laricka were a woman with a single suitcase Ida might ask her to switch beds, or maybe even switch rooms, but with all those trunks...

Thinking of the rosewood bed made Ida remember the Previously Loved Treasures shop. Peter Pennington said he'd have whatever she needed. *Okay,* Ida mused, *Let's see if you can come up with another beautiful bed, Mister Pennington.*

Ida looked forward to returning to the shop. Although she had only been there once it held a strange fascination, a kind of magic calling her back. It wasn't a fancy store, but stepping inside was like losing yourself in a dream. It was something she wanted to share with a friend, so she called Roberta Maslowski.

"Remember that Previously Loved Treasures shop I told you about?" Ida asked.

"I remember," Roberta said, "but I've never been there."

"Well, I'm going back today. Want to come along?"

"I've promised to watch my grandbabies today, but if you was to go tomorrow…"

"It's got to be today," Ida said. "I need a few things for my granddaughter's room."

Roberta had been friends with Ida for forty years, and this was the first mention she'd ever heard of a grandchild. "What granddaughter?"

Ida told her the full story of Sam Caldwell's search and finding James's daughter. "She'll be here on Friday, and the room has to be perfect."

"Well, I've got a perfectly good bunk bed if you need it."

"Bunk bed? Why, that's used furniture! I need something special for Caroline."

They spoke for a few moments longer then hung up. Roberta was left wondering what exactly the difference was between a used furniture bed and a previously loved bed.

Ida called two more friends, but Deb Vaughan had to work and Ilene Goldberg had a bridge game. In a last-ditch effort to find someone to come along, she asked Laricka.

"So sorry," Laricka replied, "but today is my day with the boys."

The boys, Ida knew, were Laricka's two noisy grandsons who banged in and out of the front door a dozen times a day. "Can't you skip seeing them for one afternoon?"

"No, no, no," Laricka replied. "Children grow up too quickly. Miss one day of being with them, and by the next day something's changed." She told Ida of a time five years back when she'd missed seeing the boys, and it turned out to be the very day one of the lads lost his first tooth. "I've never forgiven myself for missing that," she said with a sigh.

"Okay." Ida shrugged; then she walked off. Laricka's comment had struck a nerve and resurrected thoughts of all the things she herself had missed, all the days of being together that could never be recaptured. At that point, Ida was no longer interested in having company. She climbed into her car and drove cross-town alone.

Peter Pennington stood in front of the store, almost as if he was expecting her. "Welcome, welcome," he said and took her hand in his.

As they walked into the store, Ida said, "I'm hoping you have another beautiful bed."

Peter stopped, turned, and looked at her with an expression of puzzlement. "Bed? You don't need a bed, you need a lace coverlet and a lamp."

While it was true that she'd need a new coverlet, Ida replied, "I do so need a bed."

Peter shook his head. "The four-poster you have is fine. All it needs is a coat of polish."

Ida's mouth dropped open. "How did you know…" Before Peter could answer she shouted, "Roberta! Roberta Maslowski told you, didn't she?"

"No one told me." Peter gave a mischievous grin. "As I've said before, I have a gift for understanding what customers need and don't need."

"So you're an expert on what people need?" Ida said facetiously.

"Actually, yes. People often confuse wanting and needing. It's my job to make that distinction. When a person says I need this, that, or the other thing, they honestly believe if they get what they're asking for they'll be happy."

Ida, a practical woman not easily tricked, found herself drawn into the conversation. "And are they?"

"Once in a while," Peter said, "but more often than not they simply move on to wishing for something else."

"Well, you may be right about other people," Ida replied, "but I really do need a bed. My granddaughter is coming to live with—"

"I know," Peter interrupted. "But once it's polished the four-poster will look fine, and she'll appreciate that it was her father's."

Ida crinkled her nose and began thinking. There was a possibility Peter could be right. Maybe the bed could give Caroline back a tiny piece of her daddy. Maybe it would—

While she thought it over, Peter said, "There's no maybe about it."

Having him give voice to her thoughts was a bit scary. "Are you some kind of magician? A mind reader, maybe?"

Another mischievous grin and a shake of the head. Peter reassured Ida that what she needed was a lace coverlet, which he happened to have. While Ida stood there wondering how he came by such information, Peter grabbed his bright yellow stepstool and reached for a number of things on the higher shelves. In less than five minutes he'd gathered them into a grouping that he placed on the counter.

"How's this?" he asked.

The lace coverlet was one of the most beautiful Ida had ever seen, and the silk pillow with its threaded tassels was the ideal complement. The globe lamp was delicate and feminine, a far cry from the old lamp with a broken switch. But the teddy bear was something she didn't understand.

"I guess you don't know everything," she said to Peter. "My granddaughter's twenty-eight years old."

"I know," Peter replied, "but I'll bet she had a bear just like this when she was a child."

Ida gave a big hearty chuckle. "And you're going to tell me it will bring back good memories, right?"

Peter came back with a shrug that suggested it couldn't hurt to try.

Ida bought almost everything Peter offered, but she again said no to the young man's picture. "I've no place to hang it."

"Seems to me it would be perfect above the bed," Peter replied.

Ida again shook her head. "This time you're wrong. It's not something I need."

Before Ida left she found a snow globe that played "Silent Night" and bought it for herself. She had always longed to see a snowy Christmas, but in southern Georgia such a thing almost never happened.

As she gathered up her things to leave, Peter suggested he could deliver them. "That room also needs to be painted," he said. "I'm thinking a pale lavender." He promised to pick up the paint and stop by later in the afternoon.

When Peter Pennington arrived at the house it was four in the afternoon, and he was still wearing that same black suit.

"Afternoon," he nodded. Then without any direction he walked up the stairs and set the brown bag and a can of paint in what was to be Caroline's room. "Nice," he said. "Very nice." He pushed open the window, removed his suit jacket, and rolled up his sleeves.

Ida, who followed behind with the crocheted coverlet, asked, "What are you doing?"

"I'd think it rather obvious," he replied and pried off the lid of the paint can.

"I can't afford to have you——"

"No charge," he said and continued working. He unfolded a long handle and attached it to the end of a roller he'd pulled from the bag. As he started pouring paint into the tray, he turned to Ida. "I'd love a glass of milk and a slice of that peach pie you're baking."

"Well, of course," she said and hurried down the stairs. She wasn't gone long, perhaps long enough for him to have a single wall half-done, certainly not more than that, but when she returned Peter had finished painting the entire room and he'd already slid most of the furniture back in place. She gasped. "How on earth..."

"Mmm, that pie looks good," Peter said and took it from Ida's hand.

She turned to take in all he'd done, and when she turned back the pie was gone and the milk glass empty.

"This is just marvelous," Ida said. "I don't know how to thank you."

"That delicious pie was thanks enough," Peter answered. By then he was back to wearing the black jacket. As he headed down the stairs Ida noticed that there was not a single splash of lavender paint splattered on it. "Unbelievable," she said.

After supper that evening, as everyone lingered over coffee and peach pie, Ida told the story of what happened.

"He did it in twenty minutes, maybe less," she said, "and without getting a drop of paint on anything but the walls."

"Yeah, sure." Louie laughed. "And nobody but you saw this Peter Pennington, right?" He gave another loud guffaw.

"No one else was here," Ida explained. "I was going to introduce Peter and looked for y'all, but there was not a soul around. Honestly."

"Well," Laricka sighed, "If I'd have known ahead of time, maybe...but I'd promised the boys I'd treat them to a movie."

Louie guffawed even more loudly. "Don't ya get it? She's pulling our leg. My bet is she had a painter here all day."

"No," Ida argued. "It's the truth." But she might as well have saved her breath, because the more she protested the louder they all laughed.

When everyone rose from table and headed to their rooms, Wilbur stayed behind. "How about I give you a hand with these dishes?" he said, and before she could answer no he was on his way to the kitchen with a stack of dirty dessert plates.

Ida followed behind balancing four mugs and a handful of silverware.

She washed, Wilbur dried. When Ida finished the last of the cups, she turned to him and asked, "You believe my story, don't you?"

Wilbur gave a gentle smile. "If you ask me to, I will."

TRAVELING SOUTH

On Wednesday morning thirty minutes after Greg left the apartment, Caroline loaded two suitcases and her computer into the trunk of the car and headed crosstown. Ever since he stopped coming home for dinner and started finding fault with most everything, she'd thought about leaving him. But it was a thought she was afraid to move past. She imagined the emptiness of a life with no one and pictured her heart so heavy it would have the weight of a bowling ball in her chest.

Oddly enough, that wasn't the way it was.

Caroline felt lighter than she could ever remember. Lighter than when she ran through the streets of New Orleans, lighter than when she spent long months caring for her mother, and much lighter than when she pretended not to notice the cloyingly sweet perfume that clung to Greg when he came home late.

She didn't just feel lighter, she *was* lighter. She'd rid herself of the things that made the days seem dreary and the nights seem long. Gone was the apartment with its windowless walls and empty bed. Gone was the thankless job with no future. Gone was the man she once thought she couldn't live without.

When the afternoon mail arrived, letters would be dropped on each person's desk. Short letters that said for personal reasons she found it necessary to leave town. She'd given no mention of where she was headed but stuck to succinct paragraphs stating that she was resigning the job, giving up the apartment, and leaving the man who in truth had left her a year earlier. Although the letter to Greg was longer than the others, she left many things unsaid. She'd thought about the words for a long time and in the end decided that detailing each and every heartache would pain her more than it would him. It would be twisting the knife he'd stuck in her heart.

She snapped on the radio and eased into the line of cars headed south on Route 95. The traffic was sluggish going through Philadelphia, but once the skyline faded into the distance she picked up speed.

As she crossed into Delaware Caroline tried to picture the woman who would be her grandma, but there was nothing. She could barely remember her daddy; how could she possibly know what his mama would look like? Caroline thought about the conversation with Ida Sweetwater and remembered the sweetness of the woman's voice. *My son James is your daddy,* she'd said. Not maybe or perhaps, but with certainty. The call had come at a time when Caroline was feeling alone and empty, and she'd rushed into believing such a thing could be true...but what if it wasn't? What if she got there and Ida Sweetwater asked for proof that James was her daddy?

The only thing she had was one small black-and-white photo taken with the man who'd been her daddy. Her mama claimed the picture was taken the Easter Sunday before he left, but couldn't say for sure. Caroline had smiled when the picture was snapped, but the man standing next to her did not. He wore a brimmed hat that shaded his eyes, but you could see the sense of annoyance tugging on his expression. Was it something she'd done? Was it because of her he'd left? A thousand times Caroline had pushed deep into her memory trying to recall that day, but she couldn't.

My son is your daddy, Ida Sweetwater said. She'd claimed it openly and laid an offer of love on the table. Caroline accepted it without question. The issue of whether the rebellious son who left Ida and the angry man who left her mama were one and the same was of no significance. Ida Sweetwater was now her grandma, and despite any questions or misgivings that lingered in her thoughts, Caroline had decided she would be the granddaughter Ida wanted.

As she drove through Maryland, hunger pangs poked at Caroline's stomach. She continued driving for a while longer, then exited and went in search of a place to eat. Three miles from the highway she found a roadside stand with outdoor tables. She pulled in and parked the car.

Before she'd taken two steps, a brown dog darted from behind the garbage cans and ran to her wagging his tail. "Well, hello there," she said and squatted to pet him.

The dog lapped her arm.

As Caroline ran her hand along his back, she felt the protruding rib bones. "Aw, poor baby," she said. "You look like you could use a meal. Where's your mama?"

The dog seemed to understand—whether it was the words or simply the act of kindness there was no way of knowing—but he stood on his hind legs and nuzzled into her neck. "Well, now, aren't you just the sweetest thing," Caroline cooed. She played with the dog for a few minutes, then stood and walked toward the building. The dog followed along. As she entered the restaurant, he squeezed through the door behind her.

The guy behind the counter looked up. "Hey! You can't bring your dog in here!"

"He's not my dog," Caroline answered.

"I don't care whose dog he is, he ain't allowed in here!"

Caroline looked toward the couple sitting in the back booth. "Is this your dog?"

The man and woman both shook their heads.

The only people in the restaurant were Caroline, the counterman, and the couple. She looked back to the counterman. "Well, then, who does the dog belong—"

"I don't know or care!" the counterman snapped. "He came in with you, so get him out!"

"Okay, okay," Caroline answered. She turned back to the door, and the dog followed. She pushed it open and pointed a finger. "Out."

The dog lowered his head and started toward the door. He stopped halfway through and looked back at Caroline.

"Go on," she said, trying to sound firm. Once the dog was outside, she stepped to the counter and ordered an egg sandwich and coffee to go. A moment later she added, "Also, give me a hamburger and a cup of water."

"The half-pounder or the quarter-pounder?"

"Half-pounder," she answered. "No pickles."

The dog was waiting at the door when she left. "Come on, scruffy," Caroline said, "I bought you lunch."

Before she ate her food, Caroline unwrapped the hamburger. Afraid a dog that hadn't eaten in a while would get sick on a big meal, she broke it into bite-size pieces and slowly hand-fed them to him. When the hamburger was gone, she set the cup of water on the ground. The dog lapped the water then curled up at her feet, not sleeping, but attaching himself to her.

Earlier in the day Caroline had been in a hurry—a hurry to get going, a hurry to move beyond Philadelphia, a hurry to get to Georgia. But now, like the dog, she was content to sit and let the sun warm her back. When she finished her meal she bent to pet the dog. His fur was matted in spots, and he had the smell of day-old rain. She felt for a collar, but there was none. No collar. No tag. "You poor baby," she murmured and continued to pet him.

The dog nuzzled closer.

After almost two hours, Caroline stood and scuffed the dog's head one last time. "I'm sorry, sweetie, but I've got to get going." She dropped the lunch wrappings in the garbage can and started toward her car. The dog followed.

"You can't come with me," Caroline said sadly. "I'm sure you've got an owner who's going to be looking for you."

The dog whined.

"I don't even have a place of my own," she explained. "How can I give you a home when I don't have one?"

The dog sat back on his haunches and raised his front paws.

"Oh, sweetie," Caroline said, "you're begging, aren't you?"

The dog gave a short yap and held the position.

"But I don't have a home to give you," she reiterated.

The dog remained in position.

Twice Caroline turned toward her car, and twice she turned back. Each time the dog was still begging. She opened the car door and turned back one last time. The dog was still begging. "Oh, all right." She laughed. "Come on."

The dog darted across the lot and jumped into the car.

As Caroline pulled back onto the highway, she glanced at her new friend. "If we're going to be traveling together, I suppose I should give you a name." She drove for miles trying out names like Max, Fido, Buster, and even Scruffy. Nothing was right. Like her, the dog was getting a new start and he needed the right name. She was passing through Richmond when it came to her clear as day.

"Clarence!" she exclaimed.

Caroline was a firm believer in Providence. Just when she'd begun to feel low the dog had come along, an angel of some sort, scruffy perhaps, but a sure sign she was headed for a wonderful life.

When she crossed into South Carolina they stopped for the night. After they'd scarfed down another round of hamburgers, Caroline found a K-Mart and spent twenty-six eighty-one on dog supplies. That evening they showered together, and afterward she spent nearly two hours combing the tangles from his fur. That night they slept in the bed together, and, unlike Greg, Clarence pressed his body close against hers.

CAROLINE

I *never had a dog before and never really wanted one, but now that I've got Clarence it makes me realize what I've been missing. He isn't the cutest dog that ever lived, but he's sweet as pie. Last night when he was leaning up against my thigh, I started wondering what kind of person would run off and leave a sweet dog like this. After a long while, I figured it out. Whoever left Clarence there with nothing to eat and no place to go is probably a lot like my daddy.*

The truth is you're better off without people like that, whether you're a kid or a dog. In life there's good people and bad people. Mama wasn't either one, she was just plain unlucky. She used to say, "Caroline, if I hadn't met your daddy, I could've lived my life a happy woman." She said it in a sort of joking way, but I think it was probably true. Once in a while Mama would forget missing Daddy and she'd be happy as a kid. It didn't happen all that often, and when it did it didn't last very long. We'd be joking and having a good time, then she'd spot some little thing that reminded her of Daddy and slide right back inside her misery.

The difference between Clarence and Mama is that he got treated badly then bounced back, but Mama, she never bounced back. The best you could hope for was a hop, skip, and a jump every now and again.

I've only known Clarence for a day, but already he's my best friend. You know why? Because me and that dog are equals. I feel like he's as glad to be with me as I am with him. It wasn't that way with Greg.

Given the fondness we've got for each other I can't see myself getting rid of Clarence, so I sure hope Missus Sweetwater doesn't have a dislike of dogs.

I'm saying Missus Sweetwater, because the thought of having a grandma hasn't settled in my head yet. I keep wondering about that first moment, when she opens the door and sees me standing there. Do I say, Hi, Grandma, *or* Good afternoon, Missus Sweetwater?

Maybe she'll be the first to speak; then I can just go along with whatever she says.

THE ARRIVAL

Wednesday night sleep was impossible for Ida to come by. The excitement of having a granddaughter made her heart flutter with anticipation. It brought the kind of happiness that wiggled in the tips of her fingers and made her feet feel like dancing. At times it almost took her breath away. When she closed her eyes, instead of drifting off she started picturing all the things she and Caroline would do together: leisurely lunches on the back porch, long conversations and shared dreams. She could already envision the girl peeling apples for a pie as she rolled the dough.

Ida had created her own image of Caroline. It was a softened version of James, his dark hair and eyes, his happy-go-lucky laugh, his charm—yes, the girl would definitely have his charm. *This old house will come alive again*, Ida told herself, and she believed it.

Were she to look at the situation through other eyes, Ida might have noticed that the house was already alive. It overflowed with people who had developed a fondness for one another, and on any given evening you could hear the laughter circling the dining room table from miles away.

In the wee hours of the morning Ida began to think through the list of things that needed to be done. It had all been taken care of. The bedroom where James once slept was now transformed. It was bright, cheerful, and styled for a young woman. Peter Pennington was right; the room didn't need a new bed.

Ida breathed a sigh of relief. She was definitely prepared. If Caroline arrived early she'd serve a lovely lunch of stewed peaches and sliced ham.

And if she didn't get there until suppertime, it would be the most festive meal imaginable. Ida had laundered the Irish linen tablecloth and napkins, even though they'd never once been used. She folded the napkins into triangles and with a hot iron pressed them flat. As she thought through her checklist, Ida could almost smell the sizzle of the roast beef she'd cook. And for dessert she'd made her specialty: a three-layer chocolate cake with frosting so rich a single bite could carry a person to utopia.

After she'd reviewed the checklist for the ninth time Ida closed her eyes, but seconds later the thought came to her: What if Caroline didn't like chocolate? What if she was a vegetarian? Ida bolted up and climbed out of bed. Trying to make as little noise as possible, she hurried down to the kitchen and started mixing up a carrot cake. Before she put it in the oven, a sleepy-eyed Wilbur stumbled into the room.

"What's all the noise about?" he asked.

"I got to thinking," Ida said, then explained her fears.

"Nonsense," Wilbur replied. "If she doesn't like chocolate, give her a slice of that wonderful peach pie you served at supper."

"Serve leftovers to my granddaughter?" Ida said incredulously.

"That pie's not just leftovers, it's the best peach pie I've ever tasted."

Ida slid the carrot cake into the oven and turned back. "And what if she's a vegetarian?"

"Ida," Wilbur said, chuckling, "you worry about the most foolish things. Caroline coming here has nothing to do with the food. She's coming because she wants to be with you."

Wilbur poured himself a glass of milk and stood watching Ida bustle across the kitchen. "This Caroline's a lucky girl," he said. Then he drained the glass and returned to his room.

It was almost dawn when Ida climbed back into bed. She'd baked and frosted a carrot cake and prepared a casserole of creamy potatoes and vegetables. Now she was prepared for anything—so she thought.

Most mornings Ida woke when the first rays of light filtered through the blinds, but then most nights she was sound asleep by ten o'clock. On Thursday when the sun rose, Ida didn't. She was sound asleep and having the loveliest dream, a dream in which she walked hand in hand with Big Jim and shared the sweet kisses they'd shared in their youth. It was the kind of dream from which no one wants to awake.

It was after eight o'clock when Louie hollered up the stairs, "Hey, Ida, there's no breakfast!" He called out three times with no response. Finally Harriett Chowder, who couldn't start the day without a cigarette and a strong cup of coffee, volunteered to go rap on Ida's door.

Twice Harriet gave a soft knock on the door, but there was no response. The third time she banged hard with her fist and yelled, "Wake up, I need coffee!"

Ida woke with a start. Casting one sleepy-eye at the bedside clock, she saw it was twenty minutes until nine. "Good grief!" she shouted and jumped out of bed. Pulling on a robe and slippers, she hurried downstairs.

The first thing Ida did was set a pot of coffee on to brew. Then she pulled the eggs and bacon from the refrigerator. Eggs and bacon took time to make, but she had no choice. A week ago she'd tried setting out a breakfast of cereal but there'd been a considerable amount of grumbling, especially from Louie.

"This ain't hot," he'd said. "I signed up for hot, and that's what I'm expecting."

It was the last time she'd given them cereal.

Ida scrambled the eggs and pulled out a large frying pan. She glanced at the clock and tried to hurry. It was almost nine; there was no telling what time Caroline would arrive and she needed time to dress.

Ida poured the eggs into the skillet, then stretched out slices of bacon on the griddle. She was scooping the pile of eggs onto a platter when Laricka walked into the kitchen.

"I thought maybe I'd lend a hand," she suggested. "I know you're saving that fancy chocolate cake for dinner, but if you've got any cocoa I can whip up one of my black cakes in no time at all."

Louie, with his uncanny ability to zero in on anything food-related, heard the comment. "I don't want cake! I want eggs and biscuits!"

"Oh, dear," Ida murmured, "I've forgotten about the biscuits."

By the time Ida got breakfast on the table, fed Bobo and Miss Abby, then cleaned up the dishes it was twenty after ten. She had just gone upstairs to dress when the doorbell rang.

"I'll get it," Max called out. When he opened the door, a lovely young lady stood there.

"Well, hellooooo," Max crooned.

Expecting Ida and having not been warned about the other residents, an astonished Caroline asked, "Who are you?"

"Max Sweetwater," he said, relaxing his body into a lumpy looking swagger. "I live here."

"Live here?" Having heard only the Sweetwater in his name, Caroline blurted out the first thought that came to mind. "Granddaddy?"

"I am most certainly not your granddaddy!" Max replied indignantly. Having an eye for the ladies as he did, he was tempted to tell her he was way too young to be her granddaddy but settled for saying, "I'm a boarder."

"A boarder?"

"Yes," Max nodded. "A paying boarder who contributes generously to the financial well-being of this homestead."

Still a bit confused, Caroline asked, "Isn't this Ida Sweetwater's house?"

Before he could answer, Ida came flip-flopping down the staircase in her housecoat and slippers. "Get away from my granddaughter, Max!" she yelled as she scuttled across the foyer. Pushing Max aside, she reached out and folded Caroline into her arms.

"Grandma?" Caroline mumbled, but by then Ida had her squished up against an ample bosom that left little space for words.

After several minutes of near suffocation, Ida released Caroline and held her at arm's length. "Happy as I am to see you, you're not what I was expecting."

An icy cold shiver slid down Caroline's back.

"Outside of those brown eyes," Ida said, "you don't look a thing like your daddy." She hesitated a moment then added, "Your mama must have been a beautiful woman."

"She was." The words were tentative, riddled with fear. Was Missus Sweetwater going to say *Nice to see you, stay a day or two, then be on your way?* "I'm sorry if I'm a disappointment," Caroline said, but before she could go any further Ida interrupted.

"Disappointment?" Ida gave a chuckle that filled the foyer with happiness. "Shoot, honey, you're no disappointment. You're what I've been praying for all these years."

"Besides having red hair like Mama," Caroline said, "there's something else you ought to know. I've got Clarence with me."

"Clarence? Is he that fellow you've been—"

It was Caroline's turn to laugh. "Clarence is my dog."

"Well, if that's don't beat all." Ida chuckled again. "A dog named Clarence."

Although less than an hour had gone by since Ida finished cleaning up the breakfast dishes, she happily announced they'd be having an early lunch. "After driving all the way from Pennsylvania, Caroline needs some hot food and rest!" She jangled the bell that announced mealtime, and people began emerging from their rooms.

"Oh, my gosh," Caroline whispered. "Are all these people boarders?"

"They all live here," Ida replied, "but I don't think of them as boarders. They're more like resident friends."

One by one Ida introduced them to her granddaughter, and they settled around the table. When Max plopped down in the chair next to Caroline, Ida suggested he move to the other side of the table.

"Laricka's sitting here," she said.

"Gimme a break," Max grumbled. He gave Ida a slant-eyed look then moved.

Although Ida had planned a simple lunch of sliced ham and peaches, her happiness carried her away and lunch became grander than a Thanksgiving dinner. Once she'd discovered that Caroline did indeed love chocolate and was not a vegetarian, she brought out the carrot cake and creamy potato casserole alongside the ham, peaches, coleslaw, and biscuits.

The residents had never before seen such a luncheon. Louie filled his plate three times and then decided he had just enough room for another slice of that delicious carrot cake. While everyone heaped on second and third helpings, Caroline told them of herself: her days in New Orleans, the move to Cherry Hill, and then to Philadelphia. She gave voice to the good memories. The time she and Joelle went to the Mardi Gras parade, the Easter James gave her a giant chocolate bunny, the first Christmas she celebrated with Greg.

"So where is your young man?" Laricka asked.

"Oh, we've parted ways."

Laricka's eyes grew round and big. "After living together?"

Caroline nodded, but before she was forced to explain her grandma came to the rescue.

"Enough about him," Ida said. "Did you know Caroline is writing a novel?"

Doctor Payne raised his eyebrows and nodded. "Now, that really is impressive."

"I like novels," Harriet volunteered. "Mostly detective stories and trashy stuff."

"I doubt that you'd like mine." Caroline laughed. "It's a love story."

"Love story?" Max echoed. "Well, if you need any help with research—"

Ida looked across with a frown that silenced anything else Max had in mind.

After lunch they all settled in the parlor. For Caroline it would have been the living room, but for Ida it always was and always would be the parlor. "Sit here," she said, guiding Caroline to the high-backed leather chair. "It used to be your granddaddy's favorite spot. He'd sit there to read the evening paper, and before he was halfway through he'd fall fast asleep."

"I know the feeling." Wilbur laughed.

One story led to another; then mid-way through the afternoon Ida disappeared up the stairs and returned with a stack of family albums. Page by page Caroline saw her daddy change from a baby to a child and ultimately to a young man. He was not yet twenty when the last picture was taken, younger than her by nearly a decade. In that picture there was no brimmed hat. His face was bathed in sunlight and his smile bright, eager looking almost. It was the same person but not the daddy she had known. There was no anger, no bitterness.

Caroline studied the picture and wondered what had changed him. Was it her? Was he simply not ready to be a father? She could still hear Joelle's voice telling of the good times they'd had in their early years together. What changed?

Caroline looked up at Ida. "I know it's asking a lot, but I would love to have this picture."

"It's yours." Ida pulled the picture from its corner mounts and handed it to her.

"Thank you, Grandma." The word fell from Caroline's lips easily, not at all forced or awkward as she thought it might be.

CAROLINE

*L*ooking at those pictures was fun, in a strange sort of way. It was like a story of the world before I was born. In the picture of Daddy's christening Grandma looks younger than me, and Big Jim has a puffed out chest like he's the proudest man on earth. You could sense how in love they were and how much they loved that baby. Looking at the picture made me feel sort of sad. Not sad they were happy, just sad I wasn't part of those good times.

I don't remember one day of Mama and Daddy being happy together. I'm sure there was a time when they were happy and in love, but somewhere along the line whatever love they had fell by the wayside and meanness slipped through the door. I can't say who was at fault, and the sorry thing is I doubt either of them could either.

Seeing Daddy smiling as he did in those pictures makes me think he wasn't at all the way I remember. In Grandma's photographs he looked like life was a party and he was going to be the first one there. I wish I could have known him back then. The only time I remember Daddy being real happy was the day he left. He was wearing a big smile when he turned around and waved to me one last time. After that he just kept walking.

Mama started crying before Daddy was out the door, and she kept right on crying 'till the day she died. Whatever happiness Mama once had most likely left town with Daddy. Being she was so crazy in love with him, I've got to believe they met when he was that happy-go-lucky guy in Grandma's pictures.

I think back on all those years when it was just me and Mama, and I can't help but wonder if maybe she was once a smiling-faced, happy-go-lucky person too.

I don't know much about Daddy because he was gone for most of my life. But the saddest part is I never got to know much about Mama either, because after Daddy left she closed up like a clam and quit living.

SETTLING IN...

It was after six o'clock when they closed the last picture album and Caroline heaved a great sigh. For as far back as she could remember her daddy had been little more than a shadowy figure in the background of life, a tall man with a brimmed hat that shaded his eyes. But as Ida moved through the pictures and retold stories of James in his youth, he became flesh and blood. In her mind's eye Caroline could see him young, vigorous, and driven by wanderlust.

"James always wanted to travel," Ida said. "He made a list of places he was one day gonna see."

"What places?" Caroline asked.

"Australia was one of them. He used to say it was a wide-open land made for adventurers like him." Ida gave a soft chuckle. "Of course, he said the same thing about China and Paris, France."

"Did he ever go?"

Ida shrugged. "I hope so. I'd hate to think he had all those dreams and didn't chase after any of them."

"Mama told me when Daddy left he was headed to Mexico."

"So I've heard," Ida answered. She tried to remember if Mexico was one of the places James planned to visit. She could picture the list but it was blurry in spots, vague and unyielding.

When the clock sounded seven loud gongs Ida jumped up. "Oh, my gosh, I've forgotten about supper. Louie is going to be furious." She pointed a finger toward the hallway and asked Caroline to go rap on Louie's door. "Tell him dinner's going to be a bit late. Say it will be ready by seven-thirty."

Caroline knocked twice before Louie woke and stumbled to the door. When she delivered the message, he rubbed his eyes and glanced down at his watch.

"I think I'll pass on dinner," he said. "I'm still full from lunch."

"Okay," she answered and turned to leave, but before she was halfway down the hall he called out.

"I suppose I could do with a sandwich or two of that sliced ham."

As it turned out none of the residents were very hungry, so Ida returned the roast beef to the refrigerator and simply set out two platters with the makings of sandwiches. With there being little interest in the food, a lively conversation bounced back and forth across the table. The main topic of discussion was Caroline's novel.

"Being a novelist is an admirable profession," Doctor Payne said. "It's not like being a doctor, but it's certainly admirable."

Louie seldom missed an opportunity to trim the pompous Payne down to size and piped up. "You wasn't never a doctor, you was a dentist!" A snicker hung onto the word "dentist."

"Dentists are doctors," Wilbur replied. "It's just a different doctoral degree."

"Hardy-har-har," Louie chuckled. "No matter what you call a mule, he's still a jackass." He had a few more comments on the tip of his tongue, but when Louie saw the look Ida gave him he went back to talking about Caroline's novel. "So, you got an agent for this book, or a publisher maybe?"

"Not yet," she answered, then explained the book was only three-quarters finished. "I've got my computer with me, and I'm hoping to complete it while I'm here."

Ida raised a hand to her forehead. "Oh, no. I thought I had everything ready, but I've forgotten to put a desk in your room!"

"That's no problem," Caroline replied. "I can work on the kitchen table."

Of course Ida would not hear of it. "I know of a wonderful little shop that has anything and everything a person could want. Tomorrow morning we'll take a drive over and pick out a lovely desk for your room."

Although Caroline insisted such a thing was not necessary, Ida's mind was made up.

It was after nine when Ida finally suggested Caroline get settled in her room.

"Sounds good," Caroline said and called for Clarence to come along.

Ida went first, taking the stairs one at a time and pausing to catch her breath after each step. Caroline followed and Clarence padded behind. When Ida opened the door to the room, Caroline peered in. "Oh, Grandma, it's beautiful!"

"It used to be your daddy's room." Ida's words were threaded with a mixture of joy and sadness. "Of course it looked a lot different then."

Caroline lifted the worn teddy bear off the bed. "Was this Daddy's?"

Ida teetered on the edge of truth for a moment, then decided there was no harm in a small lie that could bring happiness. She nodded. "Yes, indeed, and I know James would want you to have Teddy."

"Teddy," Caroline repeated wistfully.

She then turned, wrapped her arms around Ida, and whispered, "Thank you, Grandma."

That's when Ida knew she had done the right thing.

That night Clarence again climbed into bed with Caroline and pressed his back against her thigh. After they'd settled into place, she reached for the nightstand to turn off the light. Teddy sat alongside the lamp, and Caroline could almost swear the bear was smiling. That smile was the last thing she saw before the room went dark.

The next morning a soft rap on the door awakened Caroline. When she opened the door, Ida stood there with a steaming mug of coffee.

"Breakfast will be ready in about twenty minutes," she said, "but I thought you might like an eye-opener first." She handed the mug to Caroline then disappeared back down the stairs.

"But wait," Caroline called, "don't you need help fixing—"

"Nope," Ida answered as she crossed to the hallway and disappeared from sight.

It was early March, and while the afternoons were becoming warm there was still a chill in the morning air. Caroline dressed in jeans and a light sweater then hurried downstairs. She had no sooner slid into a chair when Ida came from the kitchen with a large platter of scrambled eggs and sausage links. That was followed by baskets piled high with homemade biscuits and pieces of honeydew melon cut into tiny squares.

The platters were passed around the table and everyone, including the bone-thin Harriet, shoveled a good-sized portion onto their plate. Louie scooped up twice as much as the others. "Nothing like a good hot breakfast," he said and passed the platter to Wilbur.

When everyone finished eating there was not even a stain left on the platters and only one biscuit left in the basket. As Ida began stacking the dirty dishes, Caroline joined in. "They sure are a hungry bunch," she whispered.

"That they are," Ida replied, "but it's mighty nice having them." She told Caroline how Big Jim's sickness had depleted their bank account.

"The only thing of value I had left was this big old house, so I started renting out rooms. Max was first." She turned to Caroline. "Did you know he's your granddaddy's baby brother?"

Caroline shook her head. "Up until a few days ago, I didn't know I had any family."

"Well, you sure do now." Ida smiled. "You've got me, and I still think one of these days your daddy is gonna come walking through that door hollering he's back home."

"That would be nice," Caroline said, "but I'm not holding out a lot of hope."

"You never know." Ida grinned. "You just never know."

Caroline had to admit that was true. If an unknown grandma could come from out of nowhere, it was possible her daddy would one day come home.

As Ida washed the dishes, Caroline dried them and breathed in the smell of sausage and biscuits that lingered in the air. "You sure are a wonderful cook."

Ida gave a big hearty laugh. "Shoot, honey, this's nothing but down home cooking. Anybody can do it."

"Not me," Caroline replied. "I wouldn't know where to start."

"Didn't you cook for your young man?"

"Hardly ever. He wasn't home much, and when he was we generally got take-out."

"Take-out?" Ida repeated. "Like pizza?"

"Unh-huh. Pizza, fried chicken, Chinese. Stuff like that."

"Well, if that don't beat all," Ida said.

"It's not because I'm not willing," Caroline said. "I just never learned how."

"Your mama didn't teach you?"

"Mama?" Caroline giggled. "Why, she couldn't boil a pot of water."

Although she said nothing more, Caroline began to wonder if maybe it was the endless dinners of pizza and canned soup that drove her daddy to leave.

THE DESK

That afternoon Ida climbed into the passenger seat of Caroline's Toyota, and they went in search of a desk. "We'll start at Previously Loved Treasures," Ida said, "because Peter Pennington always has exactly what you need." Although she was careful not to mention the teddy bear, she told of finding the rosewood bed and the new lamp for Caroline's room. "Peter not only seems to know when you're coming, he also knows what you're looking for."

"I doubt that he *knows*." Caroline laughed. "It's probably just a good guess."

"It's not a guess," Ida replied. "He knows."

Caroline laughed again.

A few seconds later Ida waggled her finger and pointed to the storefront a few doors down. "There it is."

When they pulled up in front of the store Peter Pennington stood alongside the door, just as he'd been on Ida's previous visits. He looked exactly as she'd described him. Thin, elfin almost, with thick round glasses perched on the bridge of his nose. Caroline would have considered him bird-like, were it not for the black suit he wore. The dark heavy fabric seemed to anchor him to the earth.

When the engine rumbled to a halt, Peter walked to the curb and opened the passenger door on Ida's side of the car. He bent and leaned toward her.

"I thought you'd be coming in today," he said.

"Hello, Peter," Ida replied. She turned and gave Caroline a sly wink. "See." She nodded confidently.

"And this must be your lovely granddaughter." Peter smiled.

Caroline laughed. "Yes, and I suppose some magical power told you that."

"No," he answered. "Your grandma did. She was in last week getting a few things for your room." With a mischievous twinkle in his eye, he said, "And now I'm guessing that you're back to pick out a desk?"

Caroline looked at Ida. "Did you tell him about the desk?"

Ida shook her head.

"Your grandma's been bragging about how you're going to be a famous author," Peter explained. "So it stands to reason a writer would need a desk."

"Oh, okay."

The logical explanation settled comfortably in Caroline's head but not in Ida's. Yes, she'd told Peter that Caroline was coming to live with her, but she couldn't recall mentioning her granddaughter writing a book. While Ida stood there trying to remember, Caroline followed Peter to the back of the store.

"I've got exactly what you need," he said and pushed aside a standing mirror blocking the way.

Behind the mirror sat a small wooden desk. It was old, scratched in a number of places, and missing a knob on the bottom drawer.

"I know it's not much to look at," Peter said, "but it's perfect for your needs."

Ida, who'd followed behind, peered around the mirror. "It's not very fancy. Don't you have something a bit nicer?"

Peter shook his head. He got ready to explain the desk was exactly what they needed but didn't have to. Caroline had already taken a liking to it.

"I love it," she said. "It looks so sturdy, like it's been around for a hundred years and could be around for a hundred more." She walked to the desk, slid several of the drawers out and back again. "How much is it?"

"Seventeen dollars."

Ida gasped. "Seventeen dollars! That beautiful rosewood bed was only five dollars, and it came with a brand new mattress!"

"Yes," Peter replied, "but this desk comes with stories."

"Stories?" Caroline echoed.

Peter nodded. Although there was no one else in the store, he leaned in close and whispered, "This desk once belonged to Samuel Clemens."

Caroline's eyes grew big and round. "Really?"

Before anyone could say anything more Ida scowled. "Poppycock! This is nothing but an old desk that's overpriced."

"Not true," Peter replied. "This desk is filled with stories. You can't see them, but I'll bet your granddaughter can."

Caroline laughed. "I doubt Mister Clemens left any untold stories in this desk, but it is just right for my needs." She pulled the wallet from her purse. "I'll take it."

"Overpriced," Ida repeated.

Before they left the store Peter promised to deliver the desk that very afternoon. "Delivery's free," he said. "And I'll include a few more things you'll need."

"A few more things?" Caroline asked.

"Yes," Peter nodded. "A desk blotter, a ceramic jar for pencils—"

"A seventeen-dollar desk ought to include a chair," Ida muttered.

In addition to knowing what a person needed, Peter also had excellent hearing. He turned to Ida. "Okay, I'll include a chair."

"Free?"

"Yes."

Ida gave a smile of satisfaction. As they left the store she leaned close to her granddaughter and whispered, "Honey, you've got to learn how to negotiate."

True to his word, Peter did deliver the desk that afternoon. He arrived in the same green van still wearing the same black suit. He pulled the desk from the van, hoisted it on his back, and carried it up the stairs as if it were nothing more than a sweater draped over his shoulders.

"Wait, I'll help you," Caroline offered, but Ida assured her that Peter Pennington was a lot stronger than he looked.

"He brought that big rosewood bed in by himself," she whispered.

After he'd set the desk in place Peter returned to the van and carried in a chair. A high-backed desk chair such as Caroline had never seen. The leather was soft as a glove, and in addition to the wheels that would make it easy to slide in and out it had an overstuffed lumbar pillow.

Still smarting from what she felt was too high a price, Ida smiled.

"Well, now, this is more like it."

Before Peter Pennington was back in his van Caroline had unpacked her computer and placed it atop the desk. She powered up the computer and opened the file for her novel. It was still there, waiting for her to finish it. But it was a love story, a story of passion and shared dreams. She scrolled down to the last few pages she'd written and sat there looking at the final paragraph

He took her in his arms and begged forgiveness. "I've been a fool," Matthew said. "Take me back, Claire, and I'll spend the rest of my life making you happy." With that he scooped Claire into his arms and caressed her with an abundance of passion. The heartache she had endured for so long was forgotten when he touched his lips to hers.

The words on the screen now seemed trite, unrealistic. Love didn't simply repair itself in a single act of contrition. It clung to anger and pushed bitter resentment into every word. Obviously the story needed work. Men like Matthew were nothing more than fairytale princes. He needed a few flaws. And Claire—poor, gullible Claire. She would have to see life as it was; she would have to be rewritten with more determination and grit.

Caroline leaned back into the chair and stared at the screen for a few moments longer. Then she closed the file and logged off the computer. Tomorrow she would start rewriting the story, rewriting it with truth woven through the words. But for tonight she would simply enjoy being here.

Bounding down the stairs, Caroline called out, "Grandma, need some help fixing dinner?"

IDA SWEETWATER

I had to laugh when Caroline came in asking if she could help with dinner. The poor child doesn't know a skillet from a stew pot. Not that it's her fault; she just never had anyone to teach her those things. Cooking is something you learn from your mama, and from what I can gather Caroline's mama didn't do any.

And as far as James is concerned, Joelle not cooking doesn't justify his behavior. The two of them were a pitiful excuse for parents, if you ask me.

Right is right, and what they did wasn't right. Regardless of what they were feeling about each other, they had a child they should've been thinking about.

I can't give back the years Caroline lost with a no-good daddy and a mama full of self-pity, but I can make the future better. I'll make sure she's got a good home and plenty of love.

It may take a bit of work, but I'm going to teach her to cook. At least I'll try.

When I think back on all the years I blamed Big Jim for what happened with James, I feel real sorry. I thought Jim was being too strict on the boy, but I can see now he wasn't strict enough. I guess Jim saw a selfish streak in James that I wasn't willing to see. I was like most mamas: blind to my child's faults.

I hope Jim and God can both forgive me.

Where There's A Will...

Ida began with letting Caroline set the table. "Knife on the right, fork on the left," she explained. But at breakfast the next morning a spoon was included, and Caroline came running back for further instructions.

During the week that followed Caroline boiled spaghetti, dipped chicken breasts in egg and rolled them in breadcrumbs, then chopped lettuce for a salad. And when the timer sounded she pulled on oven mitts, removed the biscuits from the oven, and piled them into a basket. None of those things could actually be considered cooking but Ida felt it best to start with a familiarity of the kitchen, which in and of itself was proving to be a challenge.

In the midst of preparing a lemon meringue pie, Ida asked Caroline to fetch the zester and she came back with a jar of paprika. At that point Ida suggested Caroline should be upstairs working on her novel. "After you become a famous author," she said with a laugh, "you can hire someone to do the cooking."

As someone who for years had considered a bag of pretzels a meal, Caroline had no love of being in the kitchen and apparently no talent for cooking. Once the suggestion was made, she scurried from the room before Ida could change her mind. In the days that followed, that became the routine. Ida cooked and set dinner on the table while Caroline labored over a novel that now seemed stale and unimaginative. After several days of struggling with a single sentence, she turned to writing letters to friends she hadn't spoken with since leaving Philadelphia. On numerous occasions she volunteered to help in the kitchen, but Ida said help wasn't necessary.

On the last Wednesday of March, Ida cooked up a breakfast that bordered on being a banquet. Not only did she serve omelets chuck full of peppers, onions, and tomatoes, she served thick slabs of ham, stacks of sausages, big bowls of hash browns, and a homemade cinnamon crunch coffee cake. When everyone had eaten to the point of gluttony Ida said, "I have some business to attend to, so I won't be here at lunchtime—"

"Whaddaya mean you won't be here?" Louie cut in.

"It means just that," Ida answered. "I won't be here to make lunch."

"No lunch?" Louie moaned.

"I didn't say that," Ida replied patiently. "Caroline will prepare lunch."

"Caroline?" a chorus of voices echoed dubiously.

Ida assured everyone that her granddaughter was perfectly capable of preparing lunch and promised to be back before dinner. When they finished the breakfast cleanup, Ida wrote out a list of what was needed for lunch and handed it to Caroline.

"It's just a platter of cold cuts and some potato salad," she said. "Nothing needs to be cooked or prepared."

"Sounds simple enough." Caroline pocketed the list and headed upstairs again to tackle the love story that had gone sour.

When Ida climbed into the car and headed toward South Rockdale, she knew exactly what she would do. She felt certain Big Jim would approve and as for James…well, James would no longer have a say in the matter.

The white stone building sat crosswise at the end of Main Street. It stood three stories tall, not large by many standards, but the biggest in South Rockdale. Ida parked the car, crossed the street, and entered the building. Opposite the door was a building directory. Ida traced her finger along the names: Cohen, Diamond, Elkins, Morrissey, and, there at the bottom, Susan Deuel Schleicher, attorney at law.

Ida stepped into the elevator and pressed three. When the doors whooshed open she moved into the hallway. The door on the left was an accounting firm; the law office of Susan D. Schleicher was on the right. Ida twisted the door handle and walked in.

There was nothing friendly about the office; everything was either black or white. Like the law. "I have an appointment with Miss Schleicher," Ida told the receptionist.

The girl turned her head, whispered something into a small mouthpiece, then turned back. "She'll be with you shortly. Have a seat." She pointed to the black leather sofa.

Ida could have gone to Jack Muller, the only attorney in Rose Hill. But she was never comfortable with Jack. He wasn't a person she could talk to easily. She'd be in the middle of explaining a problem and Jack's eyes would be darting back and forth, like he was looking for somebody better to talk to or lightning to strike.

For years Big Jim did business with Jack Senior and everything was fine. Then Jack retired, and Junior took over the law practice. Junior wasn't like his daddy. Jack Senior measured every man by his own worth, but Junior was the type to butter his bread on both sides. He'd gone to school with James, and if push came to shove he'd have his hand out ready to side with James. No, it was better this way.

Susan Schleicher had a good reputation, and she'd come highly recommended. Georgiann Hennley swore without Susan's help her father-in-law would have lost his business. And Linda Moore said Susan single-handedly prevented a highway from slicing through Maryellen Pallow's backyard.

This wasn't something Ida was jumping into blindly. Five different people had said the same thing. Susan Schleicher was ethical. Susan Schleicher was reliable. If you needed a lawyer, Susan Schleicher was the person you wanted.

Within minutes, an attractive blond woman came from behind the wooden door. "Good afternoon, Missus Sweetwater." She extended her hand. "I'm Susan Schleicher."

Ida knew immediately she'd made a wise choice.

When they settled in Susan's office Ida explained her intent. "The only real asset I have is the house Big Jim built, but it's sturdy and strong…"

Susan's eyes focused on Ida's face as she spoke, but her right hand moved with short quick strokes as she noted the things that were said.

When Ida finished speaking, Susan said, "I doubt there's a problem here. Are you certain you feel comfortable with the girl's claim that she's your granddaughter?"

"She didn't claim it," Ida said. "I sought her out."

"And your son is not, or was not, married to the girl's mother?"

Ida shook her head sadly. "You raise kids thinking you've taught them right from wrong, believing you've done the best for them, but sometimes our best just isn't good enough."

Susan reached across the desk and covered Ida's hand with hers. "I know this is hard, but once the doctor cuts the umbilical cord that baby is no longer part of you. They grow up with their own likes and dislikes, and when they wander off it's through no fault of ours." Her words had the sorrowful sound of someone who had lived through such an experience.

"We'll specify a token inheritance for your son," she said, "which will acknowledge that he was taken into consideration. Then you can bequeath the remainder of your estate, including the house and land, to your granddaughter."

And that's how Ida Sweetwater's will was drawn up. Thirty dollars would go to her son James, one silver dollar for every year of heartache he'd caused. Thirty pieces of silver, it was written.

Everything else she owned would go to Caroline.

When Ida left Susan's office she stopped at the bookstore and purchased a copy of the new Betty Crocker *Good and Easy Cookbook*. It was time for Caroline to learn to cook.

That evening when Caroline asked if help was needed in the kitchen, Ida answered yes and handed her the cookbook.

"We'll start with something simple," Ida said. "A macaroni-and-cheese casserole."

Caroline's eyes lit up. "I can make that! I've done it for years."

For a moment Ida was optimistic, thinking she'd misjudged the child, but when she set the ingredients on the counter Caroline stood there with a confused look.

"Where's the package?"

"Package?" Ida said. "What package?"

"The one with the macaroni and cheese mix."

Ida gave a chuckle, then explained how food tasted so much better when it was made from fresh ingredients. She opened the cookbook to "Dinner in a Dish" and thumbed her way through to page 42. "This is a good recipe and easy to make."

Although Caroline had a dubious look on her face, she took the cookbook and began reading. Twice she read it through, then started. Whereas Ida cooked with a dash of this, a pinch of that, and handful of something else, Caroline measured every single ingredient right down to a few granules of salt or a single peppercorn.

"You don't need to be that exact," Ida suggested, but Caroline replied that she wanted to make certain it turned out right.

When the clock chimed six, Caroline was just sliding the casserole into the oven.

"Oh, dear." Ida sighed when she saw Louie already sitting at the table. She pulled some sliced chicken from the refrigerator, tucked it between two slices of bread, and carried it to the dining room. Offering him the sandwich, she said, "Caroline is making dinner, and we're running a bit late. This will tide you over."

Louie scowled at the plate. "A sandwich for supper?"

"It's not supper," Ida said. "It's just an in-between snack."

"Oh. When's supper?"

"In about a half-hour," Ida replied. "I'll ring the bell."

With Caroline trimming the ends off the string beans one at a time, it took considerably longer than Ida expected and it was almost seven when she finally jangled the dinner bell. Other than a bit of grumbling about the time and Louie's comment that Ida's macaroni was a lot cheesier, the dinner went along fine.

As she was drying the last of the dishes, Caroline puffed up with pride and said, "I guess I'm not such a bad cook after all."

Ida laughed and wrapped her arms around the girl. "Don't you worry, honey. In a year or two you'll be better than me."

Although she enjoyed the vote of confidence, Caroline doubted such a thing was true.

CAROLINE

*H*ave you ever been in a place where everything seemed so perfect you started thinking it was too good to be true? Just about time you start pinching yourself and wondering if it's real, that's when it all blows up in your face and what you thought was the worst that could happen, happens. That's how I'm feeling right now. Mostly happy but a little bit scared.

I love being here, and Grandma Ida is really good to me. She makes me feel like she's loved me all my life. She says she did. She tells me stories about how she used to dream of having a little granddaughter and all the wonderful things they'd do.

I sure do wish she'd found me when I was a kid. We would have done all those wonderful things for sure, but like Mama used to say, if wishes were horses, we'd be riding instead of wearing out our shoe leather.

Grandma Ida is really patient about teaching me to cook; that's why I don't have the heart to tell her I don't like it. I like being with her and doing things but not the cooking. It's such a temporary thing. You slave over a hot stove and spend hours making a delicious meal. Then you dress up the table with a fine linen cloth and fancy napkins, thinking it's going to be a wonderful event. But it isn't. People come, eat dinner, then leave to go do whatever pleases them, and all you've got is a big pile of laundry and a bunch of dirty dishes.

One time I asked Grandma if it wouldn't be a lot less work to send out for a pizza or something, and she laughed like I'd told the best joke ever.

She said cooking wasn't work. It was her way of showing people how much she loves them. With all the cooking Grandma does, it's obvious that she's got plenty of love to give.

Right now I'm lucky to be getting a share of that love, but I'm hoping this isn't another one of those times when I'm gonna wake up and find out it really was too good to be true.

In The Days That Followed

Three days after Ida returned from South Rockdale, the notarized will appeared in her mailbox. Her intent was to discuss the matter with Caroline, explain that regardless of what happened in the future she'd be taken care of. Ida slid the envelope from Susan Schleicher between the stack of kitchen towels and potholders at the bottom of a drawer.

"Later," she said and moved on to slicing peaches for the day's pies. The subject she'd have to discuss was death, and she simply wasn't ready to look death in the face.

That evening Caroline's cooking lesson was spaghetti with fat, round meatballs. It was a recipe Ida perfected over the years. Perfected, yes; written down, no.

"It's easy as pie," she said, but since Caroline had witnessed Ida's pie-making ritual that did little to dissuade her fears. Having had a fairly good response with her Betty Crocker macaroni and cheese Caroline would have felt far more comfortable with returning to something that had carefully measured ingredients, but Ida seemed intent on the spaghetti.

"Start with a few cans of tomatoes, a can or two of paste, some fresh basil—"

"Few? Some?" Caroline repeated. "By a few cans, do you mean two, three, or four?"

"It all depends on how much sauce you want to make."

Although Caroline finally got the sauce mixed and simmering on the back burner, she was nowhere near comfortable with the process. The meatballs fared no better. With pinches and dashes of one thing or another, Caroline knew she could never again prepare such a dish without written instructions. Next time she'd bring a pad and pencil to the kitchen and copy things down in a step-by-step manner.

The following evening Caroline came carrying a pad and pencil, but stopping to write down every single step proved cumbersome and time consuming. That evening supper was again late.

"Maybe we'd better return to using the cookbook," Ida suggested.

Caroline agreed.

And so it went for the next two weeks. At times the sauce was runny or the meat well done, but Caroline was learning and the residents could be forgiving because Ida always served one of her delicious homemade pies for dessert.

The night Caroline cooked up a pot of chili with beef chunks everyone agreed it was her best yet, but the dish gave Ida a serious case of indigestion. After chewing a handful of Tums, it was no better. Figuring a good night's rest would take care of the problem, Ida retired early.

For a long time she could not fall asleep; the acid roiled through her chest and angrily pushed its way into her throat. At midnight Ida climbed from the bed, chewed another handful of Tums, and swallowed the last sleeping pill Doctor Morgenstern had prescribed after Big Jim's death. When she finally fell asleep Ida was thinking of Jim, remembering the good times and lonely for the warmth of his body beside her.

He was in her mind when she drifted off, and he reappeared in a dream sweeter than any she'd ever known.

In the dream they were both young and so very in love. Jim wrapped his arm around her, and she held an infant in her arms. They were encased in a protective bubble where the air was filled with happiness. It was a world of their own, a world where none of the happiness could leak out and nothing bad could seep in. The young Ida looked up at Jim, and he bent to touch his lips to hers. In that single moment, the infant became a boy and the boy turned into a young man.

Then everything changed. Angry words filled the bubble, and the young man shot a fist through the glass that held them together. As the glass shattered, Ida felt a sharp pain ricochet through her body. It lasted for a few moments, and when the pain stopped the boy was gone. Jim was once again holding her in his arms.

"It's okay," he whispered. "It's okay."

Ida felt herself relax into his arms, and the peaceful happiness returned.

When Ida was not in the kitchen the next morning, Caroline set a pot of coffee on to brew. Although she knew how to make it, the residents often complained that her coffee was thick as mud or weak as water. As the coffee brewed she set the dishes on the table, scrambled a dozen eggs in a bowl, unwrapped a pound of bacon, and placed the strips side by side across the griddle.

It was almost eight when Louie came into the kitchen and found Caroline sitting in the chair leafing through a recent issue of *Home and Garden*.

"Why ain't there no breakfast on the table?"

"I'm waiting for Grandma," Caroline answered. "She does the biscuits."

"It's eight o'clock!" Louie said. "Go get her."

Caroline wrinkled her brow. "If she's still sleeping, I don't think—"

"Look," Louie replied impatiently, "if you don't go get her, I will!"

"Okay, okay." Caroline stood and started toward the hall. "Looks like you could be a bit more patient," she grumbled.

Louie's words followed her up the stairs. "I been patient for an hour!"

Caroline rapped on Ida's door, softly at first, then firmly. After several minutes of getting no answer, she cracked the door open. "Grandma?"

No answer.

"Grandma?" she repeated in a loud voice.

Still no answer.

Caroline pushed the door open and rushed to the bed. "Grandma?" Her voice turned panicky and fearful. She bent to shake Ida, but her hand touched icy cold skin. Caroline let out a scream that could be heard several towns away.

Within moments several of the residents stood behind her.

"Call an ambulance!" Caroline shouted. She was still trying to shake Ida awake.

Doctor Payne pushed through the group and reached for Ida's arm. He may have only been a dentist, but he knew how to take a pulse and he knew that when one was missing the person was already dead.

"It's too late," Payne said. "Ida's gone."

"No!" Caroline screamed. "It can't be!" She threw herself across the bed and clung to Ida's body. "Please wake up, Grandma," she begged. "Please…"

With streams of tears rolling down his face, Wilbur stepped forward and reached for Caroline. He lifted her from the bed and pulled her into his arms. "Go ahead and cry. I know how much it hurts." The sorrow in his words was as great as hers.

That morning the coffee went untouched, the bacon remained uncooked, and the eggs sat in the bowl until they started to give off an odor. No one had any appetite, not even Louie.

Caroline was inconsolable. After the ambulance came and took Ida away, she ran to her room and slammed the door shut. All afternoon and for miles around you could hear her howling like a wounded bear.

By morning of the next day, a silence had settled over the house that was in many ways worse than the howling. It was the kind of sorrow that spread from person to person and carved deep scars in everyone it touched.

The residents of the house gathered in sad little clusters, grieving for what they'd lost. Each of them had come to the house looking for a bed to sleep in, nothing more. But through the months they had morphed into a family. Ida's family. Now she was gone, and the pain of having loved her was everywhere.

Caroline's heartbreak was visible in her swollen eyes, the dryness of her lips, and the unkempt look of her hair. Wilbur's pain was great, equal to Caroline's, but he stood strong. It's what Ida would have wanted, he told himself.

He thought back on the evenings they sat together on the porch swing, long after the others had gone off in pursuit of their pleasures. He had fallen in love with Ida. Not the youthful type of love that flared with passion, but an elderly love. A love that softened the ravages of time and disguised itself as a helping hand or listening ear. A love that was different but no less deep.

Not once had he told Ida of his feeling, and now it would remain forever untold. It was too late for words. The only way Wilbur could again express his love would be to watch over Ida's granddaughter, a girl blinded by the same grief he felt. Yes, he had to remain strong; it was his final act of love.

WILBUR WASHINGTON

*T*he problem with life is that it's so damn temporary. You always think there's going to be another day following the one you're enjoying, but sometimes there isn't.

There were a million things I wanted to say to Ida but never did. Not big flowery statements but mentions of all the little everyday reasons I loved her.

A few days ago I was watching as she got a peach pie ready for the oven. It was all put together, but before she slid it in to bake she pressed a fork around the edge of the crust and made fancy-looking ruffles. I wanted to say doing things like that is what's so special about her, but Louie walked in and I swallowed my words. Now I could kick myself for not speaking up. I should have said what I had to say and let tongues waggle if they wanted to.

The irony of life is that we're quick to tell people what we don't like about them, but we hold back on saying how special or wonderful they are. Instead of letting someone know what's in our heart, we wait until they're gone then stand around crying and thinking of all the things we should've said.

I'm just like everybody else; I spent all these days waiting for the right time to say something special. Then when that time came around I let it pass me by. Once a moment is gone, it's gone forever. You can wait and hope it will come around again, but it seldom does.

The painful truth is I should have spoken up while I still had the chance. I should have taken hold of her hand and said, Ida Sweetwater, I'm in love with you.

I held off because I thought it might sound silly, a man of my age speaking such words. Looking back, I can see how wrong that thinking was. You're never too old to love someone, and there's never a wrong time for telling them so.

I never said it, but I hope to God Ida knew how much I loved her.

WILL OR WILL NOT

After Ida's funeral a gloom settled over the house, a gloom bigger and darker than was imaginable. The residents no longer gathered for meals. Instead they sat in mournful little groups and occasionally nibbled on the leftovers from a week earlier, funeral food brought to the door and delivered along with condolences. The lone exception was Max Sweetwater. He wore a smug look of contentment and from time to time could be heard whistling a merry tune.

Caroline paid little attention to Max and seldom left her room. The novel she had been working on was forgotten, and the computer screen remained dark. Days earlier she had been overflowing with the joy of life but she was now little more than a shadow, a dark shape that moved solemnly through the hallway, going from the bedroom to the bathroom and then back to the bedroom without ever speaking.

After three days had passed, Wilbur, who'd come to care for Caroline as he cared for Ida, grew concerned. That morning he brewed a pot of coffee and knocked on her door with a mug in his hand. She opened the door, accepted the coffee, then left it to sit and grow cold.

That day and another one passed, but Caroline remained in her room. Wilbur sat in the parlor and waited to hear her door squeak open, but it didn't happen. As evening approached he set aside the newspaper he'd feigned reading, walked up the stairs, and rapped on Caroline's door.

When there was no answer, he rattled the doorknob and said, "We've got to talk."

"I don't feel up to talking." Caroline sniffled.

"I know you don't," Wilbur replied. "But this is about your grandma."

It was the one and perhaps only reason that could pull Caroline from her bed. She cracked open the door and said, "What about Grandma?"

Without waiting for an invitation, Wilbur pushed open the door and wrapped his arms around Caroline. "This has got to stop. Your grandma wanted you to be happy. It would break her heart to see you acting this way."

Caroline stepped back and lowered her eyes shamefully. "I can't help how I feel."

"Do you think your feelings are more important than your grandma's?"

It would have been better to be scolded. Caroline could have stood there and taken it then curled herself under the blankets and continued to cry. Instead he'd challenged the loyalty of her love.

"Of course I don't," she replied.

"Your grandma was mighty proud of this house," he said. "It was the one thing she had to give you. And now here you are—"

"The one thing she had to give me?"

"Yes," Wilbur answered. "A few weeks back Ida told me she'd made up a will leaving the house and everything she owned to you."

Tears filled Caroline's eyes but she didn't speak.

"Ida wanted you to be happy here." Wilbur's words were soft and tender. "Don't you think you could try to do that for her?"

For a long moment Caroline said nothing. The tears overflowed her eyes, and, sobbing, she leaned her head against Wilbur's chest.

"I'll try," she whispered.

Later that evening Caroline appeared in the kitchen, and the residents heard noises they hadn't heard in many weeks. It was the sound of a large pot clattering down from the shelf. After nearly three hours Caroline clanged the dinner bell that sat on the dining room sideboard.

One by one, the residents came. They walked slowly and with little happiness in their step, but they came. It was after nine o'clock when Caroline dished out helpings of macaroni and cheese and carrots. Wilbur said a prayer of thanksgiving and they ate. Although the cheese sauce was thin and watery and the carrots underdone, everyone said the meal was just like Ida would have served.

"Your grandma would have been real proud of you," Laricka said.

Although it was offered as a compliment, Caroline's tears started again and that's when Max took over the conversation. "Don't worry, Caroline. As the new owner of this house I'll see to it that we have adequate kitchen help. My plan is to—"

"New owner?" Wilbur cut in.

Max nodded. "Although nothing's been finalized yet, as Big Jim's brother I'm next of kin and obviously in line to inherit my brother's estate, which includes the house."

"You're not taking Caroline into consideration," Wilbur said pointedly.

"Oh, she'd be welcome to stay here," Max replied. "If she pays rent like everyone else." Before anyone had time to question him, Max swung into a lengthy explanation of how he planned to hire a cook for food preparation and a housekeeper to do the cleaning.

"Of course," he said, "it means I'll be raising the rent."

"Raising the rent?" Laricka shrieked. "I can barely afford what I'm paying now!"

"Then you'll have to move," Max answered.

Harriet echoed Laricka's thought. "I can't afford to pay more. We don't need a housekeeper and cook."

"And what?" Max said. "We'll continue eating this kind of slop?" He gestured at the swirl of watery macaroni on his plate.

Up until that point Wilbur had held his tongue, figuring Max's words were nothing but pompous pondering and not worth arguing over, but the macaroni comment pushed him into action. He glared across the table and in a loud commanding voice said, "Hold on there!"

Ignoring the bristle in Wilbur's voice, Max continued, "My intent is to make this house a high-class residence, a place we can be proud to call home."

In a frail thin voice Caroline said, "I'm already proud to call it home."

"Me too," Laricka echoed.

By then Wilbur was on his feet and leaning across the table with his nose nearly touching Max's. "You ought to get your facts right before you go spouting off about what you'll do or not do. It so happens Ida left the house to Caroline."

"Impossible," Max stuttered. "She's not a real Sweetwater!"

"Caroline is Sweetwater enough for Ida to believe in her!"

A bright red flush started on Max's neck and crawled up his face.

"Bullshit! She's a phony, an imposter, a bastard child!"

"Enough!" Wilbur yelled back. "One more comment like that, and I'm coming across this table!"

Although he was up in years, Wilbur was taller and wider than Max and the bristle of anger made him seem menacing.

"Caroline and I had a talk today," he said, "and she's decided things will remain exactly as they are."

Several of the residents applauded, and Harriet said, "Good!"

Max's face grew even redder that it was. "Caroline can't decide crap. I own this house, she doesn't!"

Wilbur looked square into Max's face. "Yes, she does. Ida had a will that left everything to Caroline."

"Bullshit!" Max repeated. "Ida was a Sweetwater; she'd never cut out her own kin." He hesitated a moment then said, "How come I ain't seen no copy of this so-called will?"

Wilbur turned to Caroline. "Do you know where Ida kept her important papers?"

"No, I don't," she answered. "We never talked about things like that."

Wilbur lowered himself into his chair, his shoulders now a bit slumped. At that point he had to admit he'd never actually seen the will, but he'd heard about it from Ida. "It was about two weeks ago," he said. "Ida told me she'd had a lawyer draw up a will leaving everything to Caroline."

"A lawyer?" Max echoed dubiously. "No name, just a lawyer?"

"She might have mentioned a name, but offhand I don't recall it."

"Ha," Max sneered. "Another bullshit story."

Wilbur glared at Max. "I've got no reason to lie. I'm just repeating what Ida told me."

"So you say," Max snapped back. "But I think you're in it with her." Max shook a thumb toward Caroline. "This one's figuring to sell the place and walk off with a nice fat profit!"

"I'm not looking to sell anything," Caroline said defensively. "This is my grandma's house, and I'd like to keep it the way she wanted."

Max angrily turned to Caroline. "Grandma, my ass! You don't have a shred of evidence proving James was your daddy!"

"Grandma said I've got eyes just like Daddy."

Harriet, who'd been drowning her sorrow in the bottle of bourbon kept in her nightstand, said nothing, but her eyes bounced back and forth as the argument raged on.

"Brown eyes? That's your evidence?" Max gave a resentful grunt. "I'm Big Jim's blood brother, born of the same mama! If anybody's got a right to this house, it's me!"

Doctor Payne stood and rapped the handle of his knife against the table. "Listen up!" he shouted. When everyone else stopped talking he lowered his tone. "This is easily enough settled. Tomorrow we'll call Jack Muller and ask him."

"Call who?" several voices echoed in unison.

"Jack Muller," Doctor Payne repeated. "He's the only lawyer in Rose Hill. Everybody uses Jack."

As he listened to the argument circling the table, Wilbur thought about his conversation with Ida. Jack Muller did not sound like a familiar name, but maybe he was wrong. Rather than continue what was rapidly escalating into a territorial war, he'd try and see if he couldn't remember the name of Ida's lawyer. He started with A and one by one went through the letters of the alphabet, hoping to trigger a memory and call up a name.

Why was it, Wilbur wondered, that when you really needed a piece of information, it got stuck in the back of your mind? In cases like this, the only thing he could do was wait and hope it would reappear.

A WAR OF WILLS

Before the supper table was cleared the battle lines had been drawn. Although such a thought had never before been mentioned, Max insisted he'd moved in fully expecting to one day inherit the house built by his brother. It was noticeable how Max no longer referred to Big Jim by name; he was now "my brother."

Doctor Payne, a stickler for formalities, stood squarely behind Max. As the others squabbled across the table, Payne stood and cleared his throat loudly. "Given the absence of a will, the court would have no recourse but to turn the estate over to a blood relative."

"Ah," Louie grumped, "so now you're a brain surgeon *and* a lawyer?"

"That remark was uncalled for," Payne shot back. "I am simply stating a fact."

Although generally not one to step into the fray, Laricka spoke up. "Even if there is no will I know for a fact Ida wanted Caroline to have the house."

Payne held his adversarial position and stood firm. "And how exactly do you know that?"

"Ida was a grandma just as I am," Laricka answered, "and there isn't a grandma in the world who'd choose her brother-in-law over her grandchild." She leaned back into her chair, obviously pleased with the rationale.

"Garbage!" Max shouted. "Irrational, bullshit garbage! It was my brother who built this house and—"

"Hold on!" Wilbur held his hand up. "Doctor Payne may not be a lawyer, but I was and I can say with certainty that who thinks what is of no relevance. This is not an issue of opinion. Ownership of the house will eventually be determined by the legal document stating Ida's intent. Right now we don't have a copy of her will. I know it exists but——"

Harriet drained the glass of bourbon she'd brought to dinner and hiccupped. "Sorry."

Wilbur completed his thought. "The challenge will be to find it."

Caroline sat at the end of the table with her plate of runny macaroni untouched. So far she had said but a few words, and as the others argued her eyes filled with tears. Her thoughts drifted back to other angry voices: Mama, Daddy, Greg. The sound of anger was always the same——harsh, unrelenting, ugly. Anger never resolved itself it just led to more anger, and in time whatever love there had once been was gone.

When she finally spoke her voice quivered like jelly thickened with sorrow.

"Stop arguing. I didn't come here for the house. I came here because I wanted to be with Grandma. Now that she's gone there's no reason for me to stay. Max can have——"

"No, he can't!" Harriet jumped up so quickly her chair toppled backward. Seemingly sober as a judge, she turned to Caroline. "You know damn well what your grandma thought of Max. Why, she'd roll over in her grave if she thought you'd let him grab hold of what was intended for you!"

"But if it's rightfully his——"

"It isn't," Wilbur said. "We don't have an in-hand copy of Ida's will yet, but I know it exists. *I'm going to make sure Caroline is taken care of*——those were her exact words. She loved you just as she loved this house, and she intended for you to live here."

Laricka agreed, and Louie insisted Caroline had to stay because she was the only one who knew Ida's cooking secrets.

"But until this issue of the will is straightened out," Wilbur said, "someone has to manage the house. Collect the rents, pay bills, and——"

"See to meals," Louie added.

It was after ten when the residents began to discuss a vote on who should be the interim house manager. With the right side of his mouth curled into an argumentative sneer, Max maintained that since Caroline did not pay rent she was not entitled to vote so she voluntarily stepped aside.

"No deal," Louie said. "Caroline gets a vote. She does the cooking, and that's worth more than the measly rent you pay."

It was common knowledge Max paid less than the other residents. He'd bragged about it, claiming "family benefits."

"I agree with Louie." Laricka nodded. "And if Caroline needs help with the cooking, I can whip up one of my black cakes."

Louie groaned. "Enough with the black cake. Nobody wants burnt cake."

Laricka puckered her lips into a pout. "Black cake isn't burnt."

"He knows that," Payne said, "but Louie thinks he's funny."

Before it became ugly, Wilbur called for a vote on whether Caroline was entitled to vote. Without her vote it was five to one, Max being the only dissenter. The others agreed preparing meals was adequate compensation for not paying rent.

After the issue of Caroline voting was settled, they moved to voting on the management of the house or, as Max described it, temporary custody.

He expected Wilbur to side with Caroline but thought Harriet would back him up. For three nights in a row he'd slipped into her room, poured any number of drinks, and stayed for far longer than was respectable. On those occasions Harriet giggled and flirted in a way that made him believe she'd not only stand with him but maybe even swear to whatever he said. The earlier outburst, he'd decided, was a reaction to too much bourbon. Plus, given the friction beteeen Louie and Payne, they'd most certainly be on opposite sides.

The way Max saw it, Caroline had Wilbur and Louie; he had Payne and Harriet. And after Louie's comment about the black cake, it looked like Laricka might swing to his side. She would probably be the deciding vote.

"All in favor of Max taking over management of the house," Wilbur said.

Doctor Payne and Max raised their hand. Max looked at Harriet and nodded.

Nothing. If she noticed, she gave no indication of it.

"Anyone else?" Wilbur asked.

Still nothing. Neither Harriet nor Laricka moved.

"Okay," Wilbur said. "That's two for Max."

"All in favor of having Caroline manage the house," Wilbur said.

Louie, Laricka, and Harriet's hands shot up, then Wilbur and Caroline followed suit.

"Okay," Wilbur said, "that's five for Caroline. Looks like she wins."

Although there was little Max could do about it, he sputtered and spat for a while, then stomped off toward his own room. As he passed by Harriet, he snarled, "Don't expect me to be stopping by this evening."

The next morning Caroline rose before the sun crossed the horizon. She went down to the kitchen, set a pot of coffee on to perk, and pulled the iron skillet from the cupboard. That morning when the residents came to breakfast there was a platter of fried eggs with broken yolks and half-cooked bacon. The basket previously used for biscuits was filled with slices of Wonder Bread, and Caroline had a bandage wrapped around the palm of her left hand.

CAROLINE

*L*ast night Wilbur came to my room. I suppose he did it because he heard me crying. His room is just across the hall from mine, and it's easy enough to hear what's going on. If it was anybody else I might've said go away and leave me alone, but talking to Wilbur is like talking to Grandma. He doesn't ask anything of me, he just listens like he really cares.

He told me he was telling the truth about Grandma's will and said it was just a matter of time until we come across it. I hope he's right, because living here feels like I've still got a piece of Grandma with me. This morning when I went down to the kitchen I could almost see her standing behind me, telling me what to do. If I leave here she'll be like Daddy, stuck in my mind for a while then growing fuzzier with every day that passes.

When I first came to Rose Hill I figured Clarence was my best friend and maybe even the only friend I'd have here. Then I met Grandma. It seems impossible I could come to love her so much in such a short time, but if you knew Grandma you'd understand. She had a way of making you feel good about yourself even if you did something stupid. One time I was supposed to be keeping an eye on the biscuits and got to thinking about my story; next thing I knew smoke was coming from the oven. Grandma had to mix up a whole new tray of biscuits, but instead of yelling at me she laughed and said she'd done the very same thing a number of times. Knowing what a good cook Grandma was I doubted that was true, but hearing her say it made me feel a whole lot less stupid.

I sure hope we can find that will, because if we don't I doubt Max will let me stay here. He might tolerate me for a short while, but he'd be looking for a way to get rid of me. Probably he'd say my cooking is no good, which is true. But I'm trying to get better.

If I do have to leave, Clarence will go with me. That's the good thing about having *a dog. No matter where you go or how worthless you are to other people, the dog still loves you.*

Sad. I never realized that before.

THE SEARCH

At the breakfast table Max announced he was going to Jack Muller's office to check on the existence of a will. He'd planned to go alone, but Doctor Payne suggested he go along. "As a witness," he said.

"Some witness," Harriet grumbled. "You're on his side. He'd lie and you'd swear to it."

"There is no lying about the existence of a will," Wilbur said. "It's a legal document that either exists or doesn't."

"Yeah, well, what if he goes there, snags the will, then says there ain't none?"

Laricka nodded. "Harriet has a point."

After fifteen minutes of discussion, it was decided that Laricka, who claimed to be reasonably neutral, would tag along as an unbiased observer. The three of them left the house at five minutes before nine.

At four minutes before nine Wilbur, Harriet, Louie, and Caroline began searching the house for the will. "A copy has got to be here somewhere," Wilbur said. Throughout the night he had racked his brain and run through the letters of the alphabet a dozen or more times trying to recall the name of the lawyer Ida mentioned, but nothing came. The name had disappeared from memory, so it was imperative they find the will.

"Caroline, you and Harriet go through Ida's room," Wilbur said. As much as he wanted to be there and touch the remainders of a woman he'd loved, he felt it unseemly to go through things of such an intimate nature. Louie took the kitchen, and Wilbur searched the rest of the house.

In the kitchen Louie flipped through the pages of every cookbook, searched the vegetable bins, and rummaged through the freezer. He checked beneath the trays of silverware, removed the dishes from the closet, then replaced them. When he came to the drawer containing a stack of dishtowels and potholders, he lifted the stack from the drawer and checked beneath them. Nothing. He lifted the corner of a few towels, peeked beneath them, then set the stack back into place.

When Max and his entourage reached the office of Jack Muller, a receptionist informed them that he was in district court and wasn't expected back until late afternoon.

Visibly agitated by such news Max asked, "What time?"

She shrugged. "Could be three, could be four, could be later."

Max suggested they sit and wait, but Laricka and Doctor Payne responded with a resounding "no."

"I've got better things to do," Payne said.

"And my grandsons are coming to visit," Laricka added.

Max then suggested they take the thirty-seven-mile drive to the courthouse and was again voted down.

"We'll come back tomorrow," Payne said, and although Max objected to the wait he was left with no alternative.

By the time Max returned home, Wilbur and the others had finished searching the house but found nothing.

Lunch was a somber affair with most everyone thinking on what they might have missed. Most everyone, but not Caroline. Her thoughts were focused on the work at hand. For lunch she'd made a tuna salad but neglected to drain the oil from the can, then mixed in way too much mayonnaise and chopped the onions into a size more suitable for apple chunks. Again a basket of Wonder Bread was placed on the table.

"Not bad," Louie said and scooped a large pile onto his plate.

The others picked at the edges of the bowl and then settled for bits of bread and butter. Max used the disastrous salad to repeat the fact that Caroline was poorly qualified to be manager of the house.

"What we need is a professional cook," he said. "Someone who knows how to prepare meals properly."

Once Max said that, the other residents began loading scoops of the salad onto their plates.

"Actually it looks pretty tasty," Laricka lied.

Before everyone left the table, the bowl was empty.

That afternoon Wilbur collected the rent checks; all except Max's. When he'd broached the subject, Max snarled, "Pay rent for living in a house that I own? No way!"

"You don't actually own the house," Wilbur replied. He was going to mention that the likelihood of Max ever owning it was non-existent, but given the ugliness in Max's attitude Wilbur said only there were expenses to be paid and everyone had to help.

That only served to make Max angrier. "Poor management! If she knew how to run a boarding house, she'd have managed without harassing me for a measly week's rent."

"It's two weeks," Wilbur replied, but Max ignored the comment and continued on his tirade. After going back and forth for several minutes, Wilbur turned with an air of disgust and walked away.

That afternoon he gave Caroline an envelope containing the rent checks and twenty-five dollars in cash. "The cash is Max's rent for one week," he explained. "He'll catch up with the rest next week."

Caroline had a look of surprise. "Max paid cash?"

Wilbur nodded, then quickly changed the subject.

All too often he'd seen Ida sitting at the table totaling up columns of figures and trying to make ends meet. It was always a stretch. Caroline was less capable of managing than Ida; still, if she knew Wilbur had put the money in for Max, she would have refused it. Charity, she would have said, and handed the money back.

As it was, Caroline pocketed the envelope with no further questions.

Fifteen minutes later she loaded Clarence into the car and pulled out of the driveway.

Standing at the window and watching, Max grumbled. "Bunch of jerks, giving a girl like that their money. That's the last we're gonna see of her." Laricka, who'd been the only person within earshot, gave him an angry glare then turned and left the room.

Caroline drove directly to the bank and opened a checking account in her name. She deposited all five checks plus one hundred-and-twelve dollars of the money she'd brought from Pennsylvania. She held back the twenty-five dollars in cash for necessities.

From the bank she continued to Food Lion. Instead of picking the snacks she usually bought, she filled an entire shopping cart with items Ida was likely to select: chopped meat, pork chops, fresh ears of corn, ripe tomatoes, and a ten-pound bag of potatoes. She also added several packages of ready-to-bake biscuits. Caroline knew her grandmother would never have bought those, but until she learned to make a decent biscuit these would have to do. When she got to the checkout line there was not one bag of pretzels. No chips. No TV dinners.

That evening when Caroline served dinner, the pork chops had places where the breading had come loose and dropped off and three pieces of corn had bits of silk still caught between the kernels, but there was a basket of biscuits on the table.

Everyone but Max smiled. Although there was a round of compliments stating that Caroline's cooking had dramatically improved, Max said nothing.

Three days passed before Jack Muller finally made time to speak to Max, and when he did it was a five-minute meeting in the reception room of his office.

"I haven't heard from Ida since Big Jim's passing," Muller said. "I believe she's taken her business elsewhere."

"Was there an earlier will, one written back a year, maybe two?" Max asked.

Muller shook his head. "The last one I did was five or six years before Jim passed."

Max's eyes brightened. "Do you have a copy of it?"

"Just a file copy. The will was probated and settled when Jim died."

"By who?"

Muller began looking at Max with a suspicious eye. "What's going on here? And what gives you the right to be snooping in Ida's business?"

"I'm Jim's brother, and I've got every right to look into what's happened with my brother's estate."

"Afraid not," Muller said. "Jim left everything to Ida. And now that she's gone I guess you'll have to talk to James if you want to know what happened to the estate."

"He's been gone for thirty years. Nobody knows where he is or even if he's alive."

"Did he have any children?"

Max curled his lip. "That's the problem. This girl showed up claiming James was her daddy, but I'm thinking she's a phony."

Muller had dealt with enough no-goods to sense when a person had the stink of trouble on their skin. Max Sweetwater was ripe with it.

"That's a pretty strong accusation. Unless you've got proof positive, I can't help you." He turned and walked away.

That didn't stop Max; he trailed behind Muller. "If proof is what you want, proof is what you'll get."

Without bothering to answer, Jack stepped back into his office and closed the door.

As Max stormed out the door, the receptionist said, "Have a nice day."

Laricka and Doctor Payne, who'd both witnessed to the conversation, agreed that Max had not proven there was no will any more than Wilbur had proven there was.

So things remained at a stalemate. And Max did not hand over a rent check even when the others did.

In the days that followed, Caroline was up early and had breakfast on the table by nine o'clock. Although the residents had become accustomed to eating at seven, no one complained. By week's end Caroline had mastered scrambled eggs, little sausage links, and biscuits. When Doctor Payne suggested melon with cottage cheese might be a pleasant change, four pairs of eyes glared at him angrily and Max gave a self-satisfied nod.

Just learning as she was, it took Caroline twice as long to cook and three times as long to clean up the kitchen. Struggling to get the platters ready to serve, she ignored the thrown-about dishtowels and splatters of grease that dotted the stove. A week after she'd begun making breakfast, Caroline left the sausage simmering on the front burner of the stove and went to the pantry in search of salt. In less than a minute, the grease caught fire and spread across the spills and splatters. Seconds later it caught hold of the potholders she'd left lying there. Caroline was moving a large bag of flour aside when she heard Laricka scream, "Fire! Fire!"

Caroline rushed back, grabbed the pitcher of orange juice ready to go on the table, and poured it over the flames. By then Wilbur and Louie had arrived in the kitchen.

The fire sputtered, spit, and finally fizzled out, becoming a greasy, sticky goo that dripped down the front of the stove and onto the floor. Bits and pieces of the tattered potholders melted and were now cemented to the stove.

Caroline gave a mournful sigh. "I'm never going to get this right."

Seeing the girl hunched with the weight of responsibility as she was prompted Wilbur to once again lie. "This is nothing. Why, one time your grandma set fire to a pan of bacon twice this size!"

"Grandma did?"

"Sure she did. It's a thing that can happen to anybody." Wilbur turned to Louie and Laricka. "Right?"

They both gave blank-faced nods, even though neither of them remembered Ida ever doing such a thing.

"The important thing is just to get this cleaned up," Wilbur said. He pulled open the drawer of dishtowels and handed three to Laricka. "Wet these and let's get started."

Without being assigned tasks, Louie and Laricka began wiping and cleaning. Wilbur carried the skillet now full of orange juice to the sink.

It took almost twenty minutes to clean the kitchen, and in the process of doing so they dirtied seven kitchen towels. After she'd rinsed the towels and carried them to the laundry room, Caroline tossed the charred remains of the potholders in the garbage can.

By then it was nine-thirty and breakfast was still uncooked. Getting ready to start over, she reached into the drawer and pulled out four fresh towels and two new potholders. That's when the envelope Ida had so carefully hidden fell to the floor.

"What's this?" Laricka asked and handed Caroline the envelope.

It was a thick white envelope that had been mailed to Ida, but it now had Caroline's name scrawled across the front in a handwriting they had all come to know. In the upper left hand corner was the return address for Susan D. Schleicher, Attorney.

FINDERS KEEPERS

Once the will was found, Max turned uglier than imaginable. He insisted the will was a forgery, and if perchance the signature was authentic Ida had apparently been coerced into giving a total stranger the house *his brother* built. He copied down the name and address of Susan D. Schleicher and warned he would take a trip to South Rockdale and check out this *supposed* lawyer.

By time the excitement died down it was nearly ten-thirty, and no one had eaten breakfast. Wilbur, feeing victorious and vindicated, offered to take everyone to the diner, his treat. Everyone nodded yes, except Max. He skulked off, saying he'd get to the bottom of this.

Louie laughed. "You're at the bottom of it."

Max didn't bother to respond. The thought of losing something that rightfully belonged to him crawled under his skin and caused an itch that was impossible to scratch.

Two days later Max announced that he had an appointment with Susan Schleicher and planned to uncover the truth about the will. This time Laricka refused to tag along as a witness, saying it was a waste of time and her grandsons were coming to visit.

"They're here all the time," Max said. "Can't you skip a day?"

"Not with my precious grandsons!" Laricka replied. She reminded everyone within earshot how children were only young once and you had to take advantage of every moment you could spend with them. "Just look at what happened to poor Ida," she said and shook her head sadly.

Only Doctor Payne was willing to accompany Max on the trip, and even he was skeptical as to whether such a venture was worthwhile. "What is there to prove?" he asked, but Max's answer had been just a sly nod of his head.

On the drive to South Rockdale there was very little conversation. Max drove and Doctor Payne leafed through the pages of the *Today's Dentist* magazine he'd brought along.

After Max had suffered in silence for nearly two-thirds of the trip, he said, "How long's it gonna take you to read that thing?"

"I don't know," Payne replied. "Is there some kind of hurry?"

"Not so much a hurry," Max said, "but I was figuring on you giving me some kind of encouragement. Bolstering my spirits a bit."

"Encouragement?" Payne repeated. "For what? Going on a wild goose chase and making everybody's life miserable?"

"What wild goose chase? I'm just trying to set things straight."

"Stop kidding yourself." Payne looked up from his magazine. "That will's legitimate, and you know it. You're just too much of a pompous ass to admit it."

"Me?" Max's eyes grew big and round, and his nose began twitching side to side. "You're the one! Everybody *says* you're pompous. Not just me, everybody!" Max angrily floored the accelerator, and they arrived in South Rockdale forty-five minutes before their appointment with Susan Schleicher.

Up until now Payne had considered Max a principled man who could at times be difficult. But that last comment was something he couldn't brush aside. "I'll meet you back here in forty-five minutes," he said and walked off. A second later he turned the corner and disappeared.

"Well, if that don't beat all," Max grumbled. "I figure him for a friend, and he gives me this kind of crap." The anger inside his head swelled and pushed against his brain. It was difficult enough to think through the questions he had to ask, and Payne was making it harder. "I should never have brought him," Max said with a groan as he paced back and forth across the lobby of the building. He thought and rethought what he should say to Susan Schleicher, but in between every thought was the echo of Payne's words.

With not a minute to spare, Payne returned carrying two new magazines. "Let's get this over with," he said. Without another word passing between them, they entered the elevator.

When they walked into Susan's office, all of the well-planned arguments Max had practiced disappeared. A red-hot ball of anger aimed at Caroline Sweetwater had replaced them. She was to blame for everything. She was the reason he'd have to pay rent to live in a house that was rightfully his. He pulled a copy of the will from his pocket and waved it in the air.

"Did you do this?" he shouted accusingly.

"Sit down," Susan commanded. "And do not use that tone of voice with me, or I'll have you thrown out of my office."

Max took a seat and mumbled, "Sorry. I'm just a bit overwrought about this will." He passed the copy to Susan.

She leafed through the pages then looked back at Max. "What's wrong with it?"

"Wrong? Everything's wrong. I doubt this is even a legitimate will!"

Susan's voice grew quite a bit testier. "On what basis?"

"This girl is not Ida's granddaughter!"

Susan chuckled and leaned back in her chair. Since Max had introduced himself only as Mister Sweetwater, she'd assumed he was the son. "Ida suspected this would happen," she said. "That's why she left you the thirty silver dollars."

With his face growing redder by the minute, Max shouted, "I'm not Ida's son! I'm Big Jim's brother!"

"I don't care if you're Santa Claus," Susan said. "One more outburst, and you're out of here."

Max, unaccustomed to being bossed about by a woman, came right back at her. "You can't talk to me this way! I have rights!"

He probably would have said something more, but by then Susan had already called for security. Within the minute an armed guard appeared and took Max by the elbow.

"Let's go," the guard said and eased Max toward the door.

Standing behind the desk with her arms folded across her chest, Susan chided, "And for your information that will is completely valid and will stand up in court, whether Caroline Sweetwater is Ida's granddaughter or not."

Before Max reached the outskirts of South Rockdale, Susan had already walked across to the courthouse and filed the will for probate.

On the drive back to Rose Hill, Doctor Payne did not say a word. When Max asked if he was going to tell the others what had transpired,

Payne feigned interest in a magazine article about high-rise buildings in Panama City. The silence angered Max more than a simple yes or no. The angrier he got, the harder he pressed the accelerator. At one point they sped through a stretch of farmland going ninety miles per hour, and Max came within inches of hitting a cow that had wandered onto the roadway.

When they arrived at the house, Payne climbed out of the car and slammed the door with such finality the car vibrated for a full ten seconds.

That evening when the residents gathered at the dining room table there was no mistaking the fact that Doctor Payne had moved to Caroline's camp.

"Unfortunately, Susan Schleicher was of no assistance," Max said. "She was under the mistaken impression I was James and—"

"It's over," Payne cut in. "Over. There is no grey area. No 'yes, but.' No 'what if.' Ida left her entire estate to Caroline, and that's that."

In an effort to save face, Max said, "It may come to that, but I didn't actually get to finish my conversation with—"

Payne leaned across the table and stuck his face in Max's. "It's over! The woman threw your pompous ass out of her office! Can you not understand that—"

"She threw him out of her office?" Harriet snickered.

"Whoa, boy," Louie guffawed. "That's what I call an ass-kicking!"

Max banged his fist against the table. "Enough!" Then he stood, kicked his chair over, and left the room.

It was more than a week before he returned to the table.

The anger settled on Max like black coveralls, and he went for days at a time without venturing from his room. When Caroline rapped on the door asking if he'd like a sandwich or slice of a store-bought pie, he told her, "Stop bothering me!"

In the days that followed Max seldom came to breakfast, and on the rare occasion when he did come to supper he was foul-mouthed and nasty. He told Laricka her grandsons had the look of pigs and implied Harriet was easier than a street prostitute. Caroline he called a swindler and a disgrace to the Sweetwater name.

For more than two weeks Max's anger simmered at a hair's breadth below the boiling point, but it exploded the night Caroline made a beef stew. Max, having had several shots of vodka before dinner, was in an ornerier than usual mood. He took a large piece of beef in his mouth, then moments later spat it onto the floor. "You call this a stew? It's not fit for dogs."

Clarence rushed over and gobbled the meat on the floor, then approached Max and nosed his arm looking for seconds. Without thinking twice, Max backhanded the dog and sent him sliding across the floor.

Caroline jumped out of her seat and rounded the table in three long strides. In that single moment all conversation and the clatter of silverware came to an abrupt halt.

Taller than Max and quite possibly stronger, she reached out, grabbed him by the front of his shirt, and yanked him from his seat. "Clarence is my dog!" she screamed, her face hovering over his. "And if you ever lay a hand on him again, I'll run a knife through your miserable heart!"

Panting hot angry bursts of air in his face, she held onto Max for a moment, dangling him in the air. When she finally let go, he dropped into the chair with a thud.

Too much water had passed beneath the bridge. Too much anger had built up. The weeks of resentment bubbled inside of Max, and he lashed out.

"Some shithole dump this is," he said bitterly. "You care more about a dog than you do the people who live here."

As angry as Max was, Caroline was now angrier. "Yes," she answered through clenched teeth. "I do care more about Clarence than you!"

Max mumbled something under his breath, and then Caroline finished her thought. "If you don't like it, leave!"

Max rose from the table and walked off.

The next day Max installed a deadbolt lock on his bedroom door. From that day forward the room remained locked, whether he was inside sleeping off another bender or outside stumbling toward the Owl's Nest to tie one on.

CAROLINE SWEETWATER

Yesterday if you told me I could get angry enough to do what I did, I would have laughed in your face. Me? I'd say. A person whose very nature is to be peaceable?

I've spent my life stepping back to avoid an argument, and I always believed I as doing what needed to be done to hold life together. Now, looking back, I realize I was just being stupid, sticking my head in the sand and hoping trouble would pass me by.

The thing is trouble doesn't pass you by. It stays and hovers over your head like a storm cloud full of teardrops and heartache. I've been living under that cloud for way too long. I should have given voice to my anger a long time ago, but I didn't. Stupid, I know.

I think back on how Greg did things that should have been unforgivable and how I squashed my own hurt just so I could forgive him. Not only did I forgive him, most times I didn't even argue the point. The sad truth is I was afraid of losing Greg the way Mama lost Daddy. The thought that I'd be better off without a man like him never even crossed my mind.

Wimpy as it may sound, I've never had enough courage to stick up for myself. But defending somebody you love is a whole lot different than sticking up for yourself. It makes you able to do things you didn't think you could do. When I defend Clarence, I'm fighting for somebody I love. And I love Clarence way more than I ever loved myself.

Yes, I know you're going to tell me Clarence isn't a somebody, he's a stray that I picked up along the highway. But to me, he's a somebody.

We're kind of alike, Clarence and me. We're both strays abandoned by someone we thought loved us. I saved Clarence just like Grandma Ida saved me.

I know Grandma is gone, but I feel like she's still here. I go day to day pretending *she'll be back tomorrow or maybe the next day.*

It's hard doing all the things that need to be done in this house, and if I let myself accept that Grandma will never be back I'd fall to pieces for sure.

THE LAMP

After Caroline's threat, Max stayed clear of her and most everyone else in the house. If he happened to pass one of the other residents, they stepped aside and said nothing. For the remainder of that week he spent the days sleeping, and when the sky turned dark he left the house and headed for the Owl's Nest. After long hours of sitting at the bar and pulling bits of conversation from strangers with no interest in talking, he'd stumble back to his room. By that time the house was dark and most of the residents sleeping.

On several occasions Caroline heard him lumbering about the kitchen, obviously pilfering leftovers from the refrigerator. Since her room overlooked the center hallway she could see the glow of the refrigerator light coming from the kitchen and hear the clattering of dishes. In the morning she often discovered half a roast chicken or large slabs of ham missing, along with a basket of biscuits.

An edginess that hadn't previously existed began to creep into the house.

The first to notice it was Wilbur. He took Caroline aside and suggested she might want to ask Max to leave. "He's trouble," Wilbur warned.

"Not Max," she answered. "He's harmless. He's just acting up to prove how mad he is. In time he'll get over it."

Wilbur gave a rather doubtful shrug. "Maybe so. But if I were you, I'd keep a wary eye."

Of course, Caroline didn't. She couldn't, because in her mind Max was family. He was Big Jim's brother, her great uncle, her only living relative. Whenever one of the residents suggested Max should leave, she thought about how Ida had taken her in. "He's family," she'd say and drop the subject without any further explanation.

She was certain that given time Max would come around.

Wilbur knew better, and when he went to his room at night he remained awake for a long time listening, waiting to hear the lock click shut on Max's door. Once he was certain Max had gone to bed, Wilbur allowed himself to sleep.

As the days passed, Caroline settled into becoming as much like Ida as was possible. She started early in the morning, cooking pots of oatmeal and frying platters of eggs. As soon as the table was cleared and the dishes washed, she'd begin tidying up the house. On a chilly morning when she rose fifteen minutes late, she threw on a housecoat that had once belonged to Ida and hurried downstairs to start breakfast. When Laricka rushed past the kitchen she caught a glimpse of Caroline and let out a gasp that could be heard in the attic.

"Oh, my Lord," she said, "I thought that was Ida's ghost standing there."

"No," Caroline answered. "It's just me."

That afternoon Wilbur talked to Caroline as a grandfather might.

"You're too young to be living a life of cleaning and cooking for old folks," he said. "You should be getting out, having fun with young people your own age."

"I am having fun," Caroline answered. "I'm doing what I think Grandma Ida would want me to do."

Wilbur heard the weight of responsibility in her voice and gave his head a sad shake. "I doubt this is what your grandma wanted for you. I know it's not what I'd want for my grandson." He thought about his own grandson, a year older than Caroline, living in Paris and enjoying a carefree life.

"Maybe you should think about selling the house," he said. "You could take the money and move to Paris."

"Paris? What would I do in Paris?"

"Finish the novel you're writing,"

"Oh, that," Caroline said dismissively. "I'm not sure I'm cut out to be a writer."

It had been more than a month since she'd turned on the computer, and the images she once had of a love story were long gone. Lost, perhaps, in a pile of oven mitts and dishcloths.

"If not Paris, maybe New York," Wilbur suggested.

Caroline shook her head. "I don't think so," she said, and that was the end of the conversation.

On the second Thursday after the incident, Caroline was upstairs dusting the loft when she heard a loud crash. Fearing the worst, she came flying down the stairs.

Huge tears rolled down Laricka's face. "I am so sorry, so sorry…" Standing behind her were the two grandsons. Fragments of what was once a lamp lay scattered across the parlor floor. "Don't run, I told them. A thousand times I said, don't run." Laricka turned and glared at the boys. "But did they listen? No, of course not!"

"We're sorry," the boys said in unison.

"Sorry?" Laricka repeated. "Sorry won't fix the lamp!"

Caroline stepped into the fray. "No problem. A lamp is easily enough replaced."

"But this was Miss Ida's favorite," Laricka replied mournfully.

Caroline knew there was no replacing a thing someone had treasured, so she began gathering the pieces from the floor. "Maybe I can have it fixed."

After she'd scoured the floor on her hands and knees looking for stray splinters of glass, Caroline placed all thirty-six pieces in a box and headed for town. She planned to take the lamp to a jeweler she'd seen on the far end of Main Street, but as she drew near the shop where she'd bought the desk something caused her to pull over and park.

Although she hadn't noticed it being on the window during her first visit to the store, it was there now. Right beneath Peter Pennington's name the lettering read "Lamps Repaired."

Caroline climbed out of the car and circled around to retrieve the broken lamp from the trunk. Before she could gather the box into her arms, Peter Pennington stood beside her.

"Let me help you with that," he said and lifted the box from the trunk.

"But how…" Caroline stammered.

"Where else would you bring a broken lamp?" Peter said and gave a mischievous grin. He started for the store and Caroline followed behind.

"I don't know if this is fixable," she said. "But it was my grandma's favorite, so I'd really like to…" Her words trailed off. Maybe it was hoping against hope, expecting someone to repair a lamp with pieces as small as a splinter. Caroline held her breath as Peter peered inside the box.

"It's repairable," he said and promised to have it by noon of the next day.

"Oh, bless your heart," Caroline replied gleefully.

"Indeed," Peter said, then asked about the desk she'd bought.

"I'm afraid I haven't been writing," Caroline said. "I think I've lost the inspiration."

"Lost the inspiration? Impossible. That desk is full of stories waiting to be written!"

"With Grandma gone, I've got a lot of responsibility and not much free time."

Peter nodded knowingly.

"And it's difficult to write about a romance when—"

"Romance?" Peter peered over the top of the thick glasses he wore. "That's not what you're supposed to be writing." He pushed his glasses back onto the bridge of his nose. "Haven't you listened to the desk?"

"Listened to the desk?" She laughed.

Peter nodded. "I know you think it's a silly idea, but try it. Sit there and wait. Let the desk tell you what it has to say."

He was such a sweet little man, and since he was willing to repair the lamp Caroline didn't want to jeopardize their friendship by laughing at how ridiculous such a thought was. "I'll give it a try," she said and, promising to be back tomorrow, left.

Peter watched her leave, sad because he knew his advice would go unheeded.

On Friday afternoon Caroline came back to pick up the lamp.

"Ready and waiting," Peter said. He pulled out the same yellow step stool, climbed up, and retrieved the lamp, which sat on the top shelf. "Here you go," he said and handed it down to her.

The lamp was perfect, exactly as it once was. No glue lines, no mismatched pieces, no evidence that it had ever been repaired. "How on earth…" Caroline wondered. She opened her purse and asked how much she owed him.

"One dollar."

"One dollar? But this must have been hours of work…"

"Not so much," he answered, then asked if she'd tried sitting at the desk.

"Um, not yet," Caroline said. "I'm still learning to cook, and I spend most of my afternoon—"

"I know," he said and gave a sad nod. "It's a complex thing to let your thoughts fly free when your body is tied to the labors of life."

"That's true, but I believe it's what Grandma would have wanted." Caroline smiled as she thought back. "Grandma loved the residents, and I know she'd want me to take care of them."

"Generous gesture," Peter said. "Very generous." He gave a thoughtful nod, then followed with a smile. "I've got something intended for your grandma, but now I'm convinced you should have it." He pulled the yellow footstool to a stack of shelves in the far back of the store and climbed up.

From where Caroline stood the shelf appeared empty. Peter stretched his arm to the far back and pulled down a picture covered with dust.

"Mercy," he said, "this looks like it needs a cleaning." He pursed his lips, blew a few puffs of breath across the picture, then climbed down and handed it to her.

The picture was old, a faded black-and-white portrait from the 1920s or maybe the '30s. Caroline looked at the smiling face of the young man. "Was this someone Grandma knew?"

"No," Peter answered wistfully. "Your grandma never knew him, but I did. I knew both Will and his twin sister, Abigail. The picture belonged to Abigail and it was something she treasured." Peter chuckled. "After she died the picture was tossed in the garbage. Knowing how precious it was I couldn't let that happen, so I rescued it."

Caroline smiled. "I'm sure she appreciated—"

"She certainly did. But having the picture was a big responsibility. It meant I had to find the right person to give it to."

"Why was Grandma the right person?"

"In time you'll understand." Peter laughed. "Now that Ida's no longer here, I believe you're the right person."

"Me?" Caroline held onto the picture for a moment, then passed it back to Peter. "I don't think so. What with buying food and household expenses, I'm kind of strapped for cash. Maybe next time—"

Peter handed the picture back to her. "It's a gift. Hang it over your desk, and it will give you the freedom to write."

"Oh, you mean like a source of inspiration?"

"You could say that," Peter replied. "Like a source of inspiration."

WILBUR WASHINGTON

*H*aving boys is a whole lot easier than having girls. I know, because Martha and I raised two boys. When one of them was staring trouble in the eye, I'd say, Toughen up, kid. Act like a man! That works fine for boys, but what do you say to a girl?

Especially a girl who isn't ready to listen.

I know she's not really my granddaughter, but I think Ida would want me to think of her that way. That's how Ida was. She took care of any needy soul who came her way. She was the sort who'd take a mongrel dog from the street and treat him like he had a pedigree.

No question Ida had a big heart, but she also had a misplaced sense of loyalty when it came to Max. Being he was Big Jim's brother she felt she owed him, and that's why she let him move in. Of course, she had no way of knowing what would happen after she was gone.

Damn, I miss that woman. We all do. Louie misses her because of the cooking, but I miss her because she was someone I could be with and talk to. I never said so, but in the way old folks come to care for one another, I was in love with Ida. It wasn't the kind of love I had with Martha, or, for that matter, the kind Ida had with Big Jim. But we certainly were fond of each other. When you get to our age, love is an easygoing thing; it's not steeped in passion but found in a touch or a smile. It's simply knowing someone is there for you and they've got an ear to listen. There were many evenings when the two of us sat on the porch swing creaking back and forth, not saying a word. We didn't have to; just the touch of our bodies next to one another felt sweet as warm honey. Lord God, how I miss those times.

With Ida gone Caroline needs someone to watch over her. Max is her uncle, but I can assure you he's not looking out for her best interest. It's unfortunate that she doesn't see the truth of what he is. She believes because he's her granddaddy's brother, he'll eventually get over being mad. I've met men like Max before and I'm warning you, they don't get over anything. They might make you think they have, but in the long run they'll get what they want, even if it means stepping over your body to do so.

That's something Caroline is too young to realize.

I haven't got a whole lot to give the girl, but the one thing I can give her is the wisdom of my years. For whatever that's worth.

THE WATCH AND THE WASH

In early May Wilbur's pocket watch mysteriously disappeared. He searched the house, looking in even the most unlikely nooks and crannies, but found nothing. He asked each of the residents if they'd happened upon his watch, and when they answered no he lifted the sofa cushions and peered beneath the beds.

Sixty years of pulling the watch from his pocket to check the time was a habit Wilbur found impossible to break. And once the watch was gone it seemed he reached for it all the more often. His hand would slip to his vest pocket and feel the emptiness; then a look of longing would drift across his face.

Caroline noticed.

On the third Tuesday of May, she returned to the Previously Loved Treasures store in search of a pocket watch.

"With large numbers," she said, "and a chain."

"Got it," Peter Pennington replied. He climbed onto the yellow step stool, pulled a box from the shelf, and removed a watch that could have easily been the one Wilbur lost. It wasn't just similar to the missing watch; it was an exact replica.

When she asked the price, Peter said, "One coin."

"One coin?"

He nodded in that strange way he had of bobbing his head without taking his eyes from hers. "Reach in your pocket and pull out a coin. Whatever that coin is will be the price of the watch."

"What if it's a penny?"

"Then that's the price."

Caroline laughed. With little to lose, she stuck her hand in her pocket and pulled out a quarter.

"Oh, dear." Peter furrowed his brow. "I thought it was going to be a dime."

"Isn't a quarter better?"

"No, it's way too much."

Caroline eyed the watch. It ticked with the precision of Big Ben and was without flaw. "Too much?"

"It's used," Peter explained. "Previously loved."

Sticking with his opinion that a quarter was overpriced, Peter scrambled back up the yellow step stool and brought down a music box. "I'll include this," he said. He twisted the key, and the angel atop the box turned round and round as the music tinkled.

With great delight Caroline watched and listened. When the music stopped, she said, "I don't recognize this song."

Peter laughed. "In time you will. In time."

Before she left the store he asked if she'd hung the picture.

"Yes, I have," Caroline answered, but as she spoke the bitterness of the lie tripled in size and stung her throat.

"Good." Peter nodded. "Very good."

On the drive home Caroline made a mental note to hang the picture. She thought it charming that Peter Pennington believed it might inspire her; unrealistic perhaps, but charming. Obviously he had no knowledge of her schedule. From early morning until near bedtime she rushed around cooking, cleaning, buying groceries, running errands, paying bills, and a dozen other things. Writing a novel had been a foolish idea to start with.

"Maybe someday," she told herself. "Maybe someday."

When she arrived home Caroline slipped into Wilbur's room, left the watch on his nightstand, and said nothing. At supper that evening he wore a grin so wide it almost swallowed up his nose. He waited until everyone was seated, then pulled the watch from his pocket.

"I found my watch," he announced. "It was right where I'd left it." He looked at Max. "I'm afraid I owe you an apology."

Max, who had grown suspicious of everyone, asked, "For what?"

"I thought you'd taken it," Wilbur admitted.

"Gimme a break," Max grumbled. He looked down at the plate of food in front of him and shoveled in a large chunk of potato.

Max avoided looking at Wilbur throughout the remainder of the meal. Before the others finished eating, he stood and walked away from the table. Minutes later he left the house and headed for the Owl's Nest.

Seeing the watch had shocked Max. The pawnshop where he had sold it was more than six miles away. Not only was it in another town, but it was also a place you wouldn't go to unless you had good reason. Wilbur couldn't possibly have found the watch, yet there it was back in his pocket.

"It's a trick," Max muttered. It had to be a trick. As he walked, he convinced himself they were all working together, plotting against him. Trying to force him out. "That's what this is about," he said. Before he pushed through the door of the Owl's Nest, he'd decided they weren't going to get away with it.

When Max returned home, the house was dark. He bypassed the kitchen, stumbled to his room, and fell fast asleep.

The next day was Wednesday, the day Caroline stripped the beds and washed all the sheets and towels. That morning she rapped on Max's door several times asking for the bedclothes that needed laundering. The first two times there was no answer, so believing him still asleep, she waited. It was near noon when he finally answered with a gruff, "Go away!"

Waiting for Max meant washday got off to a late start. It was nearing three-thirty when Caroline pulled the first load of sheets from the washer and placed them in the dryer and after four when the buzzer sounded for the second load. Returning to the laundry room, Caroline opened the dryer and found the first load still damp. She reset the dryer, switched it from warm to hot, and went back to the kitchen.

Moments after she'd put a tray of biscuits in to bake, Caroline smelled smoke. She opened the oven and eyed the biscuits. Nope, they were still balls of white dough. She sniffed the air and followed the scent. It led to the laundry room. When she opened the door, flames shot up from behind the dryer.

"Fire!" she screamed and yanked the plug from the wall.

Louie, who'd moments earlier sat to read the newspaper, jumped up and came running. He pushed past Caroline, grabbed a sopping wet towel from the washer, and threw it over the flames. The fire spit and sputtered for a minute, then died out. Louie shook his head as he watched a cloud of steamy smoke rise from beneath the towel.

"I wouldn't try using that dryer again."

Caroline had to agree. She glanced at the pile of wet laundry. "Is there a Laundromat around here?"

"Not close by," Louie answered. "I think there's one over in Mackinaw."

Mackinaw was forty-five miles east of Rose Hill, a nothing town, a truck-stop place with little to offer other than gas stations, motels, and a Laundromat. Caroline thought of Mackinaw and the dingy Laundromat she'd passed on the trip to Rose Hill; then she looked back at the dryer. "Maybe it can be repaired."

"I doubt it," Louie replied.

Thinking the Laundromat would be less crowded later in the evening, Caroline went back to preparing supper. Delaying the inevitable, she sat down and ate with the residents.

"Sorry about the dryer," Laricka said sympathetically. "Do you think it's still under warranty?"

"That dryer?" Louie replied skeptically. "It's fifteen years old, if it's a day."

Caroline nodded. "I'm pretty sure it has to be replaced." Her bank account had dwindled to a little more than one hundred dollars, and the thought poked at her like a sharp needle.

"Since we all use the washer and dryer," Wilbur said, "why don't we each chip in twenty bucks towards a new one?"

"Good idea," Doctor Payne said, and all but one agreed.

"It's not my house," Max said angrily, "so why should I pay to fix something?" Although he'd taken just a few bites of the food on his plate, Max stood and left the table.

He wasn't paying rent, he reasoned, so why should he be expected to pay for repairs? That thought was one of many Max stored up. Added together they gave him justification for revenge.

After dinner Caroline cleared the table. She washed and dried the dishes, then stacked them in the cupboard before she carried the laundry baskets to the driveway. With a two-year-old copy of *Ladies Home Journal* tucked in her purse and three loads of wet sheets in the trunk of her car, she started for Mackinaw.

Max left the house moments after Caroline.

MAX SWEETWATER

*I*t irks me that everybody treats Caroline like she's something special. She's not. She's a conniving scam artist. A nobody.

I'd bet my bottom dollar she ain't one ounce related to James or anybody else in the Sweetwater family. She probably saw his name somewhere and cooked up this bullshit story about being his daughter. I knew James, and I can say for sure he wasn't one for settling down, never mind having kids.

Miss Caroline might have pulled the wool over poor old Ida's eyes, but she's sure as hell not pulling it over mine!

I ain't your run-of-the-mill dumb patsy; I know what she's up to. I met her kind before. She figures to run me off, then sell the place and walk away with a pocketful of money. Well, it ain't gonna happen.

This house is rightfully mine, and come hell or high water I'm gonna get it. Watch and see.

Nobody screws Max Sweetwater and gets away with it.

The Danger of Drying

It was after ten when Caroline pulled up in front of the You Wash Laundromat. A neon green "Open 24 Hours" sign lit the front window, and beyond it was what appeared to be an empty room. Caroline gave a sigh of relief. With a row of empty dryers, she could do all three loads at one time and be out of there within the hour.

One by one she carried the baskets in and set each one in front of a dryer. The basket of wet laundry claimed ownership of the machine if someone else happened by, although at this time of night such a thing was unlikely. Caroline loaded all three dryers, slid her quarters in, and watched the sheets start tumbling. She looked around for a comfortable chair, but there was none. The only place to sit was a long wooden bench running the width of the back wall.

Pulling the magazine from her purse Caroline started toward the back, flipping through the pages as she walked. She believed herself alone until from the corner of her eye she saw something move and gasped.

"Good grief! You startled me!"

On the dark end of the bench sat a woman with a young girl sleeping in her lap. "Sorry," the woman said.

She was young, in her twenties maybe, but bone thin. Even though the overhead light in that area was dark and the woman kept her face lowered, the large purple bruise was obvious. "Are you all right?" Caroline asked.

"Unh-huh." The woman nodded.

Caroline eyed the bruise again. "You ought to put ice on that."

"It'll be okay."

"No, it won't." Caroline set the magazine aside, stood, and walked toward the woman. "There's an all-night bar down the street. I can get some ice and—"

"Please don't. I'd rather nobody know we're here."

Caroline heard the fear threaded through the woman's words. "I'm not gonna tell anyone you're here, but you really ought to—"

"No. Please. I'll be okay."

The voices caused the child to stir, and she woke with a whimper. "Mama, I'm hungry."

The woman gathered the child closer to her. "In a while, Sara. We'll get something to eat in a while."

"I can run down to the bar and get takeout," Caroline suggested.

"No," the woman replied, this time more emphatically.

Something was definitely wrong. "Who are you hiding from?"

"Daddy," the child answered innocently.

"Shush, Sara." The woman hugged the child closer to her chest.

Caroline looked at her aghast. "Your husband did this?"

"He didn't mean to; it was an accident."

"If it was an accident, why are you hiding? Why didn't *he* get ice for your face?" Caroline's voice turned hard and unrelenting. Bitter memories of her own mama with similar bruises ran through her thoughts, and it became impossible to back away. "If this was an accident, he would have taken you to the hospital!"

"It *was* an accident," the woman said apologetically, "but when Joe's drinking—"

"Don't be a fool," Caroline said angrily. "And don't make excuses for him."

"Joe loves me, but lately he's had a run of bad luck and—"

"A run of bad luck doesn't excuse this!"

"He's not a bad man. Tomorrow morning, Joe will see what he's done and—"

Caroline narrowed her eyes suspiciously. "This isn't the first time, is it?"

The woman kept her face lowered and gave no answer.

"Why don't you leave?" Although there was still no answer Caroline didn't give up. "Are you waiting for him to kill you or maybe your daughter?"

The woman gave a sorry shake of her head. "We've got nowhere to go."

"Come home with me," Caroline suggested. "I've got room enough and—"

"Thanks," the woman said, "but that's not a good idea. When Joe finds us, he'll just take it out on you." She told how three years earlier she'd left and gone to her sister's house.

"Evelyn ended up in the hospital. Joe warned if she told who did it me and Sara were good as dead, so Evelyn never told."

"Men like that are crazy," Caroline said. "If you stay with him, you and Sara could both end up dead!"

"Joe wouldn't kill us," the woman replied. "He loves me and Sara. It's just that—"

Caroline slapped her hand to her head. "You don't get it, do you?"

After more than a half-hour of discussion the woman, Rowena, agreed to go with Caroline. The convincing argument was that Caroline lived forty-five miles away, and Joe had no way of connecting her with Rowena.

Rowena and Sara remained in the shadows while Caroline pulled the sheets from the dryer and loaded the baskets into the trunk of her car. Once she'd finished doing that, Caroline looked up and down the street. Not a soul in sight. She raised her arm and waved.

Rowena and Sara dashed out of the Laundromat and scrambled into the back seat of the car.

"Duck down until we're clear of town," Caroline said as she closed the door.

The nervous fluttering in her stomach urged Caroline to floor the accelerator and get away as quickly as possible, but she kept her hands locked onto the steering wheel and held the car steady at the speed limit. No one saw them leaving, and she was determined not to do anything that would garner unwanted attention now. Although unwilling to admit it, the tale of what had happened to Evelyn was stuck in Caroline's thoughts.

When the lights of the town faded into nothingness, Rowena sat up. "You're sure no one saw us?"

"Positive," Caroline answered.

When they arrived at the house, it was nearing midnight. Caroline made sandwiches and sat mother and child at the kitchen table. Five-year-old Sara ate two sandwiches and four cookies. Rowena nervously nibbled at a single sandwich. Although she had agreed to come, the fear in her eyes was apparent. Twice more she asked if Caroline was absolutely certain no one had seen them.

"Absolutely certain," Caroline confirmed, but even as she spoke the words, fear tugged at her thoughts. What if…What if…What if?

After they'd eaten, Caroline took Rowena and the child to her room. "You can stay here," she said and offered a nightgown for Rowena and a tee shirt for Sara.

Caroline gathered her own things and moved to the loft where Ida had slept. It was small but filled with sweet memories. For a long time she remained awake, thinking through the things that needed to be done. It was nearing daybreak when she decided Rowena Mallory would become Rose Smith, a friend from back home.

Although she had never noticed clothes at Previously Loved Treasures, she knew Peter Pennington would have them. Tomorrow she would buy different clothes for both and a box of hair dye for Rowena.

ROWENA MALLORY

C aroline is a real sweet girl, but I hope to God she hasn't bit off more than she can chew. She doesn't know Joe, so she don't know what he's capable of doing. Unfortunately, I do.

She's right about me being a fool. Looking back you see things a lot clearer than when you're smack in the middle. Being married to a man like Joe is never easy, so you start fooling yourself into thinking that's how life ought to be. It's not. There was a time when I loved Joe more than life itself. That's fine when you haven't got a baby to care for, but now I've got Sara and things are different. It's not that I love him less; it's just that I love her more.

Up until now Joe never hit Sara, not once. Oh, often enough he'd come home drunk, smash things around, and start yelling so loud we were afraid to blink an eyelash. Times like that I was scared to death he'd start in on poor little Sara, but he didn't. That's not to say next time he won't. Joe is plenty mean, and meanness has a way of spreading itself around. Today it was me; tomorrow it could be her. I'm not willing to chance it.

I know you're questioning why any girl would marry a man like Joe, but he wasn't always this way. When we met I was sixteen years old, and he was twenty-three. That night when I left the bowling alley with Evelyn she said I ought to watch my step, 'cause Joe had the look of trouble. I didn't say anything 'cause I didn't want her to worry, but by then we'd already made a date for the next night. We got married a month later. I was starry-eyed in love and sure didn't see trouble. All I saw was the handsomest man who ever walked.

That first year Joe treated me like I was a precious baby doll. He never even said a cross word. He didn't turn ugly 'till after Sara was born. The first time he hit me, it was just after I'd been nursing her. He was stomping around like a bad-natured bear, and I started teasing him about being jealous of the baby. I was laughing when he *hauled off and slammed me upside the head. Less than a minute later he was on his knees begging my forgiveness. Knowing how much Joe loved me, I forgave him. I figured it would never happen again, and we'd go right back to being happy.*

I was wrong; not wrong about him being jealous of Sara, but wrong to think we'd ever be happy again.

I keep wondering if I hadn't ever touched on his sore spot, would Joe still be crazy in love with me? Some days I think yes, and other days I know it's just wishful thinking.

The saddest thing about an ugly mess like this is that you don't stop loving someone like Joe; you just keep hoping things will get better.

A Rose by Any Other Name

Early the next morning before any of the other residents got out of bed, Caroline rapped on the door of the room where Rowena and Sara were sleeping. It was a soft tap, not a knuckled knock, but Rowena opened the door cautiously.

"Thank heaven it's you," she said when she saw Caroline.

Caroline slipped inside the door. "Stay here in the room. I'll bring a breakfast tray up."

The plan was set in place, and as far as any of the residents knew it was just an ordinary Wednesday. Yes, the biscuits were a bit burnt and the bacon undercooked, but that was something they'd come to expect so no one asked questions.

Caroline sat at the table nervously nibbling on a burnt biscuit. "So, what is everyone going to do today?"

"I'm thinking I might clear the weeds out of that flower patch in front of the house," Wilbur said.

"On a day like today? Why, it's way too hot for that."

"It's not that hot—"

Before Wilbur could finish his thought Laricka jumped in. "Oh, it's definitely going to be hot! Too hot for weed-pulling."

Pleased with Laricka's answer, Caroline turned back to Wilbur. "See, Laricka thinks it's too hot too."

Laricka nodded. "You wouldn't catch me pulling weeds on a day like today. I'm just gonna sit in that nice big rocker on the front porch and read my book."

"The front porch?" Caroline repeated. Things were not working out as she wanted. Normally all the residents went their own way after breakfast. Some napped, others watched game shows on television, and Doctor Payne usually grabbed the lounge under the elm in the back yard and spent the day reading magazines about dentistry. It was a rarity when anyone sat, stood, or worked in the front of the house. Trying to come up with a plan that would appeal to the majority, Caroline suggested, "A hot day like today is when you ought to be sitting in a nice cool air-conditioned theater." When no one voiced a difference of opinion, she added, "The new Indiana Jones movie is playing at the Rialto." Although Caroline had only the Food Lion clerk's opinion to go by, she swore it was a movie they didn't want to miss.

"Sounds good to me," Louie said.

Harriet agreed. And although Wilbur stuck to the thought of weeding, he eventually gave in and said he'd go with the others.

"What about you?" Caroline asked Laricka.

"I can't go," she answered. "My grandsons are coming to visit."

Caroline thought of the grandsons, two boys who ran helter-skelter throughout the house. They popped up from behind sofas, crawled under beds, and once emerged from behind the coal bin in the cellar. They had big ears and loud voices. No secret would stay safe with them around.

"All the kids are going to see Indiana Jones," she said. "The boys would be crushed if they missed it."

The thought of depriving her grandchildren of anything struck home. "Well, yes, I suppose they would enjoy it," Laricka said. She excused herself from the table and went to call the boys.

Doctor Payne decided to pass; he'd just received a new magazine that needed reading.

With everyone out of the house this afternoon and Max still sleeping it off behind locked doors, Caroline could set the stage for her plan.

Once the table was cleared, she did the dishes in record time then jumped in her car and headed for the drugstore. In less than ten minutes Caroline was back with a box of Roux hair color. She handed Rowena the package of chestnut satin dye and a pair of scissors.

"I'll be back in an hour," she said.

It took twenty minutes to get there, but when Caroline pulled alongside the curb in front of Previously Loved Treasures Peter Pennington stood outside.

"Good morning," he said with a smile. "I was expecting you a bit earlier."

Without questioning she said, "Sorry, I had to stop by the drugstore first." Following him inside, Caroline mentioned she was looking for some children's clothing. "Girl's," she specified. "Size four or maybe five."

"Size five is what you want," Peter replied confidently. "And I've got everything you need." He carried the yellow stepstool to the back of the store, climbed up, and pulled down a box that was nearly the size of steamer trunk. "You'll also want some toys."

Peter hauled the box to the counter and lifted the lid. Inside was everything Sara would need: play clothes, dresses, underwear, shoes, even a miniature-sized pocketbook, a baby-faced doll, and several other toys.

Caroline gasped. "Oh, my gosh! This is exactly what I was looking for."

"Of course it is." Peter grinned.

When Caroline asked how much, he gave an even bigger grin and said, "Nothing."

"Nothing? How can you make money selling things for nothing?"

"I don't need money. I'm happy with what I've got." He gave his mouth a sad little twist and shrugged. "Dollars, dimes, drachmas—the world still doesn't realize they can't buy happiness."

With a look of puzzlement, Caroline asked, "Then why the store? Why not retire and take life easy?"

"This store is not for me, it's for people who need things. People like you and your grandma."

Caroline found fuzzy reasoning in such an answer, and were she not in such a hurry she would have stayed to pursue it further but time was of the essence. By four o'clock the residents would return, and everything had to be in place by then. Not that she wouldn't trust them to keep her secret, but not knowing was far better. Not knowing meant there was no chance of a slip-up.

In addition to the box of children's clothes, Peter gave Caroline a previously loved suitcase filled with jeans, tee-shirts, and sweaters that would fit her or Rowena. "It's been to Paris, France three times," he said as he carried it to her car.

Before she could pull away from the curb, he again asked if she'd hung the picture.

She'd said yes last time, but he'd obviously seen through the lie.

"Actually I haven't done it yet," Caroline confessed. "I planned to, but now that I have a guest staying in my room I doubt I'll be able to work at the desk."

"Not work at the desk?" Peter replied. "A desk with so many stories waiting to be written?" He lowered his head and gave a sorrowful shake. "Sad."

Caroline felt a sense of shame creeping over her. How could she? This strange little man had given her so much and asked so little. Peter wasn't just a shopkeeper; he was a friend.

"You're right," she said. "I know that's something I should do." Caroline smiled at Peter and it was a genuine smile, a smile that promised fulfillment. "Tomorrow I'll move the desk to my loft and hang the picture."

As Caroline pulled away she caught one last glimpse of Peter standing at the curb and waving goodbye.

When the residents sat down to dinner that night, there was a newcomer in their midst. A woman dressed in a business suit Caroline had once worn for work. A woman with short dark hair and a well-dressed daughter sitting beside her. If anyone came looking for the ragged blond from the Laundromat, they could honestly say they'd never seen such a person.

When she introduced Rose Smith, Caroline gave a slight smile. "Rosie and I go way back. Why, we've known each other since God knows when."

Rose Smith smiled and nodded.

Harriet was the only one to mention the large purple bruise on Rowena's cheek. "What happened to your face?"

Rowena, who was now Rose, gave a shallow little laugh. "It happened on the way down here," she said, then explained how on the bus her suitcase had tumbled from the rack and hit the side of her cheek.

Before there could be any more questions, Caroline jumped in. "Rose is going to be staying with us for a while. She's promised to help me with the cooking."

Louie was the first to speak. "Well, now, that's certainly good news."

"I can't say I'm a great cook," Rose replied demurely. "But I do make really good biscuits and gravy."

Everyone smiled; even Sara.

CHICKEN N' DUMPLINGS

On Thursday morning when the residents came to breakfast, they were greeted with a cheese omelet so fluffy it looked like it might float away. Alongside the omelet sat a stack of ham slices browned to perfection and a pile of juicy fat sausages.

Louie reached across the table and carved off a sizeable chunk of omelet.

"You mind leaving some for somebody else?" Harriet said.

Rose, just coming from the kitchen, set a basket of biscuits on the table. "Don't worry," she said, laughing, "there's plenty more."

Before Louie had swallowed that first bite, he garbled, "Delicious!"

For probably the first and only time Doctor Payne agreed with Louie, and Louie, with his mouth full, didn't have a wisecrack comeback.

Breakfast lasted a good half-hour longer than usual, and when the residents finally left the table they all agreed today lunch would be unnecessary.

"Why, I'm so full I couldn't swallow another bite," Laricka said.

Doctor Payne, who had begun to read medical journals as well as the dentistry magazines, added, "Overeating is bad for your heart, and given the way we've all overindulged this morning skipping lunch is a well-advised option."

Although Louie had misgivings about such a drastic move, he went along with the others. Somewhere about two o'clock his stomach started rumbling, and he regretted the decision. It was another four hours until supper. He snapped on the radio and tried listening to a Braves baseball game, but in the bottom of the third inning he started thinking about the stadium hot dogs smothered in mustard and lost track of the score.

His stomach grumbled again, and he thought back to breakfast. He could picture the platter sitting on the table at the end of the meal. There were several slices of ham left on the plate and three biscuits in the basket. What harm could there be in grabbing a few slices of leftover ham and a cold biscuit? Shortly after his stomach rumbled a third warning, Louie slipped quietly into the kitchen.

Rose stood at the kitchen counter with her back to the door. The radio played a Jimmy Buffet song, and as she snapped the ends off of a pile of string beans she sang along.

So much the better, Louie thought, and without saying a word he crossed behind her and opened the refrigerator door. He reached in, pulled out the platter of ham, a basket of biscuits, and a jar of mayonnaise. He would have gone unnoticed if at the last minute he hadn't decided to add lettuce. When he added the head of lettuce to what he was holding, the jar of mayonnaise tipped and began to fall. Louie tried to catch it, but the platter of ham went. Everything hit the floor at once in an explosion of sound.

Rose screamed and whirled around, a look of fear on her face and the knife in her hand thrust out defensively. Seeing Louie, she said, "You scared the life out of me!"

By then Wilbur had come running to the kitchen, as had Laricka.

"For shame," Laricka scolded. "We say no lunch and you do this?"

"It's okay," Rose said as she stooped to help Louie pick up the pieces of glass strewn across the floor. "No harm done."

"But," Laricka stammered, "you screamed—"

"Just startled," Rose explained, trying to calm the momentary fear of believing Joe had found her.

For the first week Rose constantly looked over her shoulder, jumped at even the slightest sound, and slept with one eye open. Despite Caroline's assurance that no one had seen them leave town together, Rose could not rid herself of the belief Joe would one day come walking through the door. The only moments of peace she found were the ones spent in the kitchen. There she could lose herself in the tasks of mixing batter, peeling vegetables, or leafing through the pages of Ida's cookbooks. When Rose came to a page that was tattered and food-stained, she would think about making that dish for supper.

After only a few days the house began to change. Burnt biscuits became a thing of the past and questions such as "Would you prefer stuffed pork chops or rosemary roasted chicken for dinner?" began to circle the breakfast table. Supper was once again served at six, and there was no longer a need for the dinner bell because the residents were seated in their chairs before the sixth chime on the clock had sounded. But the food wasn't the only change.

High-pitched giggles wafted through the hallways, and toys began to pop up in the strangest places—a Jack-in-the-Box in the hall bath, a tower of blocks on the living room coffee table, a Barbie doll with no clothes peeking from beneath a stack of newspapers,

The desk in Caroline's old room was moved upstairs to the loft, along with the picture Peter Pennington had given her. Although Peter made the desk seem light as a feather when he carried it in singlehandedly, Louie and Doctor Payne wiped beads of sweat from their faces as they heaved and hauled it up the stairs. Once the desk was pushed into place against the sloped wall, Caroline hammered a nail into the wall and hung the picture above the desk. She stepped back, eyed the picture, and looked into the face of a man who was both stranger and friend. "Welcome to your new home," she said laughingly.

On Sunday Rose made Ida's much-loved chicken and dumplings for dinner, and after Louie tasted the first bite he jumped up, darted around the table, lifted Rose from her chair, and wrapped her in a gigantic bear hug. "You're amazing!" he said. Then he pleaded with her to marry him. Laughter broke out around the table, and before long it had the merry sound of a party.

The door to Max's room was closed and locked, but sounds slid through the keyhole and picked at his thoughts. Through the weeks Max's resentment had spread from Caroline to the other residents, and such frivolity could only mean one thing: they were hatching a plot against him. With his eyes narrowed to mere slits and his mouth set in a steely straight line, Max twisted the lock open and walked into the dining room. Rose sat in the seat he'd previously occupied. With a scowl that carved ridges above his brows, he looked at her and roared, "What the hell...?"

Rose bounced up so quickly the chair fell backward. "I'm sorry. I didn't—"

Caroline might not have found the courage to speak if the angry words had been directed at her, but there was no hesitation in her defense of Rose.

"Back off, Max!" she said angrily. "I told Rose to sit there."

Before anything could happen, Wilbur grabbed onto the exchange. "Here, Max, take my seat." He stood and offered his chair.

Max eyed him suspiciously, then came around and sat.

While it may have appeared to be a lessening of Max's standoff, such a thing was not true. To Max's way of thinking, his presence prevented them from furthering whatever vengeful plans they had. He'd already imagined any number of harmful things they might do: break into his room and cart away all his belongings, plant a nest of bedbugs in the mattress, poison his toothpaste. The list was endless. He had to be on guard.

Once Max was seated at the table, the laughter ended and words came with a thin covering of wariness. The conversation turned to weather, summer flowers waiting to be planted, and a movie Harriet had seen nearly a month ago.

Max added nothing to the conversation but remained in his seat, smug in the satisfaction that he had thwarted whatever mischief they were planning. Moving forward he would be more diligent; he would be there for breakfast, lunch, and dinner.

The next morning Max came to the breakfast table. He also sat there at lunchtime and again at supper. For the first few days his presence caused the residents to be on edge, wary that a single wrong word could set him off on a tangent that could turn violent. Twice Harriet cornered Caroline and suggested it would be better for all concerned if Max moved out.

"That might be," Caroline answered. "But Max is family, and I can't ask him to leave."

In time the nervous, buckled-down conversation that took place when Max was seated at the table eased back to what it had been. Not all the way back to the frivolity of the chicken and dumplings night but back to a warm chatter that passed from one to another like a dish of butter or a bowl of peas. When the words were passed to Max he quickly moved them along, cautious of giving voice to any thought or intention they could use against him.

Hope and Fear

In the days that followed, Caroline and Rose settled into a relationship so comfortable one would pass the salt shaker before the other thought to ask. They worked side by side in the kitchen and shared the cooking duties with neither doing more than the other. Before two weeks had gone by, hearty beef stews and apple pies flavored with cinnamon began appearing on the dinner table. Biscuits, light and fluffy as a cloud, came piled high in serving baskets and were eaten down to the very last crumb.

While in the other rooms of the house Rose quietly observed life, inside the kitchen she came alive. In the kitchen there were no barriers, no subject untouchable. Caroline knew the secret of Rose's identity, and she held tight to it. As far as the world was concerned, no one in Rose Hill had ever seen or heard of a Rowena Mallory.

They seldom spoke of it but on the few occasions when they traded whispers Caroline would assure her, "There's no need to be afraid. You've got a new name and a new look. He'll never in a million years find you."

But having Joe find her was not the only fear Rose had. There was a dark corner of her heart where she hid a twisted thread of hope that he would come in search of her, and this time he would be a changed man, the man he once was. Whenever Caroline spoke of the past being forever gone, it caught hold of that thread and caused a strange weight of weariness to fall over Rose's shoulders. Times like that she would turn to remembering something pleasant. Frequently it was a story of the early days when they first dated and fell in love. Despite the purple bruise that had now turned to a greyish yellow color, she remembered only the good times, the days when he held her gently and pressed his lips to hers. In the midst of just such a reminiscence Rose said, "I know I'm doing what I have to do, but the truth is I miss Joe."

"Miss him?" Caroline asked. "How can you miss a man who would—"

"Joe's not really like that," Rose answered. "It's only because he's had a lot of tough breaks. He lost his job. He wasn't ready for a baby—"

Caroline cut in with words that were crusty and sharp-edged. "He *is* like that. You don't make excuses for someone like him!"

"I know what he did was wrong, but maybe if his life wasn't so hard—"

"So life is hard," Caroline said. "That's not your fault. He has no right to..." Her lower lip began to tremble. The memories were back, memories she believed long gone. "For Joe to do what he did was wrong. How can you forgive him for such a horrible thing? Don't you know that Sara watching her daddy hit you will stay with her forever? Do you want her to grow up like me? Fearful, afraid of everything?"

A flood of memories washed over Caroline, and she dropped into the chair. "I'm sorry if I sound harsh. But I know what that life is like. I had a daddy who was the same as Joe. He beat up on Mama until he got tired of doing it; then he walked off and left her. Left both of us. We had a miserable life with him, and once he was gone Mama kept right on being miserable."

"I didn't know," Rose stammered.

"It's not something I like to talk about," Caroline replied. "It's the sort of shame people sweep under the bed and hope nobody will notice."

For several minutes neither of them spoke; then Caroline gave a sorrowful sigh. "The funny thing is Mama's heart was so full of missing Daddy there wasn't room for anyone else. We were flat-outt miserable in that New Orleans apartment, but Mama wouldn't move because she kept believing Daddy would change his ways and come back home."

"But Joe never left," Rose argued. "I was the one—"

"Whether you leave or he leaves makes no difference," Caroline snapped. "Joe is just like my daddy. Don't think he'll change, because he won't!"

For a moment Rose stood there looking crushed. "But don't you think it's possible a man can change?"

With her mouth in a narrow hard-set line, Caroline gave her head a saddened shake. "Is that what you really think?" It wasn't a rhetorical question. It was pointed and sharp; it demanded an answer.

The thought came at Rose like a razor blade slicing away whatever possibilities she'd hidden in the closet of her mind. She closed her eyes and saw the twin images of hope and fear. They stood side by side waiting for her answer. *Choose me*, they both said. Seeing them together, so alike and yet so different, she could at last see the truth.

Rose knew she had to choose neither, for to choose one meant she got both. If she chose fear, she would stay hidden and forever live with the hope he would one day come to her as a changed man. If she chose hope, she could return to him, give him yet another chance, and forever live with the fear of what might eventually happen.

Rose could lie to others but could no longer lie to herself. It was a long time before she answered, and when she did her voice was weighted with finality.

"No, I don't suppose he'll ever change." She blinked back the tears gathering in her eyes and stood there for several minutes before turning back to stack the dishes.

That was the last time they mentioned Joe Mallory.

Rose moved through the days without voicing her fear, but it was always there. At night when the house was dark and quiet, it came and whispered in her ear. *He's coming.*

He'll not find me, she vowed. In the wee hours of morning when the only sounds to be heard were the soft whispers of Sara's breath, Rose set a plan in place to make sure she and her child would remain safe. No one had seen them come, and as long as they remained inside the house they could not be found.

For a while the child was content to sit at the table and color pictures as her mama and Aunt Caroline cooked. But Sara was five, not an age when sitting still comes easy. On occasion Rose would turn to slide a tray of biscuits into the oven, then turn back to find Sara gone. On several such occasions she found the girl chattering away with Louie or Harriet.

"You mustn't go bothering people," Rose scolded, but it was easy to see that neither of them seemed to mind.

"She's no bother," Louie said. Then he hoisted Sara onto his knee and magically discovered a piece of candy in his pocket. Two days later Harriet came home with a *Cat in the Hat* book she'd gotten for ten cents at a garage sale.

It was the same with most of the other residents. Wilbur enchanted the child with stories of boyhood adventures: fishing, camping in the woods, the Scout trip where he'd earned his Woodsman Badge. "Ah, yes," he said with a sigh, "Boy Scouts, that's the making of a man."

"I wanna be a Boy Scout too," Sara said.

"Afraid not, Missy," Wilbur replied. "But when you're a bit older you can be a Girl Scout." He told stories of the great adventures that awaited. "Why, pretty as you are, I bet you'll sell more cookies than any Girl Scout in history."

That very afternoon Sara began asking Rose to make some cookies for her to sell. "I need to practice."

"I'll make some cookies that you can sell to Mister Washington," Rose said, laughing

Little by little Sara made friends with the residents and gained greater freedom, but she was not allowed outside.

"You can go visit Mister Washington," Rose said, "or play with the boys, but do not step one foot outside the door."

"Okay, Mama."

"And stay away from Mister Sweetwater's room," Rose added.

She didn't need to warn Sara to stay clear of Max, because the child was already frightened of him. He seldom spoke to her, and when he did it was only to criticize her behavior or to tell her to get out of his way. On one particular morning he'd slept at a lady friend's house and came stumbling in as Sara ran down the hall chasing after Clarence. First the dog ran into Max and threw him off balance, and then Sara came flying around the corner and got tangled up in his legs. Max slammed into the wall and thundered, "Get the hell out of here!"

After that day, Sara avoided Max without anyone telling her to.

Max was the only resident who was off limits. The others were friends, and Sara thought nothing of tapping on the doors of their rooms. "You wanna tell me a story?" she'd ask. Even Doctor Payne would set aside the magazine he'd been reading and find time to chat with the girl.

He was sitting in the parlor with the latest *Dental News* when she wandered in and wanted to know if he was reading a story.

"Not a story," Payne said. "It's a professional magazine."

"What's a professor magazine?" Sara asked.

"It's a book of information that helps you be better at your job," Payne answered. "My job is being a dentist. What do you want to be when you grow up?"

"A princess," Sara answered.

"Princess?" he repeated. "Princess is not an occupation. Have you thought about dentistry? Now that's a fine occupation."

When a look of dismay slid across Sara's face, Louie came to her rescue. "Princess is a fine occupation, and I think you'd make an excellent princess."

Sara's smile returned.

"Besides," Louie added, "dentistry is for people who have no personality. You have lots of personality, way too much to become a dentist."

Doctor Payne gave a harrumph, then slid down behind the magazine he'd been reading.

Sara went running off to the kitchen calling, "Mama, I got a princess purse-some-ally."

On the second Sunday after they'd moved in, Laricka came to the kitchen and asked Rose if Sara could go to the Rialto. "The boys wanted to see Indiana Jones again, and I thought it would be nice to have Sara join us."

While the thought still hung in the air, Rose said, "No." Not the type of genteel "No, thank you" one might expect, but a flat, rock hard no, one without any margin of error.

Laricka pulled back like someone bitten by a snake. "Well, excuse me! I was only trying to be polite, so there's no need to—"

Caroline stepped in. "Now Laricka, don't be insulted. It's just that Sara is too young for a picture like that." She turned to Rose. "Isn't that right?"

"Yes, that's right," Rose answered, her tone softened and considerably milder.

"Well, good," Laricka said. "For a minute there I thought you just didn't want her playing with the boys."

"Oh, no, that's not it—"

Laricka gave a wave that dismissed the thought. "I know they can be a bit wild. But they're good boys, and they'd never do anything to harm Sara."

"Oh, I know they wouldn't." Rose's voice had edged its way back to normal. "And Sara really does enjoy playing with them. It's just that this movie—"

Laricka nodded. "I know." She started down the hall then turned back. "But Sara should get out more than she does. A child needs fresh air and sunshine."

This time Rose didn't need to give an answer, because once Laricka had said her piece she disappeared down the hall.

That evening when they finished putting the supper dishes back in the cupboard, Rose turned to Caroline and asked, "Do you think it's safe to let Sara play in the back yard?"

Caroline nodded. "I do. The wisteria bushes along the side of the house are so thick you can't see the yard from the street, and that big wooden fence goes the whole way around."

"Is there any other way to get back there?"

"No. The only way is to come through the house."

"Okay then." Rose smiled.

The next afternoon Sara's boundary was extended, and she was allowed into the backyard. "But only the backyard," Rose warned. "No further."

CAROLINE SWEETWATER

*H*aving Rowena here is like having a sister. When we're working together in the kitchen, that's when I feel closest to her. She's teaching me to cook, so naturally we talk about that, but we also talk about a thousand other things. After she told me she still had feelings for Joe, I explained what life was like with Mama. I think that changed her mind about wanting Joe back. Being crazy in love with a man is fine and dandy, but I don't think there's a man in the world a mother is ever gonna love as much as she loves her own child.

Rowena is awfully young to have so much responsibility, but she doesn't seem to mind. She's not like most girls who fuss about their hair and makeup. She hardly ever thinks about herself; she just worries about taking care of Sara. There's only a year or two difference in our ages, but she has a child and that makes a woman much more serious-minded.

On second thought, that might not be true of all women. It sure wasn't true of my mama. If Daddy had walked back in the door and said, Joelle, you've got to choose between me and the kid, *I can't say for sure who Mama would choose. I wish she'd been more like Rowena; I know for certain it would have made my life a whole lot better.*

I've got to stop thinking of her as Rowena, which is kind of hard to do. If I don't keep reminding myself she's Rose now, I'm liable to let her name slip. That happened day before yesterday, but luckily no one heard me. We were clearing the table and I said, Can you get the platter, Rowena? *The words were barely out of my mouth when I saw her face turn white as paste.*

Afterward I told her not to worry. I said they're safe here, but telling a person not to worry won't make them not worry. Rowena's still fearful; you can see it in her eyes. She says she's not, but if someone drops a shoe or slams a door she jumps up and starts looking around for Sara.

Sometimes I think we ought to tell the residents the truth about who she is and why she's here. You know what, I think they'd line up to protect her. They all like Rose, and they're crazy about little Sara. How could you not be?

It's been almost two weeks, and just yesterday Rose said it was okay for Sara to go outside and play in the back yard. "Don't go near the front," she warned. "Stay in the back."

Sara was out there all afternoon, and last night I saw where Doctor Payne had moved his lounge to the side of the yard and tied a tire swing onto the branch of that oak he'd been sitting under.

Imagine him doing that. Doctor Payne's one I never would have figured for being softhearted about a kid.

BACK IN MACKINAW

When Caroline drove out of Mackinaw with Rowena hunkered down in the back seat of her car, Joe Mallory was working his way through a bottle of Jack Daniels and pouring out the sorrows of his life to Ted, the bartender at Easy Aces. It was near daybreak when Joe finally stumbled back to the motel where they'd been living. After fumbling with the key for almost five minutes he pushed through the door calling for Rowena.

"Didn't you hear me trying to get in?" he yelled. "You couldn't get off your lazy ass and—"

The bed looked empty.

"What the hell…" Joe rubbed the back of his hand across his eyes and tried to focus on what he was seeing, or not seeing, as the case happened to be. Twice he squeezed his eyes shut then reopened them, but nothing changed. Rowena was not in the bed.

"Get out here, bitch!"

It was a small room, too small for anyone to hide anywhere, but the reality of that didn't register. Joe continued across the room, first falling into the dresser and then bouncing off a wall.

"Rowena," he called. "Rowena, get your ass out here!"

With almost a full bottle of whiskey under his belt, Joe swayed like he was standing on the Tilt-a-Whirl. The floor moved beneath his feet, and the walls slid away when he tried to reach for them. He smacked into the closet, then lurched toward the bathroom.

"Rowena, I know you're here!"

Still screaming her name, Joe bent to look under the bed. As he leaned forward he passed out and went down face first against the iron bed frame.

It was two o'clock in the afternoon when Joe woke. One eye was swollen shut, and his head felt like a hammer was banging against it. "I need a drink," he grumbled and struggled to his feet. For the moment, he didn't think about Rowena or Sara. He wasn't interested in where they'd gone or when they'd be back. His only thought was to get a drink and stop the pounding in his head.

Stan's Bar was two blocks over. Stan opened early, and Stan made a damn good drink. Joe needed a Bloody Mary, and he needed it now. He looked around the parking lot. The truck was gone. "Bitch," he grumbled, believing Rowena responsible.

Stan's wasn't that far; he could make it on foot. Joe started walking. Not so much walking, but just pushing one foot in front of the other and shuffling along. Twice he had to stop and lean against a lamppost to rest, but moments later he went back to moving his feet in the direction of Stan's Bar.

It took Joe forty minutes to get there, and by the time he arrived his throat felt parched and his head pounded like a kettledrum. He lumbered to the door, grabbed the handle, and pulled. The door didn't budge. He pulled again and again, then kicked the door and pounded with his fists. Nobody answered. When the throbbing in his head became unbearable, he picked up an empty trashcan from the street and hurled it through the glass window. While the bits and pieces of glass were still raining down, Joe stepped through the window and headed for the bar. He was tipping a whiskey bottle to his mouth when the police arrived.

Judge Barker was the law in Mackinaw, the only law. He was the one who said what was fair and not fair and he doled out punishment as he saw fit. Stan was the judge's brother-in-law.

Joe's head still throbbed the next day when the judge banged his gavel and said, "Fifteen days for drunk and disorderly conduct. And," the judge added, "it'll be a whole lot longer if you don't fork over the money to pay for Stan's window."

"Screw Stan!" Joe yelled. "Screw the window!" But by then the officer was dragging him out of the courtroom.

Joe didn't have the money to pay for Stan's window so his fifteen days became three weeks of sitting in the Mackinaw jailhouse. For the first five days it was pure hell. His stomach convulsed every time he thought of food, and he couldn't hold on to a cup of coffee because of his hands shaking. Twice he managed to slosh a few sips of the sludge, but both times he gagged and threw up more than he'd swallowed.

After the first five days, the hell settled into a day in/day out misery. A misery he didn't deserve. Getting drunk was a poor excuse for throwing a man in jail, he reasoned. On any given Friday, half the men in Mackinaw got drunk. Of course, those men went home and found their woman in bed where she belonged. Joe started thinking back on why he was in jail. That's when he came to the conclusion it was Rowena's fault.

For the entire three weeks Joe cursed her. If not for her, he wouldn't be here. If Rowena wasn't playing a smart-ass cat-and-mouse game, he wouldn't have had to search under the bed. He wouldn't have fallen. He wouldn't have needed a drink to nurse the pain in his head.

"This is the thanks I get," he muttered. "I take care of her and the kid, and this is how she pays me back?"

After a while he could almost see Rowena lounging on the bed back at the motel, laughing at his predicament. "Nobody shits on Joe Mallory and gets away with it," he vowed.

That's when he began to think of the various ways he could get even. When Rowena's laughter began to haunt his sleep, Joe realized that no matter what the cost he had to get out of jail. He started banging on the bars and hollering until the guard on duty finally came.

"Okay," Joe said, "tell Stan I'll give him my truck to pay for the broken window."

Two weeks earlier he'd remembered parking the truck at Easy Aces, but until now he'd said nothing about it. The truck with its bald tires and leaky radiator wasn't much, but at least with it he had a way of getting around. With it, he had a way of hauling crap from one place to another and putting money in his pocket. Without it he was screwed, but giving it up was his only way of getting out of jail.

It took another two days before Joe was released. As soon as he set foot on the sidewalk he headed for the motel figuring he'd find Rowena.

When Maggie, the owner of the motel, saw Joe coming, she flagged him down. "Don't bother going back there. I done cleaned out your room."

"Where's Rowena?" Joe asked.

"Gone." Maggie twitched her mouth to one side. It was the same expression she used when she spoke of the drifters who ran out on their bill. "Seems kind of funny, her leaving the same time you did."

"Did she say where she was going?"

"Ha, like that's gonna happen."

"Shit!"

When Maggie started complaining about the fact that they still owed her twenty-three dollars for room rent, Joe came close to jamming one of his balled-up fists into her mouth. The only thing that stopped him was the thought of going back to jail.

For the remainder of that day Joe went from place to place looking for Rowena. He tried the Food Mart, the gas station, the Laundromat, and the pool hall. He pulled the tattered picture of her and Sara from his wallet and asked if people had seen either the woman or the child. "Rowena's kind of average height, blue eyes, long blonde hair," he explained. But everyone he spoke with shook their head and said they'd not seen such a woman with or without a child.

"Damn," Joe grumbled.

At the end of a long night, when he had no place to sleep and nothing to eat, he went back to Abe's twenty-four-hour gas station and stood in front of the counter looking down at his feet.

"I need a place to stay," he said. "And I'm willing to work for it."

Abe, who pretty much ran the place by himself, agreed to give Joe a job. "Five dollars a day," he said. "You can sleep in the back and help yourself to whatever food's on the shelf."

Joe took the job and said he was mighty grateful. But gratitude was the last thing in the world he felt.

MISSING THINGS

The day Joe Mallory was released from the Mackinaw jail was the same day Louie decided to build a playhouse in the backyard of the Sweetwater residence. By then over three weeks had passed, and while Rose was still concerned Joe might find them she'd become considerably more relaxed about it. She no longer jumped at the sound of the doorbell or turned wary when she heard footsteps in the hall.

Max came to supper most every evening, but with late nights and heavy drinking he'd given up on breakfast and lunch. When he was not at the table the sound of laughter echoed through the hallways; when he made an appearance smelling of whiskey and needing a shave, little was said. The lack of conversation was noticeable, and the difference didn't escape Max's attention. Silverware clanked against plates and someone might mention a television show worth watching, but that was it.

This, of course, infuriated Max even more. Now certain they were plotting against him, he moved silently through the rooms and remained in the shadows, listening and watching. When he did catch the sound of voices, he pressed his back to the wall and inched closer to the doorway. Several times he thought he heard words like "gun" and "prisoner." And on one occasion he definitely heard Laricka say "poison." It came through loud and clear. But moments later her grandsons came barreling through the hallway, and Max had to move on. He missed knowing she had spoken of a weed pulled from the garden.

To Max each day seemed blacker than the one before. His eyes grew narrower and the set of his mouth harder. A ball of suspicion settled in his chest and grew to a size that could no longer be ignored. The anger that was once merely resentment took on the bright red glow of hatred, and Max began plotting his revenge.

He watched and waited. One afternoon when he saw Harriett leave the house, he slipped inside her room and searched for something to give warning as to what they were planning. Evidence of a sort. Of course he found nothing, but when he spied her silver cigarette lighter on the nightstand he picked it up and slid it into his pocket. Two days later he drove to Harrington and sold it for eight dollars.

"Smart-ass bitch," he'd grumbled. "Serves her right."

The lighter was the first of a number of things that went missing.

Harriet searched for the lighter for several days. It had been a gift from her first husband and was something she treasured. After she looked through the house, she called the beauty parlor to ask if perchance she'd left it there.

"Sorry, hon," Greta said. "Nothing like that's been found."

"Can you keep an eye out?" Harriet asked. "Silver with a gold heart on the front and my initials on the back. H-L-T. The T's for Thomas," she said, then wistfully added, "I got that lighter when I was married to Buck Thomas."

Greta said she'd be on the lookout, but Harriet had a feeling the lighter wouldn't turn up at the beauty shop nor at the bank. The last she remembered it had been laying on the nightstand in her bedroom.

When the residents gathered for supper, Harriet asked if anyone had seen it. Several people shook their head, others offered up a sad, "Sorry, no."

Max did neither.

Her dislike of him became obvious when she asked pointedly, "What about you, Max? Did my lighter happen to accidently fall into your pocket?"

Odd as it was for her to choose those particular words, it was purely coincidental.

Max railed in a way that only the guilty are capable of. "You've got one hell of a nerve accusing me of stealing!"

Not one to back off, Harriet answered, "Well, did you?"

"Screw you!" Max swiped his arm across the table sending his plate and a bowl of mashed potatoes to the floor. While the sound of dishes shattering still hung in the air, Max left the table and stomped back to his room.

"Oh, dear," Caroline said. "I hope this isn't going to mean trouble."
No one else said anything.

When the stack of lumber Louie ordered arrived in the backyard, Max's imagination ran wild. Convinced the residents were plotting some sort of revenge, he envisioned the possibility of them boarding his room up; locking him out or, even worse, locking him in. If they did it while he slept, he'd be trapped. Max had heard stories about people being held prisoner in their own houses, and, paranoid as he'd become, such an action seemed possible. If it did happen, there would be no way out. No way of getting food or water.

Max decided to take action. First he went out and bought two crowbars. One he hid under his bed, the other he hid behind the garage. If they boarded up his room, he'd un-board it.

That same day he began to prepare for any and all emergencies. He waited until the house was dark and quiet, then crept into the kitchen and snatched a full pitcher of orange juice along with the remaining half of a roast Caroline had planned to use for sandwiches.

The following day Louie's Atlanta Braves hat disappeared, along with the radio from the living room end table.

"Blast it," Louie grumped, "that's my lucky hat. I need it for building Sara's playhouse."

"Maybe it'll turn up," Caroline suggested.

Of course it didn't. Before Louie had the framing of the playhouse in place, he slammed a hammer down on his thumb instead of the nail he'd been aiming for. He gave a loud holler, then let go of a string of expletives that would make a sailor blush. Within minutes the thumb swelled to three times its normal size and turned the color of a storm cloud. Louie blamed the accident on the missing hat, and as he sat at the kitchen table with the damaged thumb submerged in a bowl of ice he warned what he'd do when he found the culprit responsible.

By then Max had already begun to enjoy the thrill of his nightly raids. He would slip through the dark rooms and, like a mischievous ferret, grab whatever treasures he found and carry them back to his lair. Now standing with his ear pressed against the wooden door of his room, Max heard the shouting. He heard Louie's threats and thought back on the way Wilbur's watch had mysteriously reappeared after he'd sold it in Harrington.

Although Harriet's lighter had made no such reappearance, he began to wonder if maybe Harrington was too close. He had a good thing going, so why chance it? Wilbur was a pushover and Harriet was no problem, but Louie could be trouble. Max listened as Louie raged. That's when he decided to bypass Harrington and sell the latest of his ill-gotten goods to the pawnshop in Blue Neck.

Blue Neck was fifteen miles east of Harrington, twenty-five miles from Rose Hill. It was closer to Route 95, more transients, less questions. Blue Neck was definitely a better choice.

That evening as the residents gathered around the dining room table, Max tiptoed from his room and slipped out the door with a package tucked under his arm. It took a half-hour to drive to Blue Neck and another twenty minutes to find the pawnshop located in an alleyway next to a tattoo parlor.

"Shit," Max grumbled when he saw the narrow storefront with a display of knives in the window. For a moment he considered going elsewhere, but the only elsewhere was either back to Harrington or on to Mackinaw. "What the hell," he said and walked in.

With its low-watt light bulbs and dirty windows, Max knew the pawnshop wasn't a place where questions would be asked. He pulled out the bag and dumped the contents onto the counter: the small radio, a silver-rimmed ashtray, the Atlanta Braves baseball cap, and a tortoise shell comb Laricka had forgotten to put away.

"What'll you give me?"

A Buddha-shaped man sat behind the counter and moved nothing but his eyes. He glanced down then said, "Six bucks for the lot."

"Six bucks? This stuff is worth way more than—"

"Six bucks," Buddha repeated.

Max narrowed his eyes and leaned across the counter. "You can do better than that."

"Five bucks," Buddha said, "and you've got ten seconds to either take it or get your crap out of my store."

Max didn't like being pushed around, but he couldn't make it to Mackinaw before the pawnshop closed and going back to Harrington was too risky. "I'll take it."

Without moving from the stool he sat on, Buddha reached beneath the counter and pulled out a five-dollar bill. He handed it to Max and said, "Now get out of here."

For a moment Max stood there, on the verge of saying or doing something. It was unlike him to walk away from a fight, but this one did not look promising. Buddha was four hundred pounds if he was an ounce and on home turf. Max turned and walked toward the door. He was just inches from the street when he turned back and said, "Lousy dump you got—"

Before he finished the sentence, Max felt the bullet whiz past his ear.

"Keep going," Buddha said, "and don't come back."

THE MAGGIE SUE ISSUE

When Max left the pawnshop he sizzled with rage. It was bad enough to be cheated out of a fair price for his goods and worse yet to be told to get out and not come back. Were it not for the gun, Max would have gone back and tossed a brick though Buddha's front window. Maybe he should do it anyway, he thought. He could drive by, toss a brick from the car window, and keep on moving.

Max climbed into the car and gunned the motor. The problem was he didn't have a brick. He didn't have squat. He should have had the house in Rose Hill, but he didn't. Caroline had cheated him out of the house, just as Buddha had cheated him. The unfairness of such a life roiled through his stomach and rose in his throat. Max slammed his foot on the accelerator and went roaring down the street, heedless of anything or anybody who might be in his way.

Tom Osborne was working the evening patrol shift. He was the father of a new baby, a colicky baby who'd cried through the night. For hours on end he'd walked the floor trying to quiet the infant, but she would not be quieted. Thankfully it had been a slow evening, and in less than an hour he'd be off duty.

With the patrol car parked on a darkened side street at the far end of Blue Neck Road, Tom leaned back in the seat waiting for his shift to end. He heard the roar of the car's motor before he saw it fly past. Max had not yet reached the end of the street when Tom clicked on the siren and gave chase. Max heard the siren's scream and stomped down on the gas pedal. With the patrol car in hot pursuit they traveled almost nine miles before Tom could pull ahead and force Max to the side of the road.

Believing a man who would try to outrun a patrol car capable of most anything, Tom climbed out with his gun drawn. "Get out of the car!"

Max did nothing.

"Get out of the car NOW!" Tom repeated. He stood to one side, not in front of the headlights but close enough for Max to see the gun in his hand.

"All right, all right," Max grumbled. He opened the car door and stepped out.

Still keeping his distance, Tom shouted, "Hands in the air!"

Max obligingly lifted his hands. "What's the problem?"

"You've gotta be kidding," Tom replied. "You went through town doing ninety."

"Speeding? That's what this is about?"

"And failure to stop," Tom said. "Why didn't you pull over when you heard the siren?"

"I had the radio on," Max lied, "I didn't hear no siren."

"You didn't see my lights flashing?"

Max claimed he had his eyes focused on the road ahead and swore the only reason for not stopping was that he neither heard nor saw the patrol car giving chase.

"I was trying to put some distance between me and that crazy pawnshop owner." He explained how he'd been shot at. Acting as if he were the one wronged, he added the sound of earnestness to his words.

"That don't give you the right to be endangering other people," Tom said. He holstered the gun, then asked for Max's license and registration. When everything checked out he handed them back to Max. "The pawnshop owner's harmless. He's just overly cautious about being robbed again."

"Overly cautious?" Max repeated. "He was trying to kill me! You wanna arrest me for speeding, and you're gonna let him get away with attempted murder?"

After a good half-hour of back and forth, Tom regretted he'd given chase. Max was a fired up nut-ball, and arresting him would mean hours of paperwork on a night that couldn't end quickly enough.

"Look," he said, "all this is getting us nowhere. What happened at the pawn shop is just gonna be your word against his, so how about I'll cut you a break on the speeding and failure to stop violation, and you just move on?"

Although the thought of getting even with Buddha was already set in his mind, right now Max wanted his freedom more. "Yeah, okay," he said and climbed back into his car. Even as he drove off Max was already thinking about payback.

After the night he'd had, Max wanted some relaxation and his first thought was of Maggie Sue Somers. Maggie Sue was the kind of woman who was always up for a good time. She knew how to make a man relax, and right now she was exactly what he needed. He made a left on Elm and headed for the Owl's Nest.

When Max pushed through the door he'd hoped to find her draped over the bar, but the place was near empty. A young couple snuggled in a back booth, and behind the bar Freddie washed glasses.

"You seen Maggie Sue tonight?" Max asked.

Freddie shook his head. "Not tonight."

Max fumbled in his pocket for change, then headed to the pay phone.

After a single ring, she answered with a drawl so thick it made a man feel antsy just listening to the sound.

"Hey, baby," Max said. "I'm at the Owl's Nest. If you ain't doing nothing come on down, and I'll buy you a drink."

"One drink?" Maggie Sue giggled. "Why, one drink ain't hardly worth a girl's time."

"How about I'll keep buying long as you keep drinking?"

"Oh, Maxie, you're such a tease." She gave another breathless giggle, an unwritten invitation. "Twenty minutes. I'll get all prettied up."

"Wear that red dress," Max suggested, "you know, the one I like."

After he hung up the phone, Max settled at the bar and ordered a bourbon. "I'm gonna run a tab," he told Freddie. "So when Maggie Sue gets here, keep 'em coming."

Freddie rolled his eyes. "You gonna actually pay this tab, or is it going to be another night when you forgot and left your wallet home?"

"Shithead," Max grumbled.

Maggie Sue showed up a half-hour later.

"I thought you said twenty minutes," Max grumped.

"So I'm a little late." Maggie Sue flashed a smile and twirled herself around. "Ain't this worth waiting for?"

She scooted herself onto the stool alongside Max, then ordered rye and ginger. "Double up on the rye," she added, and Max smiled.

Before the first drink was downed, Max had his hand on her knee and edged it upward. They drank too much, laughed too loud, and stayed until Freddie announced he had to close up. "You gonna settle up this bill?"

Max pointed his index finger at Freddie like it was a gun. "Catch you tomorrow." He laughed, then circled his arm around Maggie's waist and headed for the door. As they left he leaned in and whispered, "I've got a bottle of bourbon in my room, so how's about a nightcap?"

Maggie Sue nodded.

They climbed into Max's car and headed back to the boarding house.

"You allowed to have lady friends in your room?" Maggie asked.

With a considerable amount of bourbon sloshing around in his stomach, Max had a bravado that was outsized even for him. "Shit, yeah," he answered. "I can do whatever I please. My brother's the one who built the damn house."

When he pulled alongside the curb Maggie Sue looked at the house, which in the shadow of moonlight seemed larger than its size. "Wow," she said, "you own this place?"

"It ain't been decided yet," he said and slid his key into the lock.

Even though Maggie bumped up against the hall table on her way in, no one heard them or at least no one got out of bed and snapped a light on. Max's room was in the back of the house on the first floor, and once they were inside with the padlock clicked shut no one would bother them.

After a night of what Max considered a howling good time, Maggie Sue woke wanting coffee.

"Stay here," he said, "I'll go get some."

It was hours after breakfast, but Laricka and Harriet drank coffee all day long so there was sure to be a pot sitting on the back burner. Max slipped into the kitchen and pulled two mugs from the cupboard. He filled the mugs, slid two biscuits in the pocket of his robe, and started back to his room. Wilbur sat in the front parlor, and when he saw Max heading down the hall with two mugs it aroused suspicion. It was true that Wilbur had no love of Max, but neither did he go around looking for trouble from the man. That was, until now.

Ida had set down firm rules for the house. Everyone knew the rules and abided by them. Even with her gone, the rules stayed in place. It was an unwritten debt of respect that no one questioned or disregarded.

Had it not been for seeing Max with those two mugs, Wilbur would have finished the newspaper then moved on with his day. But after what he saw he remained in the parlor, waiting and watching. Two hours later, Wilbur heard the padlock click open. Moments after that Max and his friend came tiptoeing out of the room. Maggie Sue still wore the red dress, but since she'd pulled it in on in a hurry the back of the skirt was hiked up and caught in her panties.

"Good morning," Wilbur said icily.

Maggie Sue's lips curled into a broad smile. "Mornin'," she answered in her most charming voice. She stopped and turned toward Wilbur. "Nice day, ain't—"

Max grabbed hold of Maggie Sue's arm, and before she could finish what she was saying he tugged her through the hallway and out the door.

After last night's run-in with first Buddha and then a snot-nosed policeman, Max was in no mood for more grief so he avoided going back to the house for the remainder of the day. After he dropped Maggie off, he took in an afternoon movie then walked around town. As he walked he thought. And the more he thought about having to sneak in and out of a house that should have rightfully been his, the angrier he got.

When the Owl's Nest finally opened at six-thirty, he was waiting at the door.

"Ah." Freddie grinned. "So you've come to settle up that tab?"

"Yeah, yeah," Max answered. "But first let me get a drink."

One drink led to another, and Max didn't make a move to leave until Freddie again said it was closing time.

Max hefted himself off the stool and lumbered toward the door.

"Hey," Freddie called out. "Ain't you forgetting something?"

Max turned back with a bewildered look.

"The tab," Freddie said. "You told me you was gonna settle up what you owe."

"Yeah. Well, I ain't got the money right now."

"You said…" Freddie stammered.

"I said a lotta things, but it ain't working out right now." Max turned and disappeared out the door.

"That's it," Freddie said to the empty stool. "He ain't getting another drink 'til he's paid what he owes."

It was almost two when Max unlocked the door and started sneaking down the hallway. The house was dark, and he assumed everyone was in bed and fast asleep. He was wrong.

As soon as Wilbur heard the footsteps, he snapped on the parlor lamp.

"Damn!" Max shouted. "Scare the shit out a person, why don't you?"

"Sorry," Wilbur replied, "but we need to have a talk."

"I got nothing to talk about."

"I do," Wilbur said. He stood and walked over to Max. "You know the rules, and it's disrespectful—"

"Don't you talk to me about disrespectful!" Max poked a finger at the older man's chest. "Disrespectful is you and these other bozos helping that nobody swindle me outta what should have been mine!"

"Give it up, Max," Wilbur replied disdainfully. "You weren't swindled out of anything. This was Ida's house. She was free to do whatever she wanted with it."

Max went into a long spiel about his brother building the house and family being family, but before he got to the end Wilbur held up his hand.

"Enough! You know Ida didn't want you bringing your dirt here to this house. You do it one more time, and I'll personally heave your ass out on the street!"

Wilbur was twenty years older than Max, but he was bigger, stronger, and in much better shape, so it wasn't an empty threat.

"You ain't throwing nobody nowhere," Max snarled. "You ain't the owner of this house, and you got no say in what I do."

"Caroline does. And do you think for one moment she'll go against what Ida wanted?"

"Yeah, well, she ain't the one handing out threats."

"That's because I haven't told her yet. But once more and I'll—"

"Screw you," Max said and turned toward his room.

As he lay in bed that night, Max began to think of ways to get even.

He had a lot of scores to settle: Caroline, Buddha, a smart-ass cop, Freddie, and now Wilbur. As the list rolled through his mind, Max crossed off the cop; too dangerous and not worth the risk.

It was near dawn when Max finally drifted off to sleep. By then Wilbur had replaced Buddha at the top of the list, and Caroline was now number two. Wilbur would be easy. He had an upstairs room and was an old man. He could stumble and fall down the flight of stairs, and no one would be any the wiser. Wilbur had weight on his side, but Max would have the element of surprise.

Once Wilbur was out of the way, handling Caroline would be easier.

WILBUR WASHINGTON

I know, you think I'm getting involved in something that's none of my business, but honestly speaking it is my business. I told you how it was with Ida; knowing my feelings, do you think I could turn my back on a thing like this? If Ida was the one who caught Max sneaking his lady friend out, do you think she'd sit back and let it be? You know darn well she wouldn't. What kind of a man would I be if I didn't stand up for what she believed in?

Maybe having a lady friend in your room isn't the worst sin in the world, but it doesn't matter. This is Ida's house and Ida's rules.

I'm hoping a warning is enough to dissuade Max from doing it again. That would be the easiest way of dealing with the problem. It's not something Caroline should have to worry about. She's got enough problems. I see what a scoundrel Max is, but she doesn't. Caroline still thinks of him as family, and facing up to the bad side of your family is something nobody is anxious to do.

Perhaps I'm being a foolish old man, hanging on to the yesterdays of life when those days have come and gone. My mind understands the truth of what is, but my heart isn't willing to accept it. I keep imagining Ida's still here. I walk through the hallway and glance toward the kitchen thinking I'll see her there by the stove. When I'm lying in bed and hear footsteps overhead, I immediately think it's Ida. It's not. It's her granddaughter. When Rose and Sara moved in Caroline moved upstairs into Ida's loft, and the strange thing is that bits and pieces of Ida now seem to be seeping into the girl. I can hear it in her voice, in the way she laughs, even in the way she's taken Sara under her wing. When I catch a sideways glance of Caroline, there are times I can almost believe she's Ida. Maybe that's why I feel so protective of her.

Sure, I should have told Ida how I feel. I know I should have. It's too late to do anything about that now, but it's not too late to do something for her granddaughter. Max is Caroline's uncle, not me. But he's certainly not someone she can count on.

Caroline may not be a child, but she's naïve when it comes to the ugliness of life. She needs someone to watch out for her, and if she'll let me do it I'm more than willing.

I'll talk to her about it. I'll say, I may not be your real granddaddy, but I think I can be a pretty good a substitute if you'll have me. *Regardless of what Caroline says I'm going to keep right on watching out for her, because I know it's what Ida would have wanted.*

IN THE DARK OF NIGHT

T he evening after his confrontation with Wilbur, Max arrived at the dinner table acting as though all was right with the world. He'd shaved and was wearing a fresh shirt.

"You look very handsome this evening," Caroline said.

Although Max's inclination was to tell her to stick it up her butt, he nodded graciously and sat. It was important to throw them off guard, to make everyone think he'd settled into accepting she was the rightful owner of the house and everything was hunky-dory.

It was easy enough to put on the sappy act with Caroline, and the others were too dumb to catch on, but Wilbur was more of a problem. When the old man looked across the table Max could see his eyes were narrowed, his brows squeezed together, and his mouth a ruler-straight line with no up or down.

The look on Wilbur's face made Max jittery, so he focused his eyes on the pile of peas he'd been pushing to the side of his plate. He usually disappeared after dinner, but on this particular evening he followed the others to the parlor.

"Staying in tonight?" Wilbur asked pointedly.

"Yeah," Max answered and sat in the fat round chair at the far end of the room. His original intent had been to act friendly and socialize, but after only a few minutes his skin began to itch. It was the way Wilbur kept looking at him, waiting for him to make a wrong move. Twice Max readjusted his sitting position, leaning first to the left and then to the right, but the itching continued. Finally after less than five minutes, he stood and said he thought he'd retire for the night.

"Staying in?" Wilbur repeated.

If Max had a gun he would have at that moment put it to Wilbur's forehead and pulled the trigger. He tried as best he could to hide such a thought when he looked back at Wilbur and answered, "Yeah, staying in."

The problem was that once Max was back in his room, there was little he could do but remain there. At the moment he had nothing to sell and nowhere to go. He was low on cash and the Owl's Nest was out since Freddie was already bitching about the unpaid bar tab. Maggie Sue was a gal who always up for a good time but only if somebody else was buying the drinks. He was stuck.

Max lay there looking at the ceiling and thinking of ways to get money and get even.

The following night was a repeat of events, and by the third night Max was near crazy. His thoughts got tangled in one another, and his skin itched from head to toe. Even the space between his toes itched, and scratching did nothing but cause his skin to break out in raw, painful welts. Whenever a new welt rose up, Max tried to soothe it with thoughts of what he would do to Wilbur.

Four nights later, Max heard the thump on the floor and suspected he'd found the opportunity he'd been waiting for. He waited a few seconds and listened. His room was directly below Wilbur's, and he could hear everything. Max waited until he heard the second thump and the heavy footsteps that crossed the room and headed down the hallway toward the upstairs bath.

Max was quick and light on his feet. He scurried up the stairs without making a sound, then eased open the door to Wilbur's room. His thought was to come from inside the room and shove the old man toward the staircase before he knew what was happening, but once inside the room Max saw a more lucrative opportunity. Wilbur's watch lay there on the nightstand, an arm's length away.

Max snatched the watch and dropped it into his pocket, but before he could position himself for anything else he heard the toilet flush. Seconds later the bathroom door squeaked open, and a swash of light fell across the far end of the hall. Max barely made it out of there and into Harriet's room before the footsteps thudded back down the hallway.

Harriet was a heavy sleeper and although she rolled over, she never woke. Max stood with his back pressed up against the wall of her room, until he heard the groan of the box spring when Wilbur thumped back down on the bed. Slowing inching the door open, he checked the hall then eased out and slithered back to his room.

The watch was solid gold. Good for fifty, maybe sixty bucks. His luck was changing; Max could already feel it.

The next morning Max was up early and sitting at the breakfast table when the others arrived. He was like an arsonist, hungry to see the flames of his handiwork. Wilbur was last to arrive at the table, and he wore a look of concern.

Before Wilbur sat he asked if anyone had seen his watch. "I could've sworn I left it on the nightstand. But it's not there."

"Did you check the bathroom?" Laricka asked.

Wilbur nodded.

Others asked about the kitchen counter, the coffee table, and the pockets of what he'd worn yesterday. But Wilbur said he'd searched all those places.

"I can't understand it," Wilbur said. "This is the second time I've misplaced that watch."

Caroline said nothing, because she knew the second watch was not Wilbur's original timepiece. It was believable that the first watch had simply been lost, misplaced or forgotten, but this time it was too circumstantial. It wasn't likely that a person who had carried a timepiece for more than fifty years could suddenly lose not one but two such watches in so short a time. Although she said nothing, her eyes moved from face to face looking for the telltale touch of guilt that comes with evildoing.

"Don't worry," Harriet said. "It'll turn up just like it did before."

Laricka, Louie, and even Doctor Payne echoed the thought; only Max held back.

Caroline looked at the far end of the table and waited for him to say something, but there was nothing. "Max?"

Caught unaware, he answered, "What?"

As he looked up there was a brief moment before he slid back into the mask he'd worn, and that's when Caroline thought she saw the look in his eyes.

"Have you seen Wilbur's watch?"

By then it was too late; Max was already back in disguise. "Me? Of course not, I went to bed early last night."

When Caroline rephrased the question, adding, "Are you sure?" Max became belligerent and accused her of singling him out. "Why me?" he said. "Why ain't you asking the doc, or Harriet, or Louie?"

Although Caroline moved away from the question, the fleeting glimpse of what she'd seen stayed with her. Thinking back on the countless times Greg swore he was working late, she could easily recall the look of a liar. There was a telltale sign in their eyes, an ugliness that once seen was forever remembered.

As she and Rose washed and dried the breakfast dishes, they talked of the morning's events. "Do you think I'm right or wrong about Max?" Caroline asked.

Rose hesitated for a long minute then said, "I don't doubt he's a man capable of lies and God knows what else, but I can't say if this particular lie belongs to him."

Later that afternoon Caroline approached Wilbur with the same question. "I'm not willing to accuse a man without cause. But I could have sworn I saw a look of guilt on his face."

"A man like Max probably has a lot of sin in his soul, but I doubt that stealing my watch is one of those sins." Wilbur explained that while Max might have had motive, he hadn't had the opportunity.

"The truth might be," Wilbur said sadly, "I'm getting older and more forgetful. Chances are I've misplaced it, and sooner or later I'll come across it the way I did last time."

Knowing the truth of the replacement watch, Caroline heaved a great sigh and said she certainly hoped so.

For several days the residents looked for Wilbur's watch, and at some point Rose suggested perhaps a search of every room would be beneficial. Max enjoyed the day-to-day misery of the watch's disappearance and agreed. "What harm would it do," he said, confident in the knowledge that the tick of the timepiece was muffled in three layers of socks and stuffed between the bed frame and box spring where no one would possibly think to look. In a strange and perhaps slightly deranged way, he enjoyed playing this game of cat and mouse. It made him feel smarter and stronger than the others. He was the game master. They were the pawns to be sacrificed, lambs led to slaughter.

Once he found he could roam the house in the wee hours of morning with no one being the wiser, Max launched a series of nightly raids. At about nine o'clock he'd set the stage with several yawns, the kind that catches hold of others and has them following suit. Not small stifled yawns hidden in back of a cupped hand; they were big, wide open, and with arms outstretched. It was both obvious and intentional. By the time Max announced he was ready to retire, most everyone else was also.

Harriet, Laricka, Louie, and even the doc were no problem; two or three well-orchestrated yawns and they toddled off to bed. Rose was less suggestible, but she went to bed when the child went to bed and never opened the door before morning.

Caroline could have been a problem, but now that she'd gone back to working on her novel she hibernated in the attic loft all evening. A glow of light was visible beneath her door, but she was oblivious to anything happening downstairs. Max could have stumbled over a hassock or banged against the wall, and she wouldn't have heard it.

The only real problem was Wilbur—suspicious, eagle-eyed Wilbur, generally the last one to bed.

Once he closed the door to his room, Max stretched himself across the bed and waited until he heard the thump of Wilbur falling onto the mattress. Sometimes it was ten or fifteen minutes, other times it was hours, but he remained patient and after the thump he continued to wait until the chorus of muffled snores began.

Certain he could roam without interruption, Max pocketed loose change left lying on the countertop or the end table. He rummaged through the drawers of the dining room buffet and took several pieces of silver from the cupboard. He was clever enough to focus on the seldomly-used things, things that wouldn't be noticed when they went missing. When Thanksgiving rolled around Caroline might go in search of the silver turkey platter, but by then it would be too late. On a night when he could find nothing else of worth, he pocketed a still-in-the-box set of tiny salt dishes rimmed with gold.

All of the thefts went unnoticed.

When Caroline counted the blessings of Ida's love she never thought to do an inventory of the household goods, so when the silver serving spoons and salt dishes went missing she was none the wiser.

THE STORYTELLER

In the days following the Maggie Sue sighting, the Sweetwater house settled into a time of quiet calm. The disappearance of Wilbur's watch remained a mystery, but other than that there were few disturbances. Max continued his nightly raids but the things he took were not readily missed, and the thefts went undetected.

Feeling smug and self-satisfied with his endeavors, Max took on the appearance of a changed man. He came to dinner every night and was reasonably cordial to everyone including know-it-all Louie and little Sara, even though the child's constant chattering at times grated on his nerves. When that happened, he would close his ears to her voice and concentrate on what bounty the nightly raid would bring; once he'd pictured the gleam of a silver spoon or the jangle of loose coins, he could smile and nod as if he were listening.

The evening Louie announced he had finished building Sara's playhouse, Max even offered a burst of applause. The corners of his mouth curled at the edges, but it was only because he remembered Louie's smashed thumb.

The new Max was not just tolerable but at times could seem charming. It was only a few days before Harriet regained her interest and suggested he stop in some evening for a nightcap. Of course after Maggie Sue Max saw Harriet as a poor substitute, but he nonetheless returned her smile and gave a sly wink.

The only resident not fooled by Max's new persona was Wilbur. After so many years of living, he knew lions did not suddenly become vegetarians. Max was a killer at heart. He wasn't one who'd willingly give up ownership of what he believed to be his. Nor was he likely to let go of the hatred he had for Ida's granddaughter.

Wilbur kept a sharp eye on Max and a watchful eye on Caroline. When the others went to bed he stayed awake, sometimes for an hour or two, sometimes longer. He waited and listened for footsteps on the stairs. Only after he was certain the house was secure for the night did Wilbur close his eyes and sleep.

With Rose now doing most of the cooking, Caroline returned to writing. She spent long hours in the attic loft, composing paragraphs then deleting them. Although Matthew and Claire were once so vivid in her mind they had now morphed into dull, grey characters, characters without feeling or a sense of purpose. Remembering Peter Pennington's promise that the desk held many stories, Caroline would at times take her hands from the computer keyboard and place them flat on the desk, waiting for inspiration to come, perhaps spelled out like words on a Ouija board.

On the Wednesday following his encounter with Max, Wilbur sat in the darkened parlor listening for the sound of trouble and waiting for the day to end. From the corner of his eye he caught the movement of a shadow that slid silently through the hall and up the stairs. Wilbur stood and walked to the foot of the staircase, but by then the figure had disappeared. On the second floor there was a bath and the bedrooms of four people: Harriet Chowder, Rose Smith, Doctor Payne, and Wilbur himself. Up the second flight of stairs was the attic loft where Caroline slept and worked.

Without waiting Wilbur started up the stairs and continued to the attic. From inside Caroline's room he heard the sound of her voice, soft, low, muffled almost, and thick with a sorrowful undertone. He rapped on the door and without hesitation eased it open.

Caroline was sitting at the computer staring at an almost blank screen.

"I heard voices," Wilbur said. "Are you okay?"

Caroline answered with a smile and a nod. "I was talking to myself."

"Well, if you need somebody to talk to, I'm here."

"Thanks." Caroline laughed. "I wasn't actually talking to myself; I was going over the dialogue in my story." She paused a moment, then sighed, "At one time I thought this was the most wonderful story, but now..."

"Now what?"

She shrugged. "Now it sounds so silly. Fake almost. Matthew and

Claire are like plastic dolls trying to pretend they're real people." Caroline gave a weary sigh. "Maybe I'm not meant to be a writer."

"I doubt that's true," Wilbur said. "My understanding is the Lord hands out talent based on where a person's heart is. You've got a heart for storytelling, so maybe you just need to search for the right story."

"But this *is* the right story," Caroline replied. "It's exactly the way I imagined Greg would act if he wasn't so egotistical and self-centered."

Wilbur chuckled. "Oh, I get it. You thought you were in love with this Greg—"

"I was in love with him," Caroline said indignantly.

"No, you weren't." Wilbur laughed. "You were in love with the image of who you wanted him to be."

"Well, sure, I wanted him to be different, but that's only because I could see—"

Wilbur interrupted her with another chuckle.

"What's so funny?" Caroline asked.

"You thinking you were in love," Wilbur answered. "You might have been infatuated, but you weren't in love."

Caroline sputtered a few words of objection but before she could get going, Wilbur began. "Love is blind. It doesn't see faults. The man married to a fat woman doesn't see her as fat; he sees her as just right for his arms. The woman married to a drunk doesn't see him as a drunk; she believes he's a man under pressure who simply needs a drink every now and then. That's how love is."

He continued to speak, but as Caroline listened she thought back to her conversation with Rose. Although Joe was mean and abusive, Rose never stopped loving him. She was fearful of him, and yet she made excuses for his behavior and turned a blind eye. It was only because of the great love for her daughter that Rose allowed herself to leave. The sorry truth was, if Joe were to show up at the door Rose, or Rowena as he would call her, would most likely allow him to take her in his arms. However foolish or irresponsible that might be, it was the blind love Wilbur spoke of.

Caroline could not say the same about Greg. She saw his faults. They were as obvious as the nose on his face. Although it had taken time for her to come to this conclusion, she knew when she saw the Philadelphia skyline fading from the rearview mirror of her car she had already stopped loving Greg.

"I see what you mean," Caroline said. "I guess a person who hasn't known love shouldn't be writing about it."

Wilbur's voice softened. "You've known love. Maybe it wasn't the soulmate passion of a man-woman romance, but love has a lot of different faces. You loved your Grandma and she loved you. She loved you so much she wanted you to have the most-loved thing she had to give—this house. The house has its faults, but she loved it just as she loved the man who built it. The thing about love is, a person or thing doesn't have to be perfect for you to love it. It only has to be perfect for you."

Caroline's eyes began to fill with tears. "I see what you mean," she said wistfully. "I saw plenty of faults with Greg but I didn't see any with Grandma. Everything she did was generous and kind and wonderful." She stood, walked over to Wilbur, wrapped her arms around his waist, and hugged him. "Thank you," she whispered.

After Wilbur left the room Caroline sat there for a long time, thinking. It was after midnight when she closed the file she'd been working on and opened a new one.

At the top of the page she typed, "Untitled by Caroline Sweetwater."

I never knew I had a grandmother, she wrote, *until one day the telephone rang and changed my life.* It was near dawn when she saved the file and powered off the computer. Caroline climbed into bed still uncertain whether she had begun to write a novel or an autobiography. The story was without name or genre, but it had a heart as big as the house and spoke in the true voice of love.

She thought about Wilbur's words again and decided to add him to the story. He would be the grandfather she never knew. Pleased with such a thought, Caroline began assembling all of Wilbur's endearing traits and habits and that's when she remembered the missing watch.

Tomorrow she would revisit the Previously Loved Treasures shop. After nearly a week Wilbur's watch was still nowhere to be found and she had a lot of questions. Peter Pennington was generally a man with answers. He also had an uncanny ability to come up with whatever was needed. Perhaps hoping for a third replica of the watch would be asking the impossible, but then again maybe it wouldn't.

CAROLINE

I *f yesterday you asked what I was writing I would have said a love story, but it would have been a lie. The book I've been working on for almost a year is nothing more than a bunch of romantic words tied together. It's like a string of Christmas lights with a bulb missing. It's only one bulb, but without it nothing else works.*

Now I truly am writing a love story. It's about Grandma. Before last night I couldn't put my finger on what was wrong with the story, but now I can it see it clear as day. Wilbur's the one who helped me. He might not look like a romantic, but he is. It's the snowy white hair that fools you. If you look past the hair and listen to Wilbur's words, you'll see he's got the most beautiful heart imaginable. When he was talking about Grandma and how she was one of the most loving women he'd ever met, I noticed his eyes were a bit teary. I can tell he misses her, maybe even as much as I do.

Yesterday evening after he went back downstairs, I took the picture of Grandma and Big Jim and set it alongside my computer. It's just a snapshot but it gives me inspiration, and if I look at it and squint Big Jim looks a lot like Wilbur. It would be real easy to imagine Wilbur being my granddaddy.

There's not a day that goes by when I don't think of Grandma. I keep wishing we could have had more time together. I guess that's how life is—the bad things hang on forever and the good things are gone in the blink of an eye. I don't know if it's true or if it just seems that way because you miss the good things so much. I sure do miss Grandma. At least I can be here in her house with the people she loved. The residents, *she called them. It's funny but I can almost see a piece of Grandma stuck to every one of these people. Well, everyone except Rose and Sara, they don't have Grandma stuck to them because they never knew her.*

The truth is these people are more like family than any family I've ever known.

Most families squabble about this, that, and the other thing, but not the residents. They have nothing but kind words for each other. Even Max. It used to be he was angry and withdrawn, but no more. Now he's downright pleasant. Yesterday at supper, Harriet said something funny and Max laughed out loud. Up until then I'd never even seen him crack a smile.

With Rose cooking and Max being happy, I'm starting to believe things can actually work out, but I still miss Grandma.

THE WRISTWATCH

It was after ten when Caroline opened one sleepy eye and peered at the bedside clock. She'd slept through breakfast and halfway through the morning. "Oh, dear," she said, realizing that Rose had been left to handle things on her own.

It was nothing to worry about; Rose was magical in the kitchen. In less time than it would take for anyone else to assemble the ingredients, Rose could turn out a tray of biscuits golden brown and fluffy as air.

Caroline smiled a lazy smile and remained in bed thinking about the words she'd written last night. For a year she'd stumbled around the descriptions of love, dredging up adjectives like "passionate", "adoring", and "devoted". In the one hundred-and-twenty-six pages she'd set aside there was a plethora of those words, but not once had she captured the truth of love. Then last night she found what she'd been searching for and was pleased with the words. They came together the way puffs of down come together to make a cozy comforter. As she'd sat in the chair rereading what she'd written she could feel the peacefulness of Ida's presence, and it settled into her soul as if it was meant to be there.

As she climbed out of bed, Caroline touched her hand to the old wooden desk. Was it true? Were there stories locked inside the desk, stories that would in time be hers for the telling? There was a blurred line between the magical mystery and what could be nothing more than wishful thinking.

Today she would visit the Previously Loved Treasures shop and try to replace Wilbur's lost watch. While she was there, Caroline would ask Peter Pennington for the truth of the desk. But before she did either of those things, she had something important to do. Holding the seven pages in her hand, she hurried down the stairs. Wilbur sat on the front porch alone.

Caroline came up behind him and threw her arms around his neck. "Thank you," she said and squeezed tighter.

"For what?" Wilbur asked.

She plopped down in the chair beside him. "For reminding me about Grandma."

Wilbur looked at the papers in her hand and smiled. "So, is that a story about Ida?"

"It sure is." Caroline straightened the pages and began reading aloud.

As Wilbur listened, a tear fell from his eye. He also felt Ida's presence, but along with it came the heartache of longing for something forever lost. When Caroline finished reading, he said, "It's beautiful. Your grandma would be so very proud."

That afternoon after Caroline helped Rose with the lunch dishes, she climbed into her car and headed for town. When she pulled up in front of the store, Peter Pennington was not standing outside. He was also not standing behind the counter. Caroline waited a few minutes then called out, "Yoo-hoo! Mister Pennington?"

Seconds later he hurried from the back room wiping a smudge of mustard from his upper lip. "Please forgive me. I was not expecting you today."

"No problem," Caroline replied. "I wasn't actually planning to be—"

Before she could finish her thought, Peter interrupted, "But I'm supposed to know what you are going to do before you do it." His glasses slid down a bit, and he pushed them back into place. "This is highly irregular. Highly irregular."

Caroline wrinkled her nose. "That's silly. How could you possibly know what I'm going to do before I even decide to do it?"

"That's the way it is. It's the way it's always been."

Before she had time to question his answer, Peter peered over his constantly sliding down glasses and asked what she was there for. "I've nothing scheduled for you."

"Oh, I haven't ordered anything," Caroline replied. "But it seems that Mister Washington has misplaced his pocket watch again. I was wondering if you possibly might have another replacement."

"Oh, dear, another thing that wasn't supposed to happen."

"Well, of course it wasn't supposed to happen," Caroline said. "People don't intentionally go around misplacing things. I'm sure it was an accident."

Peter Pennington shook his head doubtfully. "Not an accident. Definitely not an accident."

"How can you be certain?" Caroline asked. "Wilbur's up in years, he might well have left the watch someplace and simply forgotten."

"No." Peter bunched his eyebrows together and shook his head again. "Not likely. If that were going to happen, I would have known about it."

Caroline laughed. "Mister Pennington, I love you to pieces, but you're simply not making any sense. Now about the pocket watch——"

The expression on Peter's face grew considerably more solemn. "You don't want another pocket watch. It would be asking for trouble."

"Nonsense." Caroline wanted to say that if price was the issue she'd be willing to pay more for the watch, but the look of seriousness stretched across Peter's face stopped her. "Asking for trouble, why?"

Instead of answering her question, Peter took a gray cardboard box from beneath the counter and fished through it. He pulled a gold wristwatch from the box, held it in his hand for a few seconds, then dropped it back and pulled out a clunky-looking stainless steel watch with a heavy band. "This is what your Mister Washington needs," he said and handed the watch to Caroline.

"This?" Caroline looked at the watch. It had an oversized face and glow-in-the-dark numbers. "This hardly seems like what Wilbur——"

"It may not be what he wants," Peter said, "but it's what he needs."

Caroline looked at the watch again and frowned.

"Trust me," Peter said. He reached across the counter and folded Caroline's fingers over the watch. "Take it and give it to your Mister Washington. Tell him to put the watch on and *never* take it off."

"Never?" Caroline asked. "What about when he takes a shower or bath?"

"The watch stays on."

"Won't it get ruined?"

Peter shook his head. "Waterproof."

"Oh." Caroline stood there with her eyes darting back and forth from the watch in her hand to the serious expression on Peter's face. "Are you certain about this?"

"Very certain."

"Okay." Caroline gave a disappointed sigh. She had hoped to replace

Wilbur's pocket watch with one that was exactly the same or very similar. This was at best a poor substitute. She dropped the watch into her handbag and pulled out her wallet. "How much?"

"Nothing," Peter answered. "It's a gift."

He smiled graciously, but behind the smile was a prayer that this watch would make amends for the way he so recklessly replaced Wilbur's pocket watch. Some things were not meant to be, and it would have been far better for the first watch to remain lost. When Peter thought of the trouble that lay ahead, a weight of sadness settled in his heart. "Be careful and wary of strangers."

Rose Hill was a small town, a settled-down place where neighbors knew one another, so such a warning made no sense to Caroline, but then this entire day made no sense. She turned to leave and halfway to the door she stopped and looked back. "I almost forgot. I wanted to ask you about the desk."

Peter chuckled. "You're writing again, aren't you?"

Caroline nodded. "It's the best work I've ever done. It's the desk. It has some sort of magic, doesn't it?"

Peter laughed again. "The magic is in you. Oh, it's a good desk, a strong desk, one that will be with you for years to come. But it's simply a touchstone that enables you to believe in yourself."

Caroline rolled her eyes and gave him a look of doubt. "Mister Pennington, you've got more secrets than heaven itself."

Peter stood behind the window and watched Caroline's car pull away. *Not more*, he thought, *but almost as many.*

That afternoon Caroline gave Wilbur the watch.

"Thank you," he said with an expression of puzzlement. "It's a bit heavy for my taste, but I surely appreciate the thought."

"Don't just put it in the drawer," she warned. "You've got to wear it."

"I will," Wilbur nodded. "I can use it for when I'm gardening—"

"No, you've got to wear it all the time."

"All the time?"

"Yes. Don't take it off! Not for sleeping, showering, anything!"

"Well," Wilbur said, "if it means that much to you…" He pulled the watch onto his arm and snapped the band shut.

"Promise me that you'll never take it off. Not for any reason."

Wilbur felt the urgency in her voice and nodded. "I promise." That the request seemed illogical was of no consequence. It was important to Caroline, and for that reason alone he would do it.

That afternoon Wilbur began checking the time on the clunky wristwatch just as he had done with his grandfather's pocket watch. At first it seemed an unnatural movement, something he had to stop and think about before doing, but within a day the newness vanished and he stopped fingering the pocket that for so many years had been the resting place of time.

MONEY IN MACKINAW

For two weeks Max continued his nightly raids, and the more bounty he accumulated the better he felt. Every new trinket or piece of silver he carried to his room gave him greater confidence and power. When he held a watch or serving spoon in his hands, he could feel a surge of strength move through his body. In time he would become invincible; then he would shake loose Caroline and her band of misfits. He would find a way to get what should have been rightfully his.

A triumphant gleam settled in his eyes, and a smile curled his lips.

Laricka was the first to notice. "Ah," she said eyeing Max across the dinner table. "Look at you. At last, a smile on your face." Laricka attributed it to the fact that Max had given up his late-night carousing, and he was content to let her stay with that impression.

On the fourteenth day, the excitement of what he'd done became too great for Max to contain. He decided it was time to reap the rewards of his work. Late in the afternoon when Caroline and Rose were busy in the kitchen, Laricka with her grandsons, and Doctor Payne engrossed in the latest dental magazine, Max slipped out of his room with a large bundle tucked under his arm and left the house. This time he would not make the foolish mistake of taking things to Harrison where they could eventually find their way home, nor would he go back to Blue Neck to be cheated by the insufferable Buddha. On this day he'd allowed plenty of time to drive to Mackinaw. It was far enough away for lost things to stay lost, and, given the transient nature of the town, few if any questions would be asked.

Max slid behind the wheel and laid the bundle on the seat beside him, so close that it rested against his right thigh. The touch of the bundle was cool and hot at the same time. It had an energy of its own; it gave life and strength. Holding each object and recalling the moment he plucked it from its nesting place gave Max indescribable pleasure, and for that reason he hated to part with the treasures. But the collection was worth something, enough perhaps for him to spend a full week with Maggie Sue. It was the kind of money he couldn't afford to ignore.

It was early dusk when Max arrived in Mackinaw. He needed gas for the car and directions. A pawnshop was almost never on the main drag. Places like that were down a darkened side street or tucked in the far end of an alley where people could come and go with anonymity. People who pawned things seldom came back for them, so there was no need for the shop to be located where it was easy to find. Max imagined Ida's silver serving spoons turning yellow as they waited to be reclaimed, and he laughed aloud.

A short distance from the highway Max spotted a neon sign that blinked "Abe's Gas–Open 24 Hours." He pulled in next to the self-service pump, got out, and unscrewed the gas tank cap. He lifted the hose from the pump and stuck the nozzle in the gas tank, but when he pressed the handle nothing happened. Max banged on the side of the pump and shouted, "What the hell—"

The skinny attendant standing in the doorway called out, "If you ain't using a credit card, you gotta pay first."

"You're shittin' me!" Max said.

"Nope."

"Stupid way of doing business," Max grumbled. "In Rose Hill, Harvey lets you pump the gas then come inside and pay what you owe."

"This ain't Rose Hill, and I ain't Harvey."

Although Max was none too fond of leaving his bundle alone in the car, he followed the attendant inside and handed him the money. "Five bucks, regular."

The attendant took the bills and said, "Pull over to pump two."

"Two? What's wrong with the pump I'm at?"

"It's just high test. You want high test?"

High test was thirteen cents a gallon more, and Max would not be suckered into paying more than he needed for gas. "Nah, I'll pull over."

After he'd pumped the gas, Max locked his car and returned for directions to the local pawnshop.

"Two blocks past the pool hall, make a right onto Bucket, and the next left onto Graymoor," the attendant said. "It's a block-and-a-half down Graymoor."

"Thanks." Max returned to his car and pulled out of the station. The attendant watched the car pull away and breathed a sigh of relief.

When Max had come back toward the station, Joe Mallory thought for sure he'd caught on. So far no one else had. It was an easy scam: charge a customer five dollars, set the pump inside for four-fifty, and pocket fifty cents. Do it twenty times a day, and you had some decent money. Pump two was on the dark side of the station where you couldn't see squat, let alone the numbers on the pump. People paid their money, pumped their gas, and left.

Joe Mallory watched the taillights of Max's car disappear; then he turned and went back inside the station. It would be another seven hours before he'd get off duty.

Edgar's pawnshop was easy enough to find, and with its brightly lit interior it bore no resemblance to Buddha's place. The window was filled with things like saddles, boots, and coffee pots. Max climbed out of the car and carried his bundle inside.

He set the bundle on the counter and removed the items from the pillowcase one by one. A tinkling bell over the door had announced his arrival, but no one was behind the counter. Max waited a few minutes then called out, "Anyone here?"

"Keep yer' shirt on," a voice answered. "I'm coming!"

It was yet another minute, perhaps two, before an extremely tall man with graying hair came through the door. "Everybody's in a hurry," he said with an air of impatience.

"I thought maybe you didn't know I was here," Max replied. "Sorry."

"I ain't deaf. I heard the bell."

On the inside of Max's brain he was thinking, *Then why didn't you answer it, asshole?* but his response was simply a soft chuckle and another, "Sorry." The thing about Max was that when he wanted to, he could be pleasant, charming even. It came and went at his discretion. He used it to elicit a favor or a free ride, then tucked it back inside until he had another such need.

Max spread the array of items across the counter. "What'll you give me for the lot?"

Edgar made no move to pick up anything. He eyed the merchandise, then pulled the right side of his nose and mouth into a skeptical look of doubt. "I don't get much call for stuff like this. I could maybe go sixty or seventy."

"You're kidding," Max replied. "The watch alone is worth that."

"It's only worth what I can get for it, and I done told you I ain't got much call for stuff like this."

"The watch is solid gold, and these spoons sterling!"

"Don't matter none. People 'round these parts ain't looking to buy stuff like this. You got a saddle or cooking pots? Them things sell. Fancy stuff don't sell."

"Cooking pots?" Max repeated. "That's used junk. What I got here is valuable merchandise that's worth something."

"No." Edgar leaned across the counter and glared down at Max. "What you got here is a bunch of stuff you're looking to sell, the kind of stuff that starts me thinking you might've come by it dishonestly."

Max started to sputter a response, but Edgar held up his hand. "Don't bother. I ain't in the asking questions business."

"Well, if you'd let me explain——"

"I don't much care for explaining either," Edgar said. "Seventy bucks, no questions asked. Take it or leave it."

Max took it.

Seventy bucks would show Maggie Sue a good time for three, maybe four days. After that Max would start rethinking his strategy of what to take and what to leave. "Bunch of crackpots," he grumbled as he climbed back into the car. "Don't know good from worthless."

It was after ten when Max arrived back in Rose Hill and rather than stop by the Owl's Nest, he went straight to Maggie Sue's apartment. From the street he could see a light in the bedroom. He walked up the single flight of stairs whistling "I'm in the Money" then eagerly rapped on Maggie Sue's apartment door.

She was listing to music. He could hear it coming from inside, but she didn't open the door. Max knocked again, harder this time. Still no answer. He rattled the doorknob and called out her name. No answer.

Something was wrong. Very wrong. Max thought about the last time they were together. He remembered the feel of Maggie Sue's hot breath as she whispered how she was crazy for him. It had been ten days since he'd seen her. But you don't stop being crazy for someone in ten short days. He rattled the doorknob again.

As Max stood there listening to the music coming from inside the apartment, layers of possibilities stacked up inside his head. Maybe Maggie Sue was sick. Maybe she'd fallen and lay on the floor unconscious. Maybe an intruder had gotten in and…anything was possible. Growing more concerned by the second, Max left the building, walked back to the Owl's Nest, and dialed her number. No answer.

He returned to the building and banged on the door with both fists. "Are you okay Maggie Sue?" he yelled. When there was still no answer he slammed his shoulder into the door and tried to force it open. The door didn't budge, but Max's shoulder screamed in pain.

Max left the building, got back into his car, and headed home. Once back at the house he retrieved the crowbar he'd hidden in back of the garage, then returned to Maggie Sue's apartment. He walked up the stairs and with the first swing of the crowbar sent the doorknob flying across the hall. Seconds later he had pried the door open.

A startled Maggie Sue stood there wearing nothing but a skimpy black brassiere. "What the hell do you think you're doing?"

"You didn't answer the door," Max stammered. "I thought maybe you was hurt or in trouble."

"I didn't answer the door 'cause I was busy." Maggie Sue looked like she could run a dagger through Max. "Now get on outta here, and leave me be."

Max felt the heat of shame spreading through his body. As he turned and walked down the stairs, he felt smaller than he'd ever felt before. "Screw you, Maggie Sue," he said. "There's plenty more pebbles on the beach."

Max drove back to the Owl's Nest, paid the outstanding tab, and bought drinks for the house, which was only Freddie and the two drunk fellows standing at the end of the bar. He drank until closing, then bought a bottle of bourbon and went home.

MAX SWEETWATER

Maggie Sue's a tramp. A flat-out, no-good tramp. If I had a shred of dignity I'd cut a wide circle and stay clear of the woman, but I can't. I know she's trash, I know she sidles up to whoever's got money in their pocket, but when I'm with Maggie Sue she makes me feel like a man. Nobody else ever done that.

I ain't like Jim; I never had stuff handed to me. Everything I got I had to work for or steal. Know why? Because I'm Jim's brother, that's why. People called him Big Jim, like he's some kind of god. Me they called Short-shit, thinking it was funny. Well it wasn't funny to me. Pork Berger used to say I was made outta scrapings leftover from Big Jim, and then the big jerk would double over laughing. You know how it feels to always be hearing stuff like that? Shitty, that's how it feels. Live a life like that, and pretty quick you learn you gotta grab hold of whatever fun you can get.

The truth is Big Jim owes me. He could've stuck up for me more. He could've told Pork he'd knock the bejesus out of him if he called me Short-shit again, but he didn't. You know what he did? He slapped Pork on the back and said, Stop picking on the kid. That's it. He don't never say nothing to Pork, but me he takes aside and says I ought to just ignore such name-calling. Yeah, like he'd ignore it if they did it to him. If you don't get your feathers in such a ruffle, Pork would stop doing it, Jim says. Sure he will, I'm thinking. When hell freezes over.

I just gotta forget about people like Pork and concentrate on Maggie Sue. She's what makes me feel good. All I need to keep her happy is the jingle of money in my pocket, and I'm gonna get it one way or the other. I can almost see Maggie Sue's eyes popping wide open when I tell her this house is mine. Knowing her, she'll be wanting to move in. Maybe me and her will take that big master bedroom. She'd like that.

Since day one Big Jim got everything, and I got scraps. Well, he's dead now, and I'm gonna take what's rightfully mine.

You'll see. When I get hold of this house, people's gonna respect me same as Big Jim. Ain't nobody gonna be calling me Short-shit then.

A Chance Meeting

Two days passed before Max came out of the room again, and when he finally did it was in the wee hours of the morning when darkness shrouded the house and people were lost to their dreams. During those two days he drank glass after glass of bourbon and spent endless hours recounting the misery that had been handed to him.

It began the day he was born. A tornado tore through town and blew out half the windows in the house. Bertha Sweetwater was in her early twenties at the time and expecting her second baby. She'd gone to the basement with a third load of laundry when the tornado hit and shook the house to its foundation. Furniture was tossed from one room to another, and the living sofa came to rest smack in front of the basement door. Bertha was trapped down there for six hours, and by the time a rescue team worked their way through the rubble Max had arrived. He weighed less than three pounds and was barely breathing. For months Bertha went around telling people that Max was good as dead until she found a stack of newspapers and bundled him inside the Help Wanted section.

Bertha Sweetwater wasn't ready for Max, and neither was the world. It became the story of his life. He was an out-of-place boy who came wrapped in newspaper. It was a thing that stayed with him and caused him to be the object of ridicule. A joke. Years later when Bertha would tell and retell that story, Max found himself wishing there had been no newspapers.

When Max finally came out of his room, he was more determined than ever. He'd taken a long hard look at his life and evaluated the things that could and couldn't be changed. He'd never be any taller than he already was, but he could be more powerful. Money was the great equalizer. It made small men big and caused women like Maggie Sue to come knocking on your door. In the bleakest hours of night when he'd given himself over to the emptiness in his soul, he'd thought back on the way Maggie Sue had looked at the house and sighed, "Wow."

First he would need money. With money he would get a lawyer, a good lawyer from Atlanta or Macon, someone who knew what they were doing and could get back what should have been his. Jim would have wanted him to have the house, Max was sure of it. It would be Jim's way of making up for the past. Max thought back and tried to remember their boyhood days of running and playing together, but the image was always the same: Jim, bigger than life, and Max, a dark shadow that faded into the background.

That night when everyone else was asleep, Max unlocked the door of his room and stepped into the hallway. For a full minute he stood there listening for a sound: the voice of someone speaking, the hum of a television, anything that would warn of someone still awake. There was nothing. Once he'd figured out what he had to do he'd planned another raid, one more brazen than anything he'd dared before. He was no longer fearful of being caught, because his life could be no worse than it already was.

He first eased open the door to Doctor Payne's room, and there on the dresser a scant arm's length from the door was the wallet he was looking for. Payne slept with his back to the door, so Max stepped into room and grabbed the wallet. He'd planned to pocket the whole thing but changed his mind at the last minute. He wasn't afraid of Payne, but neither was he looking to get thrown out of the house before the right time. Max pulled out a ten-dollar bill and laid the wallet back in the same spot.

He went in search of the things Edgar wanted to buy, practical things that could be sold to farmers getting by on a next-to-nothing budget. From the kitchen cupboard he took a cast iron skillet and a large spaghetti pot. From the hall closet, a stack of bath towels. He rummaged around looking for Louie's toolbox and gave up when he couldn't find it. As he headed back to his room with arms loaded, Max spied a pair of work shoes Louie had left laying in the parlor. He snatched them up and added them to the pile.

Tomorrow Max would return to Mackinaw. If the pawnshop wanted crap like this, then that's what he'd give them.

Shortly before seven o'clock the sun crested the horizon, and the residents of the house began to wake. Max heard Clarence's bark and the clip-clop of Sara's footsteps. Moments later there were voices: Rose and Caroline. Pots began to clatter in the kitchen, but Max tugged the blanket over his head and closed his eyes again. It was the first time in more than two days he'd been able to sleep, and he cursed the interruption.

After several minutes Max heard Louie's voice, louder than the others and obviously agitated.

"I left them right here in the parlor! Somebody moved them!"

At that point Max knew he could no longer sleep. He climbed from the bed, crossed the room, and pressed his ear to the door. As the frustration in Louie's voice increased, so did Max's pleasure in listening. A strange lopsided smile crossed his face when Louie said somebody had obviously stolen his shoes.

"Don't be foolish," Caroline answered. "Nobody wants those dirty old work shoes."

Max hadn't planned on going to breakfast; he had no interest in any of the residents or their boring jib-jab conversations. But he delighted in their misery. He quickly got dressed and hurried to the dining room.

On this particular morning the conversation focused on Louie's shoes. None of the other items had yet been missed. One after the other, the residents offered thoughts and suggestions.

"Could they be under your bed?"

"Maybe the hall closet."

"When was the last time you actually wore them?"

Max said nothing but sat with a smug look on his face, enjoying the party and trying not to let it show.

Rose finally looked at him and asked, "Max, have you seen Louie's work boots?"

"Me? Why, I haven't been out of my room for two days." He forced a dry cough then added, "Nursing a cold."

The discussion of where they might search continued, but there were no further questions aimed at Max. Even if there had been, he wasn't worried. He was smarter than them. Last night he'd bundled everything together and carried it to the trunk of his car, so they could search his room if they wanted and they'd find exactly what he wanted them to find: nothing.

After breakfast Max was the last one to leave the table, and from there he went into the parlor and sat in the overstuffed club chair. Sooner or later they would discover the other things that were missing, so it was important for Max to seem nonchalant. He had to give the appearance of a man with no worries and nowhere to go. The only problem was Max did have someplace to go, and he was anxious to get started.

For almost twenty minutes he sat there fidgeting with a loose thread he'd found on the chair bolster and nervously bouncing his right foot up and down. When he could stand it no longer he stood and announced, "Think I'll drive over to Harrington and visit a friend."

"Sounds good," Harriet said. "Mind if I tag along?"

This was something Max hadn't anticipated. "I don't think that's a good idea." As he spoke the words Max had no idea what he could do with them; then it hit him. He gave a shallow little laugh and added, "I'm seeing a lady friend, and I don't think she'd appreciate you being there."

"Gotcha." Harriet nodded. She turned back to reading the year-old *Glamour* magazine.

When Max left the house he was empty-handed, and he made a point of passing through a number of rooms so people would see it. In the kitchen he stopped to tell Rose it was doubtful he'd be back in time for dinner. As he passed through the house he wondered aloud if he should bring an umbrella, and as he crossed the side porch where Laricka sat he noted how tall her grandsons were getting.

Max climbed in his car and headed west toward Harrington, but before he got to the highway he circled around and pulled onto the eastbound road that ran all the way to Mackinaw. Max smiled. He had a feeling this would be the best trip yet.

When he passed the far edge of Rose Hill, Max had an urge to stop and see Maggie Sue. He could do it; he still had cash in his pocket and there'd be more coming. He passed the turnoff and continued to drive for another two miles, but then he got the itch.

"What the hell," he mumbled and made a U-turn.

It was early afternoon, and Maggie Sue was still working on her first cup of coffee. When Max rang the doorbell she answered on the first ring. Standing there in a fleecy bathrobe and not a stitch of makeup, she said, "If you're looking for anything other than coffee, it's too early."

"Coffee's good," Max replied and followed her into the apartment.

To Max's eye she looked good, even without the red dress and makeup. She looked like the kind of woman he needed. If he tried hard enough, he could imagine her living in the Sweetwater house; maybe even bringing him coffee in bed.

"Looks like I'm gonna be coming into some money," he said.

She answered with a smile.

"A lot of money," he added. "And that house you liked so much."

"The big house where you been rooming?"

He nodded.

"Wow," she said. It was the same silky soft word she'd uttered before.

"If we was together," Max said, "you could be living there."

"Together?"

Max nodded. "Sleeping in the same bed, having ourselves some fun. That kind of together."

Maggie Sue gave a big smile, the kind of smile that didn't need lipstick to look good. "You ain't fooling with me, are you, Maxie?"

Max leaned back in the chair and grinned the grin of a man with power. "Nope. I'm telling the God's honest truth."

Maggie Sue gave a squeal of delight, then left her chair and came around the table to hug Max from behind. "You're just the sweetest ever."

It was almost five o'clock when Max finally left Maggie Sue's apartment and started for Mackinaw. When he pulled up in front of Edgar's Pawnshop there was a handwritten sign taped to the door. It read, "Gone to Supper, be back later."

"Rat shit," Max said with a groan. He went back to his car and sat. He waited for almost a half hour, then figured he could do with a drink. He locked the car and walked back toward Bucket Street. Two blocks down he spotted a bar and went in.

It was little more than a hole in the wall with a handful of stools and one lone customer sitting at the far end of the bar. Max ordered a bourbon and sat. He had two more, then went back to the pawnshop.

Finding it still closed, he returned to the bar.

When Max walked in the second time, the bartender was nowhere in sight and the glass he'd emptied earlier sat right where he'd left it. Max nodded to the guy at the end of the bar. "Where's the barkeep?"

Joe Mallory shrugged. "More 'n likely gone for a smoke."

"So I can't get a drink?" Max replied sarcastically.

Joe reached a long arm across the bar, grabbed the bottle of bourbon, and filled Max's glass to the brim. "This one's on the house," he said and replaced the bottle.

Max grinned and stuck out his hand. "Max Sweetwater."

"Joe. Joe Mallory," he answered; then he turned back to his own drink.

Nothing more was said for several minutes; then Max asked if Joe knew what time the pawnshop would reopen.

"No idea." Joe shrugged. "Edgar closes up whenever he's a mind to."

"Damn," Max grumbled. "I was hoping to get out fast. I got this woman who—"

"So you'll have a few more drinks," Joe cut in. "At least you got a woman and something to sell."

"Yeah, but she ain't one who's big on waiting."

"Shit, man, none of them are. Mine left me sitting in jail and took off with my kid."

"That stinks." Max gulped down a swig of bourbon. "So, in case Edgar don't make it back tonight, are there any other pawnshops around here?"

"Nah, Edgar's it." Joe gave a slant-eyed glance at Max and realized he was the same guy who'd stopped in at the gas station asking about a pawnshop. "You been here before, ain't you?"

Max nodded. "Last week."

"If you got a bunch of stuff to sell, you sure ain't from around here. Ain't nothing here but a hard-ass sheriff and some dirt-poor farmers."

"Rose Hill," Max replied. "I got me a house there."

"Man, you must've stepped in some serious dog shit," Joe said. "You got all that, and I got nothing." He leaned his elbows on the bar and looked down into what was now an empty glass. "Damn, this is one helluva life."

A minute, maybe two, passed without anything more being said. Then Joe reached into his back pocket and pulled out his wallet. He fumbled through some papers, then pulled out a faded photograph. "If you're traveling back and forth between here and Rose Hill, maybe you seen Rowena." He passed the picture to Max. "Rowena's real pretty and she's got this long blond hair—"

Max took the photograph and studied it for a moment then asked, "Who's the girl?"

"Our kid."

"I ain't seen the woman, but I seen the kid. She's at the rooming house where I live."

"Rooming house?" Joe repeated. "I thought you said you owned a house."

"Almost own a house. Soon as I get enough money for a lawyer, I'll get what's rightfully mine."

Joe had a built-in distrust of people like Max. People who say they got this, that, and the other thing, then start looking to pick your pocket. If this guy was looking for a scam, he'd met his match. "Could be there's reward money, if you got knowledge of Rowena."

Max looked at the picture again. "I'm pretty certain about the kid, but I ain't all that sure of the woman." He turned to Joe. "How much reward you offering?"

"Five hundred." The truth was Joe couldn't scrape together five hundred if his life depended on it, but the truth didn't matter when you were scamming a scammer.

"It could be she's the woman," Max said, "but her hair's different. Dark brown and shorter."

Joe took the picture and tucked it back into his wallet. "Okay, how about you give me the address, I check it out, and if she's Rowena, I give you the five hundred?"

"I ain't no sucker," Max said. "Once you find this babe you ain't gonna give nobody nothing. I already said I'm sure about the kid, so gimme two-fifty now, and I'll trust you for the other two-fifty."

"No dice. For all I know you ain't seen neither one of them. I ain't ready to do business less you got solid proof."

"Okay, gimme a week, and I'll be back with a picture of the woman and kid."

"Yeah, that sounds good," Joe nodded. He said he'd meet Max in the bar a week from Thursday, then climbed down from the stool and walked out the door.

Max drained the last of his drink and returned to the pawnshop.

SEARCHING FOR ROWENA

When Max went back the pawnshop was open. He retrieved the bundles from the trunk of his car and carried them in.

"This time I got just what you wanted," he said. He set the big spaghetti pot on the counter, then followed it with the clang of the cast iron skillet.

Edgar smiled. "Now this is stuff I can sell." He picked up the skillet and measured the weight of it. "Seventeen bucks."

"Eighteen," Max countered.

Edgar turned the skillet over in his hand, hesitated a minute, then said, "Yeah, okay, providing the stuff ain't hot. I ain't looking for trouble with the cops."

"It's good," Max answered. "I'm just cleaning out my house."

To Max it didn't seem like that much of a lie; in a few short weeks it would be his house and everything in it would belong to him. So what if he wanted to get rid of some stuff a bit early. He was entitled.

On every item they dickered back and forth, a dollar more, a quarter less, until both parties were satisfied they'd made the best deal. After all of the household items were tallied up, Max collected seventy-two dollars. He also had the ten he'd lifted from Doc Payne's wallet, plus thirty-eight bucks from the previous trip. As he pocketed the money, he gave a grin. "I'll be back next week," he told Edgar.

With more than a hundred dollars in ready cash, Max was well on his way to having enough to hire a lawyer. Next trip he'd probably be collecting two-fifty from Joe Mallory; maybe if it was the same woman he'd get the whole five hundred. After that a few more raids and he'd be good to go.

Things were looking so rosy, he could afford to splurge a bit, maybe buy a bottle of bourbon and stop by Maggie Sue's for another visit.

Max had a grin on his face when he climbed into the car. He was already thinking about Maggie Sue. He made a U-turn on Graymoor and headed back toward the highway.

Joe Mallory didn't have five dollars to spare, never mind fivehundred, but he wasn't about to let this opportunity slip through his hands. Max Sweetwater was the first lead he'd had on the whereabouts of Rowena.

When he left the bar, Joe walked back to the gas station. Frankie, the day kid, left in fifteen minutes, and Abe never worked evenings. He'd be the only one there and slow as it was at night, Abe would never be any the wiser.

On the way back to the station, Joe kept a sharp eye out for the cars that whizzed past him. He watched for a green Pontiac, the 1960 green Pontiac Max drove. The car rattled and coughed so you could easily enough hear it coming. Joe remembered it from Max's earlier visit to the gas station, and he knew exactly what he was looking for.

Max had to pass the station. It was the only road out of town. Now it was just a question of waiting and being ready.

As soon as Joe arrived at the station, he told Frankie he could go ahead and leave.

"I got fifteen minutes yet," the kid answered.

"Abe ain't gonna know," Joe said. "So take off."

"I owe you one." Frankie gave a grin and disappeared out the door.

Joe lifted the key off the hook where it was kept and checked that the tow truck was parked out back. Then he waited. It was nearly an hour before he spotted the green Pontiac turn at the corner of Graymoor.

When Max drove past, Joe Mallory had already locked up the gas station and was waiting in the truck. He sat there until the car went a block beyond the station, then pulled out and followed at a distance. On a road that zigzagged back and forth and ran through stretches of farmland where there was not even a shadow of moonlight, it was not easy. Rose Hill was an hour away, and there were a number of times when he nearly lost sight of the Pontiac. When that happened Joe clamped his hands to the steering wheel and pressed hard on the gas pedal, edging closer until the Pontiac was again visible. Once they ran through a patch of fog, and before Joe knew what happened he was a scant two car lengths behind Max. A feeling of panic whooshed through him. He clicked off the headlights and drove for more than a mile in darkness black as pitch. To Joe driving through the dark of night was nowhere near as risky as having Max spot the headlights behind.

When the glow of Rose Hill came into view, Joe's heart began to thump hard against his chest. Rowena was here, he could feel it.

Three blocks into town Max pulled onto a side street and parked the car. Joe stopped the tow truck on a far corner where he had a clear view. He watched as Max climbed out of the car and went into a building with apartments above a row of stores that were closed for the night.

Once Max disappeared into the building, Joe got out of the truck and walked down the street. Not wanting to be recognized, he wore a baseball cap pulled low on his forehead. Backing into the shadows on the opposite side of the street, he stood and watched the building. After several minutes a light came on, and he could see shadows of people in the room. Max was easy to identify, small as he was. The woman was farther away, but Joe knew it wasn't Rowena. This woman was full and round, whereas Rowena was tall, narrow, and lean.

Joe stood there for more than an hour, but nothing changed. He heard laughter and music, but there was no sign of Rowena. "Sooner or later," he grumbled and returned to the truck to wait.

When Max left Maggie Sue's apartment it was after four in the morning, and when he pulled away from the curb Joe missed seeing it because he'd fallen asleep.

A glimmer of sunlight bounced off the fender and woke Joe. The first thing he looked for was Max's car. Gone. He glanced at the clock—seven-ten. By now Abe had arrived at the locked-up gas station and discovered the truck missing. "Shit," Joe said.

He'd figured to get the truck back before Abe got there; now it was too late. Joe knew he'd be canned for what he'd done, so he had nothing more to lose. That's why he decided to stay in Rose Hill and find Rowena. Once found, he'd toss Rowena and Sara into the truck and take them back to Mackinaw. That would be it. He'd explain to Abe and maybe even get his job back. If he didn't, so what? It was a lousy job to start with.

What Joe failed to realize was that Abe had already called the sheriff and reported the truck stolen.

WATCHING

The next morning when everyone gathered around the breakfast table, Max was missing. It was not all that unusual, because he was hit-and-miss on breakfast, and if his disposition was sour he was likely to miss dinner also.

On this particular morning the group seemed in a happier mood than usual. None of the missing items had yet been discovered other than Louie's shoes. While he maintained that someone had stolen the shoes from under the round chair in the parlor, most everyone else believed it to be simply a case of forgetfulness.

"They'll show up soon or later," Caroline assured him. Then she began talking about the new book she'd begun to write. "I've found my true voice, and I'm writing a story about Grandma."

Of course with everyone contributing bits and pieces of stories they felt should be included, breakfast stretched out until eleven o'clock. Rose served two more trays of biscuits, slices of honeydew melon, and leftovers of ham, and when everyone finally stood to leave the table they all agreed that lunch would be unnecessary. Even Louie.

"Don't worry," Rose whispered in his ear, "if you get hungry, just come in the kitchen and I'll fix you a snack."

Shortly after the residents had all gone their own way, Max emerged from his room and whooshed out the door. He jumped in the car and headed for town. This time he passed right by Maggie Sue's apartment and headed for the drugstore. He bought a fresh roll of film, then went home and loaded it into his camera. He never noticed the tow truck that pulled out behind him as he drove past Maggie Sue's apartment building.

Joe watched as Max went into the drugstore and came out carrying a small package. He stayed a full block behind when he trailed Max back to the Sweetwater house, and when Max parked in front of the house Joe circled the block. When he came around the second time, Joe parked the truck directly behind Max. He scrunched down in the seat and began watching the house. Luckily he had a bottle of Jack Daniels to keep him company.

When the clock chimed twelve, Max came to the dining room with his camera ready. He'd expected that everyone would be gathered for lunch, but no one was there. Not a single person. Doc was in the back yard snoozing behind a dental magazine, Wilbur and Louie were watching a ballgame, and Laricka could be heard threatening the two grandsons with punishment if they didn't stop running through the house. Rose was nowhere in sight. Max wandered from room to room looking for her. She was usually in the kitchen fixing lunch at this time but not today. There was no tray of chicken or ham on the counter, no dishes set out, no chopped up vegetables. Even the salt and pepper shakers were stored away.

Max walked into the center hall and hollered up the stairs. "Hello?" His voice was loud but not angry. Actually for Max it was an almost friendly sound. "Anyone here?"

Caroline came from the top floor. "I'm upstairs working. What's the problem?"

It would seem entirely too suspicious to flat-outt ask where Rose was, so Max settled for, "Where's lunch?"

"Breakfast ran really late this morning, so we decided to skip lunch," Caroline said. "I can fix you a sandwich if you want."

Anxious as Max was to get the picture taken, he couldn't run the risk of looking like he was up to something. "Oh, okay." He wasn't the least bit hungry but to decline the offer would mean questions.

He followed Caroline through the hall and into the kitchen. He sat at the counter, and as she scooped up some leftover chicken salad, he said, "Nice how you've got Rose here to do the cooking and all, huh?"

Caroline looked over and smiled. "Yes, it is nice."

"She's good for the place, gets along with everybody." Without skipping a beat Max segued into asking where she came from and whether she was married.

Caroline moved past the question without answering. "Having Rose here has certainly made it a lot easier for me. I've gone back to writing."

"Good." Max nodded. "Good to do something you enjoy." *More flies with honey,* he reminded himself.

"I'm really glad to hear you say that, Max. I've been worried that you were still angry with me because of the house."

"Nah," he said. "I'm over that. I figure if this is what Ida wanted, then it's good with me."

"I never thought of it as me or you owning the house," Caroline answered. "We're family, so I'd like to believe we own it together."

A bitter swell rose in Max's throat. "Yeah," he said in a hollowed-out voice, "except your name is on the deed." He picked up the sandwich Caroline had made and started toward the door. "I've got a few things to take care of. See you later." The tone of his voice was glossed over, not to the point where it sounded chummy but enough to hide the anger churning inside.

Max headed back toward his room, but on the way he stopped in the bathroom and flushed the sandwich down the toilet. He didn't want a hand-out sandwich; what he wanted was what should have been rightfully his anyway. He stood there and watched the last chunk of chicken swirl away; then he carried the plate back to the kitchen and plunked it down in the sink.

The afternoon seemed endless as Max waited for the dinner hour. He listened hoping to hear Rose in the kitchen, but there was no sound until almost five-thirty. When he walked into the kitchen, Caroline was preparing dinner.

"Where's Rose?" he asked.

"Sara's not feeling well," Caroline answered. "Rose is taking care of her."

"What about dinner?" The agitation in Max's voice was now apparent.

"I'm afraid you're stuck with me tonight." Caroline laughed.

"Shit!" Max turned and walked out of the room.

"But I thought you said…"

Joe Mallory sat in the truck watching the house for six hours, but he saw very little. Two women came and went, but neither of them were Rowena. Inside the house he could see nothing until the lights were switched on shortly after sunset. At first it was only shadows moving about, but gradually they took shape and came into view. Using darkness as a cover, Joe stepped out of the truck and crept closer to the window. He could see into what was most likely the parlor.

The first person to arrive was a tall man with light hair. He carried a sheath of papers and settled in the high back chair. Next came a man in work clothes, rounder than Max but only a head taller. The two women were back, but still no Rowena and no Sara. He moved closer to the house and squatted behind the azalea bushes.

When Joe heard voices, he raised himself up and peered into the window. That's when he thought he saw Rowena, not in the front parlor but walking through the back hall. She was little more than a shadow with brown hair, but he knew it was Rowena. She was unlike the others, taller, straighter, a youthful lean body. She stopped a moment and called out something; then the others rose and walked toward the sound of her voice. They disappeared into a room where he could no longer see.

Joe worked his way around the side of the house but could see nothing. Both windows were darkened. They had moved to the back of the house, he was certain of it, but there was no way around. A tall wooden fence and thick hedges surrounded the backyard. Fence or no fence, he had to see what was back there.

Returning to the truck Joe found a pair of pliers and a claw hammer. He crossed the street again and made his way toward the rear of the house. Following the fence around, he moved to the far back corner where if a board should splinter or nails pop it was less likely to be heard. He pressed his hand against several boards; they were all solid and strong. Finally he found one that wobbled ever so slightly. Using the thinnest part of the claw, he gouged the wood until he could edge the hammer's claw under a nail. He pulled the handle back, and the nail popped loose.

After he'd pulled five nails from the first board, it swung sideways. Then he moved on to the second board and repeated the process. After nearly two hours of work, he was able to push the boards aside and slip through the fence.

The back window was high off the ground, too high for Joe to look directly in. The light in the back room was dimmed, but he could see shadows. It was Rowena, and she stood close to the tall man he'd seen in the parlor earlier.

Joe heard her laugh and felt a sharp pain shoot through his heart when he watched her reach up and wrap her arms around the man's neck. "Son of a bitch," he grumbled.

For nearly a month Joe had suffered pangs of guilt, believing he'd driven Rowena away with his careless behavior. Now he realized that wasn't it at all. She'd come here to be with another man.

"You're not getting away with this," Joe growled. He crossed the yard, stepped outside the fence, and returned to the truck.

Mistaken Identity

After Wilbur said he'd be happy to read the remainder of Caroline's book whenever it was ready, she hugged him around the neck for a second time. "Thank you," she said and brushed a kiss across his cheek.

Although their relationship was new, it didn't feel new. Wilbur had come into her life just as Ida had, and when Caroline stood alongside him she could already sense he was the grandfather she'd been waiting for. After so many years of drifting through life like dandelion floss loosed from its stem, she now had roots. She had someone she cared about, and that someone cared about her.

After Wilbur left the kitchen, Caroline clicked on the radio. She was listening to Whitney Houston sing "I Wanna Dance with Somebody," which is why she missed hearing the clap of the fence boards when Joe Mallory banged his way out of the backyard.

When Joe climbed into the truck, the anger he felt churned and roiled like the fire of a volcano. The heat of it burned through his body and caused his heart to kick against his chest with such force that it took his breath away. He heaved a desperate gasp, then reached for the bottle of Jack Daniels.

He downed several swigs before his hands stopped shaking and his heartbeat slowed to an angry rumble. At first he cursed Rowena and wished her dead, but once the flow of anger crested the misery of a man who'd lost everything surfaced.

A stream of tears began to cascade down Joe's face, and he wiped them back with his shirtsleeve. When the stream became a flood, he dropped his head onto his chest and sobbed aloud.

Joe had to talk to Rowena. He had to convince her to come back. The more he drank, the more logical such a plan seemed. He sat there for hours thinking it through, and by the time the bottle was near empty he'd come to believe this was not her doing. It was obviously that man's fault. He'd turned her against Joe. He'd said things, done things, maybe even made promises. Joe's tears stopped, and the anger returned. He tipped the bottle to his lips and drained it.

"Damn him," Joe said as he stumbled down from the cab. He pulled a box from behind the seat and fished through it for a length of hose and a rag. As he searched, he cursed the man who had taken Rowena; he ranted, saying hell and damnation were too good for such a man. Once he found what he was looking for Joe circled around to the side of the truck, unscrewed the cap to the gas tank, and dropped in one end of the hose. He lifted the other end to his mouth and pulled a long sucking breath. When gasoline churned through the hose, he filled the Jack Daniels bottle then tossed the hose aside.

After he'd stuffed one end of the rag into the bottle, Joe started back across the street. He stumbled as drunken men often do, leaning forward and listing first to the right and then to the left. Putting one foot in front of the other he drew closer to the house. The parlor was now dark, and he could see no lights in the upstairs rooms. Joe followed his earlier path until he came to the opening he'd made in the fence; then he climbed through and started across the lawn. At first it appeared that room was also darkened, but then a light clicked on and a figure appeared.

Wilbur's acid indigestion was acting up again. It was the third night in a row. It didn't come from what he'd eaten; it came from an uneasiness that had settled in his mind. Vague thoughts that carried a sense of foreboding but came without an understandable meaning. He'd kept a close eye on Caroline, even walked up to the attic several times to check on her, but everything was just as it should be. Throughout the evening Wilbur had tried to convince himself it was simply reawakening thoughts of Ida that set his mind on edge, but his argument was less than convincing.

After he'd tossed and turned for nearly an hour, he decided a glass of warm milk might help. Wilbur climbed from his bed and headed toward the kitchen. From the hallway he could see a sliver of light coming from beneath Caroline's door. He smiled. She was still working on her book. With only the dim light of the hall lantern, he descended the stairs and walked toward the kitchen. Seconds after he snapped on the overhead light he heard the voice.

"Rowenaaaa!"

It was not a name, not a word, just a desperate, urgent cry. Wilbur stopped and listened.

"Rowenaaaa!"

Suddenly lights began popping on all over the house. Caroline opened her door and started down the stairs. "What was that?" she asked Doctor Payne who was already in the hallway.

He shrugged and followed her down the staircase. Harriet came seconds later.

When the cry came a third time, Caroline realized who the voice was calling for.

Wilbur did not, so he turned and walked toward the sound.

It was the sight of a man he'd come to detest that caused Joe to strike a match and light the rag in the bottle. After downing all that Jack Daniels he was so drunk he wobbled when he stood, but somehow he found strength enough to draw back his arm and hurl the bottle through the kitchen window.

The explosion shook the house and threw Wilbur to the far left of the kitchen. Within seconds the fire began to spread across the kitchen floor and up the walls, grabbing curtains, dishtowels, cookbooks, and anything else it could find. Black smoke rolled through the kitchen and into the hall.

Caroline ran back upstairs and began pounding on the doors. "Fire! Get out! Get out!" When all the upstairs rooms were emptied, she ran down and caught Max and Laricka already on their way out the door. By then lights had gone on all over the neighborhood, and a patrol car screeched to a stop in front of the house.

"What happened?" a police officer asked, but no one knew anything other than that they had heard a strange yell followed by the sound of an explosion.

In the distance the sound of a fire engine screamed through the night.

Neighbors from several houses now crowded the street, everyone asking everyone else what had happened. Caroline scanned the faces and found Rose clinging to little Sara. The fearful looks they wore said they too had heard the cry.

Caroline pushed her way through the crowd and took Rose by the hand. "Come with me."

Barbara Ann Percy, an elderly neighbor who Caroline often ran errands for, stood in the crowd of onlookers. When she saw Caroline coming, she stretched out her arms. "Oh, you poor dear—"

"I need your help," Caroline interrupted. "Take my friend, Rose, and her daughter to your house, go inside, and close the door."

"But—"

"Please."

The urgency in Caroline's voice was argument enough. Barbara Ann gave Rose a nod and said, "Follow me."

When Caroline turned back to the crowd, she began to look for each of the residents. The upstairs rooms had all been emptied out, but Wilbur was nowhere to be seen. "Have you seen Wilbur?" she asked Doctor Payne. When he shook his head she asked Max, Louie, Harriet, and Laricka. No one had seen him.

By then the fire engine had arrived.

"Wilburrr!" Caroline screamed. "Wilburrr!" When no answer came, she turned and started toward the house.

A tall redheaded fireman dropped the hose he was unfurling and grabbed her by the arm. "You can't go back in there!"

Caroline struggled to get free. "Wilbur, I've got to get Wilbur!"

"Somebody's inside the house?"

"Yes, Wilbur!"

"Do you know where?" the fireman asked. He kept his hold on Caroline. "Do you know where he is?"

Her tears overflowed. "No one's upstairs. He's got to be in the kitchen, the dining room, or the parlor."

Standing within earshot, Louie said, "He ain't in the dining room or the parlor. I come through that way, and ain't nobody in there."

"Then he's in the kitchen," Caroline said. She explained in a shaky voice that the kitchen was in the right-hand corner at the rear of the house. "Around the stairs, then straight back."

The redhead turned to his partner. "Come on, George, let's get this guy." The two firemen unfurled a lengthy stretch of hose and carried it inside the house.

Once inside, seeing became impossible. The redheaded Calvin had hold of the nozzle so he was in the lead. Staying close together, they felt their way along the right side of the wall. Following Caroline's description of the kitchen's location, they moved quickly through the hall and felt their way past the staircase. Then they crossed into the kitchen.

The moment Calvin stepped through the door he spotted the flames. George saw it also. He pressed the button on his radio. "Charge the hose!" The flat grey hose swelled with water as the two men inched forward. The smoke was so thick neither of the men could see one another, but they both held tight to the hose.

"Wilbur?" Calvin called out. "Wilbur, are you in here?" When there was no answer, Calvin passed the nozzle to George and began to feel his way along the right wall. With a heavily-gloved hand he moved around the bulk of the refrigerator and then the stove. He could see nothing. The smoke was so dense all he could do was feel.

"Wilbur?" he called again, but still there was no answer. He came near the center of the room when he saw a bright green glow a foot, maybe two, from where he was. He blinked several times, and the light came into focus.

It was the numbers on a glow-in-the-dark watch.

If it was Wilbur, he was in the path of the rapidly spreading flames. Calvin dropped to his knees and crawled toward the green glow. Before he got there he bumped up against Wilbur's foot. He reached out, grabbed the leg, pulled it toward him, and caught hold of the torso. Wilbur was unconscious but still alive. Dragging him across the floor, Calvin moved swiftly and called out to George, "I've got a survivor." George twisted the bale and aimed the nozzle upward. A powerful spray of water slapped against the ceiling and cascaded down the walls. The fire sizzled, spat, and steamed, then quickly died away.

"We've got to get this guy on oxygen!" Calvin yelled. He pulled Wilbur close to the doorway, then knelt and lifted the big man across his shoulder. Wilbur was dead weight and not easily carried. Calvin braced himself against the doorframe and stood. Following the hose line, he made his way back through the hallway and out onto the porch. When the crowd saw the firemen carrying Wilbur to safety, a cheer rose up.

"Wilbur!" Caroline screamed and ran to him. She fell to her knees alongside the lifeless body. "Please be okay, Wilbur. Please, please…" A cascade of tears rolled down her face and she began to pray, something she'd not done in a very long time. After years of disappointment and heartache she'd given up believing in miracles, but now she needed one and it was bigger than anything else she'd ever asked for.

"Please, God," she said, "I swear I'll never ask for anything else. Just please let Wilbur be okay...please..." Her voice was small and frail, but it carried a sense of urgency impossible to miss.

Caroline couldn't say how many minutes passed as she knelt beside Wilbur; she only knew it seemed a lifetime. When he finally blinked his eyes open and let go of a choking cough, the ambulance had already arrived.

As they lifted Wilbur into the ambulance, the captain's radio squawked again.

"We've got another survivor," Fred Marcaine said. Fred was part of the team that had gone around to the back of the house to wet down the wall and check for hot spots.

Hearing the call, Caroline turned and searched the faces in the crowd. All of the residents were present and accounted for. She turned to the captain. "Another survivor?"

The captain shrugged. "A neighbor maybe?"

When two firemen came from the rear of the house carrying Joe Mallory he'd already passed out. Not from injury but from a full bottle of Jack Daniels.

The captain leaned over him and caught a whiff of the whiskey. "Whew, this guy's not injured, he's drunk!"

That's when the police got involved. Once they'd pulled Joe's wallet from his pocket, it took mere minutes to learn he was wanted in Mackinaw for theft of a tow truck.

CAROLINE

I've never been so frightened in all my life. Being frightened for yourself is bad enough, but it's ten thousand times worse when you're frightened for someone you love. When I heard the sound of Rowena's name, my only thought was to get her and Sara to safety. When the police found that man in the backyard, they said his driver's license identified him as Joe Mallory. I didn't need anything to tell me who it was; I'd heard the call of Rowena's name.

With all the craziness going on I didn't stop to count heads until after Rose left with Barbara Ann; that's when I discovered Wilbur wasn't with the others. I was turning back to look for him when that fireman, Calvin I think his name is, stopped me. "Too dangerous," he said, and he wasn't about to let go of my arm.

I'm not a particularly brave person—in fact I'm not brave at all—but when someone you love is in danger, you don't stop to think about yourself. All you can think about is saving them. One summer Mama and I were at the city pool, and a little kid who'd been running around fell in the deep end. Without stopping to think about it, his mama jumped in to save him even though she couldn't swim a stroke herself. She was standing in water over her head, but she grabbed that toddler and held him up high over her head so he wouldn't drown. When people saw she couldn't swim, a bunch of bystanders pulled them both out. Well, I felt just like that mama when I realized Wilbur was still inside.

Much as it breaks my heart to see Grandma's house in such a shambles, I'm just happy to have Wilbur alive.

Later that night when I got to thinking about Rowena's husband being the cause of all this, I started wondering if I'd done the right thing in bringing her here. It didn't take a whole lot of thinking to come to the realization I had no other choice. When you know somebody's in trouble, you've got to stretch out a hand and help. If you don't you'll come to hate yourself, and that's not something anybody wants to live with.

It's funny, I came here a few months back with no family at all. Now I've got a great big family, and Rowena and Wilbur, they're an important part of it.

THE AFTERMATH

On the same night Wilbur was taken to the hospital, Joe Mallory was taken to jail. The fire had destroyed the kitchen and the back wall, and although the remainder of the house still stood it would be uninhabitable for a few days mostly because of smoke and water damage.

Once the blaze was out and the patrol cars gone, the neighbors left but Caroline stood looking at the house. She was alone when Calvin walked over and suggested she should wait until tomorrow before going back inside.

"There's still a lot of smoke in there."

"What happens now?"

"George and me are gonna stay and keep an eye on the place," he said. "Make sure there's no flare-ups, stuff like that."

"Is it ruined?" she asked tearfully.

"Not at all." Calvin shook his head. "The kitchen, maybe, but the rest of the place should be okay." He gave her a reassuring smile. "It won't look nearly as bad in the morning."

With Wilbur gone to the hospital Caroline and the seven remaining residents were homeless, but no one went without a bed. Max headed off to town saying he would spend the night with a friend. The neighbors opened their hearts and homes to the others.

Doc Payne went home with Missus Gomez, a widow with a forty-six-year-old daughter who was good-looking and extremely attracted to intellectuals. Before they even got back to the house, Mercedes had moved past the doctor title and began calling him Frank. She spoke in a throaty whisper and when she told him she was single, she leaned in so close her lashes fluttered against his cheek. It was three days before Doc returned to the house and weeks longer before he again picked up a dental magazine; he was far too busy visiting with Mercedes.

Louie stayed with the Casters who not only had a spare room but one with a television. "I don't suppose you take in roomers," Louie asked, but the answer was no. That lovely big room with a television and a refrigerator full of icy cold sodas was for their grandchildren when they came to visit.

As it turned out, Barbara Ann Percy welcomed the company. She had room enough for not just Rose and Sara, but Caroline, Laricka, and Harriet as well. With her house full of ladies in nightdress, Barbara Ann declared it a slumber party and brought out dishes of ice cream covered in chocolate syrup. After the ice cream was gone and Sara had drifted off to sleep, none the wiser about her daddy being hauled off to jail, they sat around the table and talked until there was nothing left to say.

Caroline tried to join in the conversation and she added a word or two occasionally, but her thoughts were on the house. She wanted to go inside, look around, see what had been damaged and what needed to be replaced. Although she'd never seen such things in the store, she was hopeful Peter Pennington carried refrigerators and stoves.

Max left thinking he'd spend the night at Maggie Sue's place. He parked the car in front of her building, rang the vestibule bell, then proceeded up the stairs. Once on the second floor, he twisted the knob and found the apartment door unlocked.

"Sly little minx," he said with a chuckle, believing she was waiting for him. As he crossed the living room he kicked off his shoes, then unzipped his trousers, and stepped out of them.

Unfortunately, the downstairs bell was broken and Maggie Sue had simply forgotten to close the deadbolt lock. When Max opened the bedroom door he found Herb Potter in the bed.

This time it was more than he could tolerate. Standing there in a pair of boxer shorts with his shirttail hanging loose, Max felt like a damned idiot.

"What the hell do you call this?" he screamed.

Maggie Sue said she called it an invasion of privacy and told him to get out. One word led to another, and before thirty seconds had passed he was hollering in a voice so loud the neighbors a block away heard him. Although Herb Potter was twice his size, Max demanded he get out of bed and fight like a man. By then Maggie Sue had already telephoned the police.

"She said she was gonna move in with me!" Max cried as the two policemen led him from the apartment carrying his trousers in his hand.

"You said you was rich," Maggie Sue hollered after him. "You didn't say you was crazy too!"

Hoping to circumvent any further problems, the officers suggested Max spend the night down at the stationhouse.

"It's not like you're under arrest," the older cop said. "This will just give you time enough to cool down."

"I ain't gonna cool down!" Max yelled. "That damn woman's a menace to society."

The younger cop chuckled. "She ain't a menace, she's just Maggie Sue." Which, in fact, was the truth.

While the other residents rested comfortably in neighboring houses, Max spent the night in a cell directly across from where Joe Mallory was sleeping it off.

Shortly after six Joe Mallory woke, and he was in a mood fouler than any he'd ever known before. He had no memory of being arrested and little memory of the events that preceded the arrest. Coming to the realization he was in jail, he took to banging on the bars and hollering to be let out. The racket woke Max.

The last he'd seen of Joe Mallory was at the bar back in Mackinaw. The agreement was he'd bring a picture of the girl and collect five hundred dollars. It took just a few seconds for Max to figure it out.

"Son of a bitch! You followed me here thinking you'd screw me outta that reward money!"

"Asshole," Joe replied. "There ain't no money."

"You said—"

Joe gave a cynical laugh. "You're a bigger asshole than I thought."

Of course, Max came back at him saying he'd get the money one way or another. Once the threats started, they turned on each other. Deputy

Carson overheard a good bit of the conversation and called the sheriff, and before the day was done Max had been arrested for the theft of Wilbur's watch and a lengthy list of household items.

After he was fingerprinted and booked, it was discovered that Max had a number of outstanding arrest warrants: one from Alabama where he'd swindled a woman out of her savings, a second from Tennessee where he left town with a car not rightfully his, and a third from Arkansas where he allegedly held up a liquor store.

Although Max maintained he was innocent of all those charges he remained in jail, as did Joe Mallory.

RESTORATION

Wilbur remained in the hospital for several days. For the first two days Caroline arrived before visiting hours began and stayed until long after they'd ended. On the third day she returned to the house.

Because of the situation the Sweetwater house had been considered a crime scene and cordoned off, so no one was allowed to enter for those first two days. The morning Officer Sweeney removed the yellow tape crisscrossing the door Caroline waited on the front porch.

The reopening of the house was hardly a ceremonious thing; Sweeney simply yanked the tape down and told Caroline to go on in. She did. Alone. The odor of burnt wood still lingered and it would continue for a week or more, but the house was livable. The vase on the hall table had been broken, but other than that the only real damage was in the kitchen. That was in shambles. Where there had been a window, there was now a gaping hole, and charred remnants of the curtains were thrown about the room like bits of confetti.

Caroline licked her finger and ran it over a cabinet door streaked with soot. Probably salvageable. Fighting back the tears, she reached for the bucket kept beneath the sink. That's when she saw the cover of what had been Ida's favorite cookbook. She bent to pick it up and the pages, little more than ash, fell apart.

Caroline dropped to her knees and began to sob. She cried not for the loss of things, but because those lost things had been rich with the smell and feel of the grandmother she'd come to love. Swallowed by the sorrow of such a loss, she was deaf to the sound of footsteps when Calvin came in carrying an armload of two-by-fours.

He laid the boards atop the counter and squatted next to Caroline. "I know this looks bad right now. But once it's cleaned up——"

"It's not just the mess." Caroline sniffed. "These things belonged to Grandma. They were all I had left of her."

"Oh, so you don't remember her?"

Caroline turned to him with a puzzled expression. "Of course I remember her."

"Well, then," Calvin said with a smile, "these things weren't all you had. You've still got memories."

"True," Caroline answered and gave a wistful smile. That's when she first noticed how very handsome Calvin was.

He extended his hand and Caroline took it. She stood and brushed the soot from her jeans. "Thanks."

"No problem. There's a lot to be done, so I guess we'd better get busy."

"We?"

He nodded. "I'm off today, so I figured I'd stop by and close up this hole for you."

"Thanks," Caroline repeated. This time her smile was considerably broader.

A short while later Rose came walking in. "Sara's busy making cookies with Barbara Ann, but I figured I'd help with the cleanup."

Harriet and Laricka showed up a half hour later; by then Louie had already arrived and was holding up the long end of a two-by-four Calvin hammered into place.

No one needed to be told what to do. They each moved ahead, instinctively wiping down the cupboards, scouring the stove, and emptying spoiled or soggy food from the pantry shelves. There was no job too dirty or too hard; each task was simply something that needed to be done.

Caroline broke down and cried twice that day. The first time was when she found the cookbook; the second time was when she found Ida's African violet beneath a pile of broken glass.

"It's ruined," she sobbed, thinking back on how Ida had fussed over the plant, moving it from the windowsill to the counter and then back again to the windowsill so it would get just the right amount of sunshine and diffused light.

Harriet looked at the broken flowerpot with a pile of dirt lying atop the violet. She squatted down, brushed aside the dirt, and picked up the flower. "Why, this ain't ruined at all. It just needs replanting."

"I doubt that will help," Caroline said. "Grandma said violets are very delicate."

"They ain't that delicate," Harriet answered, "they're just a bit moody." She scooped a handful of dirt from the floor and said, "Hand me that jelly jar; I'll get this fixed."

Early in the afternoon, George, Calvin's firefighting partner, showed up with three large pizzas and several big bottles of Coke. "Lunch time," he called out, and everyone stopped what they were doing.

Until the smell of hot pizza floated through the air no one had thought of food, but in less than a half hour there was nothing but crumbs left in the bottom of the boxes. Afterward, everyone went back to work.

George not only brought the pizza, he also stayed to help. When Calvin shouted out things like, "Can you put a brace under——" George had it done before he'd finished the sentence.

At the end of the day the hole that had been a window was covered with wallboard, the cabinets scrubbed down, the floor free of debris and seven bags of trash hauled to the curb. The kitchen, although it would eventually need the window replaced and a fresh coat of paint, was mostly useable.

The smell of smoke was still evident, but after a while no one noticed it. Laricka said it was a pleasant reminder of the house she'd lived in as a child, a house with a wood-burning fireplace. Harriet said it put her in the mood for another cigarette, and Louie said so long as the stove was still working he could live with the smell.

That evening they all gathered around the dining room table, including Calvin and George. Max of course was missing because he was now under arrest and confined to the Rose Hill jail. Doc Payne was still at the Gomez house, and it would be days before he could tear himself loose from Mercedes. Wilbur, although reports were good, was not scheduled for release from the hospital until tomorrow.

When everyone was settled at the table, Caroline spoke. "I don't know how to begin to thank everyone," she said. She'd thought of a dozen different things she wanted to say, but she before could get started she was interrupted.

"Thanks ain't necessary," Harriet said. "We're family."

"Yeah." Louie nodded. "Family."

"It's what Ida would have wanted," Laricka added.

Although Caroline had planned a sequence of lengthy statements saying how much she appreciated what each person had done, the words left her. For the third time that day, tears came to her eyes and she simply said, "I'm so lucky to have a family like this."

She thought back on the words Ida had once said: *Love turns strangers into family.*

In the center of the table sat the African violet, looking perked up and happy in its new jelly jar home.

It was after ten o'clock when Caroline finally trudged up the stairs to her attic room, and it was the first she'd seen the room since the night of the fire. There had been no damage in any of the second floor rooms, not even in the downstairs parlor or the dining room, but when the explosion shook the house it knocked loose the picture she'd received from Peter Pennington and sent it crashing down. The frame was split apart, and the picture lay on her desk amidst a pile of broken glass.

"Oh dear," she said.

CAROLINE SWEETWATER

*I*t's a sad thing to walk into a place you've loved and see it torn to pieces. It made me feel like the last little bit I had of Grandma Ida was gone. All those other places I lived I walked away without even a look back, but this house is different. Those places, the places where Mama and I lived, they were just apartments. One was the same as the other, and there was no special significance attached to any of them. But this house is a home. Grandma made it that way.

Calvin, that fireman, he's nice in a deep sort of way. Not many men would stop what they're doing to remind a weepy-eyed woman she's got memories to hang on to. It takes a certain sensitivity to do that, and Calvin, he's got that kind of sensitivity.

He's nice looking too. That's not something I noticed right away, but when we were having pizza I watched how he was handing everyone else a slice before taking one for himself. That's when I saw the blue of his eyes and the kindness shining out of them.

I doubt that Grandma would think a store-bought pizza lunch was something special, but this one will stick in my head for a good long time. It felt like the start of a good tomorrow. Not just one good tomorrow, but a lot of them strung together and stretching out for years to come. Grandma always said to keep a sharp eye for an omen of things to come. I think her violet coming back to life was just such an omen.

BEHIND THE PICTURE

Looking at the broken picture, Caroline felt a certain sadness in her heart. For a number of weeks the smiling young man had looked down on her, and she'd come to care for him in a strange and quite unexplainable way. She'd wondered and at times even daydreamed about who he was and what his connection to Ida had been.

There was a connection, Caroline was certain of it. She'd felt it in a number of odd ways. Not things you could touch your hand to but a feeling of familiarity, like a place she'd once been to or someone she'd known in passing. Perhaps he'd been a distant cousin or youthful sweetheart. Caroline knew nothing about him, save this single thing: his picture was intended for her grandma, and now it was intended for her. Peter Pennington had said as much, and Peter was never wrong.

He'd been right about the desk, and he'd been right about the watch. Only the picture was still unexplained.

When she pulled the wastebasket from under the desk, Caroline already knew what she'd do. She'd take the picture back to Peter and ask him to reframe it. She thought back to the happiness on his face when he'd given her the gift. Surely he'd be willing to find a new frame. Caroline chuckled as she carefully lifted the larger pieces of broken glass and dropped them into the wastebasket. She knew chances were Peter could produce the exact same frame, right down to the tiny chip on the right-hand corner. How he did it, she couldn't say, but it was mysterious and wonderful at the same time.

Caroline didn't see the large brown envelope until she lifted the piece of cardboard backing the picture. She picked up the envelope and turned it over in her hands.

It was a perfectly plain brown envelope. No markings, no name, no return address. Nothing. Thinking back Caroline remembered Peter's words: *This was intended for your grandma, and now you're the one who should have it.* Slowly and tentatively she lifted the flap and slid out the contents.

U.S. Railroad bond certificates. Ten of them. Each one with a face value of one hundred thousand dollars.

"Good grief!" Caroline exclaimed. If she had found a fifty-dollar bill she'd have been happy. If she'd found a one hundred-dollar bill, she would have been ecstatic, but a million dollars' worth of bonds was too unbelievable.

"There's got to be a mistake," she mumbled. Opening the envelope she looked inside again. Nothing. It was empty. There was no note, no explanation. The envelope contained nothing but the bonds.

"Impossible," she said and stood there staring at the stack. A dozen different scenarios ran through her head. Perhaps they were payment of a debt someone owed to Ida or maybe to Big Jim. Possibly someone in Ida's past, her parents or a lover, had intended the bonds as a gift. But who? It saddened Caroline to think that as much as she'd loved her grandma, she knew little about her life. She had no knowledge of where Ida came from or why somebody would want her to have a million dollars in bonds.

This was intended for your grandma, and now you're the one who should have it. Peter Pennington's words. He had the answer. Caroline knew he alone could explain why this gift was intended for Ida and, ultimately, her.

For a long while Caroline sat there looking through the bonds, looking at each one carefully, turning it over in her hands, and searching for some small clue: initials written in the corner, a secret message, a meaningful mark. After nearly an hour she had found nothing.

Setting the bonds aside, she cleared away the remaining pieces of glass and lifted the photograph that for weeks had been smiling down on her. "Who are you?" she asked. The photograph offered nothing more than a male version of the Mona Lisa smile. There was no mark on the photograph, no studio name, no date taken, no inscription, nothing. It was as void of clues as the envelope had been.

"Impossible," Caroline repeated. Logic warned that it was a mistake. Perhaps Peter didn't know the bonds were behind the picture. Perhaps they were intended for someone else. Perhaps, perhaps, perhaps. She could find a million reasons why such a gift wasn't intended for her but not a single rationale for why it was.

And yet…

Holding bonds of such great value in her hands did something to Caroline. It sent a shiver of excitement up her spine and ignited the spark of possibility in her mind. Although she was willing herself not to, Caroline began to think of things like buying a new washing machine and replacing Wilbur's gold pocket watch.

When those thoughts came, she tried to draw back. "Impossible," she repeated over and over again. The logic of some unknown benefactor giving either Ida or her those bonds was too overwhelming. It was simply not a thing that could be real. In the wee hours of the morning she slid the bonds back into the envelope and decided that tomorrow she would take the picture and the bonds and go back to Previously Loved Treasures. This time Peter Pennington had obviously made a mistake.

Caroline cleaned up the remaining bits of glass, then showered, pulled on a pair of pajamas, and climbed into bed. Given the long day of work, she should have been tired. She should have closed her eyes and drifted off to sleep seconds later. Were it not for that envelope she might have, but now sleep was impossible to come by. Lying in bed she tried to find a reason, a logical, explainable reason to justify her right to the bonds, but there was none. Every scenario she imagined was offset by an even more valid point proving this had to be some kind of crazy mistake.

The argument with herself was one Caroline could neither lose or win. Either was impossible because both sides knew what the other was thinking. *If only Wilbur were here,* she thought. *He'd know what to do.*

The night seemed a thousand hours long. When the first ray of dawn creased the sky, Caroline climbed out of bed and got dressed. She gathered the picture, the broken frame, and the bonds and tucked them into a tote bag.

First she would stop by the hospital and check on Wilbur. Then she'd visit the Previously Loved Treasures store.

Peter Pennington would be able to provide an explanation

PREVIOUSLY LOVED TREASURES

As soon as the breakfast dishes were dried and put away, Caroline left the house with the tote bag. She drove to the hospital and went directly to Wilbur's room, even though it was a full hour before visitors were allowed.

Breezing through the door, she said, "I've got to talk to you."

"You're early today," Wilbur said with a smile. "It must be something important."

"It is." Caroline pulled the brown envelope from her tote and handed it to Wilbur. "What do you think of this?"

Wilbur slid the contents out, leafed through the bonds, then gave a long low whistle. "Where'd you get these?"

"They were behind the picture."

"Picture?"

She nodded. "The picture Peter Pennington gave me." Caroline explained how Peter said the picture was originally intended for Ida, and since Ida was gone she was meant to have it.

"Did he say there was something behind the picture?"

Caroline shook her head. "Not that I can recall."

"Hmmm." A puzzled look settled on Wilbur's face. "Do you know what these are?"

"Investment bonds?"

"Not just bonds," Wilbur said. "Bearer bonds."

"Bearer bonds?"

Wilbur nodded. "Bonds that have no listed owner. They belong to whoever has them."

"But I have them."

Wilbur nodded again. "Yes, you do."

"That can't be right," Caroline stammered. "Why would anyone give me—"

"That's something I can't answer," Wilbur said. He slid the bonds into the envelope and handed it back to her. "You'll have to talk to your Mister Pennington."

"That's my next stop," Caroline said and dropped the envelope into her tote.

It was close to eleven when Caroline left the hospital and drove to the center of town. She parked across the street from Previously Loved Treasures but sensed something was different. Peter, who always seemed to know when she'd be arriving, was not standing out front waiting to greet her, and the interior of the store appeared dark.

Thinking her sunglasses responsible for the blackened shadows, she pulled them off and slid them into her pocket. The dark interior remained the same. Caroline crossed the street and could now see the windows were empty of merchandise. No chairs, bits of jewelry, china dishes, or lace doilies. And the window was dirty, covered with soot and grime that looked years old.

Something was very wrong. Peter Pennington kept the glass so clean it sparkled in the sunlight. Caroline reached out and tried the handle of the door. Locked.

Peter was not a young man. Possibly he was sick; maybe he'd fallen and was in need of help. Caroline rattled the door. "Anybody here?"

Silence was the only answer.

For ten, maybe fifteen, minutes she stood there banging on the door, rattling the knob and calling out Peter Pennington's name, but still there was no answer. Feeling frustrated and helpless, she walked to the dry cleaner two doors down.

"Excuse me," she said to the woman behind the counter. "I'm looking for Peter Pennington. Do you know if something's happened to him?"

The woman shrugged. "Can't help you, honey. Afraid I don't know this Mister Pennington."

"He's the man who owns the Previously Loved Treasures shop."

The woman shook her head. "Not familiar with that one."

"It's the second-hand store." A thread of impatience crept into

Caroline's words. "Two doors down, this side of the street."

The woman shook her head and shrugged again.

"The green building on the corner!"

The woman chuckled. "Shoot, sweetie, that old place's been empty for years. Nobody's been there for who knows how long."

"But he was," Caroline argued. "Peter Pennington was there and he had all kinds of stuff—used furniture, watches, clothes even."

"You sure you got the right town?" the woman asked.

"I'm positive," Caroline replied. "I've been there several times. I bought a used desk, a watch, a box of clothes—"

"Maybe you're thinking of Saint Vincent's Thrift Shop. That's two blocks down and left on Foster Street—"

"No," Caroline said hopelessly. "It was right here on the corner."

For almost a minute nothing more was said. Droop-shouldered and feeling deflated, Caroline stood there hoping time would change the answer but it didn't.

When a young man came in carrying a bundle of shirts, the woman looked at Caroline one last time. "Check with Fritzi over at the beauty parlor," she said. "Fritzi knows most everything that goes on in town."

Caroline did try Fritzi, and she also tried Herb at the hardware store and Mildred from the supermarket. The answer was always the same. No one had ever heard of a Peter Pennington or seen the Previously Loved Treasures shop.

In a last-ditch effort to find Peter, Caroline stopped at the Saint Vincent Thrift Shop. "Have you ever heard of Previously Loved Treasures?"

The girl behind the counter laughed. "Of course I have. We've got tons of previously loved things. What exactly were you looking for?"

"A man called Peter Pennington," Caroline answered.

"A man," the girl said. "Well, now, that's one thing we don't have."

Caroline returned to the little corner building and pressed her nose to the glass. "Where are you, Peter?" she said tearfully. "Were you ever really here?" A stream of tears rolled down her face as she peered into the empty store.

A stretch of bare shelves lined the wall, and the counter was covered with a layer of dust. There was no evidence that there had ever been a Previously Loved Treasures shop. And yet Caroline knew better. She could so vividly remember Peter Pennington's mischievous smile, the kindness with which he spoke, the sage advice he'd given, and his gift—the picture she carried in her tote.

Caroline cupped her hands around her eyes and looked through the window. At first the store seemed empty, totally empty, but then she saw a glint of light at the far end of the shelves. A spot of yellow. She pressed closer to the glass and focused her eyes on the spot. Slowly it took shape; it was a yellow step stool. The yellow step stool Peter used to retrieve treasures from the higher shelves.

"Thank you," she whispered through a flood of tears.

If Peter was no longer here perhaps he was somewhere else, helping another person, handing them exactly what they needed in exchange for a single coin. It mattered not that anyone else had seen or believed in Peter Pennington. Caroline did. She believed just as Grandma Ida had believed.

With a saddened heart, she climbed back into her car and drove off.

THE SECRET

Wilbur was released from the hospital the following day. The doctor indicated it would be after lunch, but Caroline arrived while the breakfast tray still sat on the table.

"I thought maybe we'd have some time to talk," she said and pulled the visitor's chair closer to his bed.

"Is something wrong?" Wilbur asked.

Caroline shrugged, "I don't know if I'd say wrong, but it certainly is confusing." She explained how she'd gone back to Previously Loved Treasures and found the store empty. "It's not like Peter to just not be there. He knew when I was coming, and he was always ready with exactly what I needed."

"Having what you need," Wilbur said with a smile. "That could be nothing more than coincidence."

Caroline shook her head. "It wasn't coincidence. He knew. I tried to buy you a new pocket watch, but Peter told me you needed that wristwatch. See what I mean?"

"Not exactly."

"The glow-in-the-dark watch saved your life."

"Saved my life?"

Caroline nodded. "The smoke was so thick, Calvin couldn't see a thing. If it wasn't for the glow of that watch…" The remainder of such a terrible thought was left unsaid.

"Who's Calvin?"

"The fireman who rescued you."

"Oh," Wilbur said, "I don't recall much of that night."

228

Pulling the conversation back on track, Caroline said, "See, Peter was always looking out for Grandma and me. He never actually said it, but I knew he was. If he cared about me, why would he leave without saying something? Goodbye, maybe? Or, I have to leave town?"

"Possibly he had no choice. He may have gotten sick or lost his lease."

Caroline shook her head again. "That's not it."

"How do you know?"

"Because I asked every merchant on the street, and they all claimed they'd never seen the store or heard of Peter."

"That is strange." Wilbur cradled his chin between his thumb and index finger, then hesitated a lengthy while before asking, "You're sure you had the right location?"

"Of course I'm sure!" Caroline answered indignantly. "I've been there five different times, and Grandma was there too."

The mention of Ida's name caused Wilbur to think back on the years of his life. He'd seen a stranger come from out of nowhere to shove a boy from the path of an oncoming car. He'd seen a silver cigarette case stop a bullet from reaching a soldier's heart. And when Ida was in need of someone to love, he'd watched her find the granddaughter she never knew she had. How many other unexplainable things had he witnessed and never stopped to think about? People sometimes offered up explanations. They'd say it was the hand of fate or perhaps a lucky break, but was that really the truth?

Wilbur gave a deep sigh. "I've a feeling Peter was there for you because you needed him, and now he's moved on."

"Moved on? As in not coming back?"

Wilbur nodded solemnly.

"But the picture and bonds," Caroline said. "They're not really mine. What do I do with them if he's not coming back?"

"Actually, they are yours," Wilbur said. "Peter gave them to you."

"The picture, yes, but it's possible he didn't know the bonds were behind it."

"He knew." Wilbur laughed. "Just as he knew I needed that watch." He reached across and folded her hand in his. "You see, Caroline, everybody deals with a certain amount of good and bad in their life, but sometimes the bad starts taking over. When that happens the Lord sends a bit of help. I think Mister Pennington might have been your help."

Caroline pictured the little man with his black suit and round glasses and laughed. "Peter Pennington, a guardian angel?"

"Despite my years, there's a world of things I don't understand. I can't say whether your Mister Pennington was a wealthy eccentric or a guardian angel, but I'd be willing to bet your grandma had a hand in making sure those bonds got to you."

Caroline gave a long sorrowful sigh. "It's sad to think I'll never see Peter again. First Grandma, now Peter. It's like there's a hole in my heart."

Wilbur gave her hand a gentle squeeze. "Don't worry. God never closes a door without giving you a window."

Caroline thought of the gaping hole in the back of the house, and for a fleeting instant she could see Calvin lifting the new window into position.

It took almost two weeks for Caroline to settle into the thought that the bonds actually belonged to her, and when she finally did it was only because she'd come to accept that they were a gift from either Peter Pennington or her grandma.

By then Calvin had replaced the window and finished the repairs. As it turned out, he was a volunteer fireman and also the owner of a building supply company. The day after Caroline moved back to the house, he began showing up every afternoon with building materials: stacks of lumber, sheets of drywall, sandpaper, nails, plaster, and tools Caroline had never before seen. He'd work for several hours, and at the end of the day he'd sit down to dinner with the residents. It was less than a week before he'd taken ownership of the chair Max once sat in.

Long after the kitchen was finished Calvin continued to stop by every evening, claiming he had to fix a washer in a faucet, straighten a cabinet handle, or touch up some tiny bit of paint in the far corner of the wall.

After almost three weeks, he began running out of things to be fixed and that's when he finally asked Caroline if she'd like to take a walk after dinner. She smiled and nodded.

That night after they settled at the table, he said, "Lucky for me I was on call that night."

"Lucky for me too," Caroline answered.

Since the bonds had matured years earlier they netted a hefty amount more than the face value, which was one million dollars. Having that much money seemed overwhelming to Caroline. Like the presence of

Peter Pennington, it was something too good to be true, something that could disappear as quickly as it came. The money sat in the bank for several months before she felt comfortable enough to start spending some of it. When she finally did, the first thing she bought was a new washer and dryer.

Two months later she hired a lawyer, and Rose, who they now called Rowena, got a divorce. It hardly mattered, because by then Joe Mallory was serving ten years in a Georgia penitentiary for attempted murder. When he got out the only thing that would be waiting for him would be the warrant officer from Illinois with a handful of other charges.

In the fall of that year, Sara started kindergarten and Caroline put an addition on the house: a spacious two-bedroom apartment.

"It's yours for as long as you want it," she told Rowena.

Rowena smiled and said she couldn't imagine ever leaving. She insisted that in exchange she would take over all of the cooking duties and management of the house. It was an arrangement that pleased the residents no end.

With plenty of time on her hands you might think Caroline finished her novel, but you'd be wrong. For months a thought had been bouncing around inside her head, and in time it became something she could no longer ignore. In February she withdrew thirty-eight thousand dollars from the bank and bought the small building on the corner of Spencer and Main.

After weeks of clearing away the layers of dust and stocking the shelves, she announced the grand opening of Previously Loved Treasures.

Once again the windows sparkled, and the shelves were stacked with things people needed. After a few short weeks the residents of Rose Hill came to know Previously Loved Treasures as a thrift shop where everything was affordable, even if a person was without a penny in their pocket. Although Caroline was by no means gifted with Peter's foresight, it was said that she could look into a person's eyes and see their need.

That Christmas Eve Caroline kept the store open until after ten. People with nothing more than a bit of loose change in their pocket came in search of toys for their children. They'd hoped for a doll, a picture book, or miniature fire truck, but they left with bicycles, wagons, fancy doll carriages, and playhouse furniture. Many of the toys still had a price sticker from one of the large department stores.

Sally Mae Wells, a woman who was dirt poor and had four kids to care for, pointed to the shiny blue two-wheeler. "You sure this is used? It looks brand new."

"Not used," Caroline corrected. "Previously loved." That wasn't a lie. Caroline had loved every one of the toys she'd bought, and she loved the thought of giving countless children a Christmas such as she'd never had.

"Looks brand new," Sally Mae repeated. She handed Caroline the fifteen cents and said, "I'll take it."

That night when Caroline finally left the store the night was crisp and clear, the moon brighter than she could remember. She crossed the street, walked to where her car was parked, then turned and looked back. The moonlight made the gold lettering seem somehow brighter than ever before. Previously Loved Treasures. Caroline looked at the sign then squinted, and just as she had so many times before she could see the tiny 2 tacked onto the last S.

No one had ever noticed the 2, which was as it should be. It was a secret. A secret she shared with Grandma Ida and Peter Pennington.

If you enjoyed reading this book, please share it with a friend.
And, if you have a few moments and wouldn't mind doing so,
please also share your thoughts in a review on Amazon or Goodreads.

Stop by and visit me at

www.betteleecrosby.com

I love hearing from my readers.

A Note From The Author

The fruit of the Spirit is love, joy, peace, patience, kindness, goodness, and faithfulness
Galatians 5:22

I have been blessed with all of these things in the friendship and support of those who helped me to make this story a reality. To list the names of all to whom I owe a debt of gratitude, would take many pages, but I believe each person knows how thankful I am for their unique support. And, I hope I have stopped along the way to express my appreciation to each of you individually.

A special thank you to the ladies of my BFF Fan Club, gals who have cheered me on and generously shared my books with their friends. Without such readers, I would be lost. And I also would be remiss if I did not mention Coral Russell, Naomi Blackburn, Ekta Garg and Kathleen Valentine—I could not do without the amazing help and guidance of these awesome women.

Lastly, but certainly not least, I thank my husband Richard. It would take a forest of trees to provide enough paper to list the reasons why I love him as I do.

Made in the USA
Monee, IL
08 May 2020

30259882R00141